About the author

Joan Conway lives in Dublin, Ireland. She works in film as a freelance location and production manager, and as a freelance script editor. She has had poetry published and has been shortlisted for radio and screenplay awards.

Praise for *Cereal Lover:*

'A warm heart, dextrous use of bathos and winning way with an outre metaphor . . . anyone nursing a broken heart or simply after an undemanding, amusing diversion should seek it out immediately' *The Times*

'Funny and entertaining' *Woman's Way*

'Light, fluffy romance . . . refreshingly unformulaic . . . undeniably well executed' *Irish Independent*

Also by Joan Conway

Cereal Lover

Bunny Girl

Joan Conway

CORONET BOOKS

Hodder & Stoughton

First published in Great Britain in 2000 by Hodder and Stoughton
First published in paperback in 2001 by Hodder and Stoughton
A division of Hodder Headline

A Coronet Paperback

10 9 8 7 6 5 4 3 2 1

A CIP catalogue record for this title is available
from the British Library

ISBN 0 340 76627 1

Typeset by Palimpsest Book Production Limited,
Polmont, Stirlingshire
Printed and bound in Great Britain by
Mackays of Chatham plc, Chatham, Kent

Hodder and Stoughton
A division of Hodder Headline
338 Euston Road
London NW1 3BH

For Howard who kindly never reads my work before it's finished and Berni who always does – that's her kindness.

For Kirsty, whose enthusiasm and support will be greatly missed: best of luck in the new job.

For Brendan Gunn and his time and talent, it's wonderful what an Ulsterman will do for a fry.

For everybody who bought the last one.

Chapter One

Somebody had just tried to kill Ciara Bowe.

Or so at any rate it seemed to her. She'd been sheltering from the rain under some scaffolding on Mary Street when a heavy piece of machinery almost landed on her. It was a close shave.

The machine thudded on to the pavement and then toppled over, trapping her foot underneath. As a result Ciara couldn't move. She didn't want to call out in case whoever had pushed the machine from the scaffolding heard her and decided they ought to come and finish the job, clamber down the rusty cement-caked scaffolding and hit her over the head with a . . . well, with whatever it was that a construction worker would hit you over the head with at 9 a.m. on a wet wintry March morning. The side streets of Dublin were quiet, the rumble of constant traffic on the main thoroughfare sounded very far off. On Mary Street there were no passers-by to come to her rescue.

If there had been Ciara wasn't sure they would take her seriously! Because she was dressed as a rabbit. A large, imposing, furry, fully padded, fluffy-tailed rabbit. So it wasn't really *her* foot that was trapped under what she now worked out to be a generator but the rabbit's. This, as it happened, didn't make much difference because she couldn't get her own foot out of the costume while the paw was trapped.

Ciara Bowe, now five days off her twenty-eighth birthday, was in a pickle.

This wasn't the only pickle she was in. It was really a pickle, in a pickle, in a pickle. Like a bubble that gets attached to other bubbles to make up one giant mutant bubble, spiralling downward under the weight of its new complexity. But it was only in the last couple of days that things had become really complicated.

Two weeks and two days before this morning's crisis Ciara had moved back in with her mother. She had done this because she'd simultaneously lost her job and her flat and it seemed the most practical thing to do. By the time she'd been there a week she wanted to kill her mother. Not kill her dead or anything; just wanted her to stop being the sort of person that she was. Though, in fact, Ciara wouldn't have minded so much her being the person she was if she wasn't her mother.

So what she actually wanted was a miracle.

This wasn't going to happen. After two weeks of her second daughter's unemployment and homelessness Mrs Bowe had taken matters into her own hands.

'Ciara, I expect you'll never guess who's been on the phone.'

Her mother's footsteps advanced along the corridor towards Ciara's bedroom. Throwing her legs off the bed and putting her feet on the floor, she looked frantically about for an occupation. There would be a huge fuss about ill health, mental and physical, if she was found lying on the bed at 6 p.m. She grabbed a tangled pile of clothes from the floor, extracted a pair of socks and quickly folded them, then laid a shirt across her lap in an about-to-be-folded position. Room tidying had always been regarded in the Bowe household as an acceptable pastime.

'No, Mum, I don't suppose I will.'

Ciara's tone veered as closely as she dared towards sarcasm. Her mother's soft but distinctive Scottish accent hardened slightly as she stood in the doorway, closely eyeing her daughter in an I'm-not-sure-I-like-your-tone manner.

'Do you want to know?' There was a dangerous edge to her mother's voice.

Ciara affected a stubborn silence and nodded. She could see that her mother was in one of her no-nonsense moods.

'John Murphy! And he's coming to dinner tomorrow. So you'll tidy yourself up a wee bit for that, won't you?'

Ciara was stunned.

Her mother was right, she certainly would never have guessed who was on the phone.

'You mean, John Murphy . . . *my* John Murphy?'

'Yes, your very own John Murphy.' Her mother's voice was a mixture of annoyance and suppressed pleasure.

Ciara groaned inwardly. As though things weren't bad enough, stressful enough, ego-destroying enough, John Murphy was coming to dinner.

John Murphy her ex-boyfriend.

Actually he wasn't just any ex-boyfriend. He was her very first. The fact was John and Ciara had shared a lot of firsts. She had first gone out with him when she was fifteen. He was the first guy she'd ever kissed. And it was from him that she first found out what a hard-on was.

Not that he had told her or anything, but after a few times snogging around the back of the local shopping centre Ciara had begun to get suspicious about him always carrying mysterious hard objects in his pocket. Having spent a lot of time deliberating she eventually made a few tentative enquiries among her more well-informed peers

4

and came up with the truth. This of course didn't deter Ciara and she and John had felt their way about each other on and off throughout the rest of her school years.

Even though he was two years older than she was they had never done anything serious, like sex, but they certainly did as much investigation as can be done standing up in what was practically a public place.

Even though he was two years older, John had left school a year before Ciara and gone to work with a local accountancy firm so it wasn't until she also left that things changed. Although she still lived at home she had moved into a new social scene and a whole other world opened up for her. John was left behind and without either of them mentioning it, during that period they saw much less of each other.

Nevertheless they kept in touch and any time neither of them was seeing someone else they would make contact, get drunk and feel each other up again for an evening, sometimes for longer, until one of them — well, Ciara really — drifted off to newer, more exciting pastures. It had all been very familiar and safe.

Although she'd never admitted it to herself Ciara used John as a sort of sounding board to check her own desirability. When they were fifteen he had declared undying love for her and had never undeclared it. So whenever there was nobody more interesting around Ciara would give him a call just to see if he was still enamoured. And, much to her ego's gratification, he always was.

Then things had changed.

Three years ago, he had called her.

'Hi, Ciara, I'm back in Dublin for a couple of days so I thought I'd get in touch.'

John had moved to America after doing his final accountancy exams, claiming there was a lot more money to be made there. They usually saw each other whenever he was home. Ciara racked her brains quickly for a way of getting out of meeting him this time. That week she was in love and every waking moment of her life was taken up with being in love. She had just met the man of her dreams so a reunion with John, no matter how casual, was nowhere on her list of things to do.

Their conversation was very short.

'Well, John, I ... um ... I'm a bit busy right now. Actually I've met somebody ... you know, a guy.'

There was silence at the other end of the line and Ciara started to become acutely embarrassed and uncomfortable.

'That is, I mean, I could meet you for lunch or something if ...' Her voice trailed off as his cold tones cut across her.

'No, Ciara, that's fine. I'm a bit busy myself anyway. *Actually* I'm seeing somebody in the States at the moment.

She keeps talking about getting married. You know how Americans are,' he finished with a stony laugh.

'Yeah,' Ciara said, putting a smile into her voice but not having the slightest notion how Americans were or indeed what he was talking about. She was at a loss what to say next. She needn't have worried, though, John was back in control.

'So, see you then, Ciara. 'Bye.'

She hadn't heard a word from him since.

Her mother, however, was not the sort to let a good man go. Mrs Bowe and John's mother, Mrs Murphy, developed a steady telephone relationship when it became apparent that their son and daughter were not playing their courtship by the accepted rules or indeed any rules. As a consequence Ciara was kept up to date on all the relevant developments in John's life, and in turn paid little or no attention to the information.

Shortly after Ciara's last conversation with John her mother passed on the news that he had moved to Eastern Europe to spearhead investment there for a giant American corporation. And now he was coming to dinner!

She racked her brains for any data about John that might fill in the enormous gap in her memory between his working in Eastern Europe and coming to dinner. Her information readout was a blank. Aware that she had more than likely just not listened to the last John 'episodes', Ciara became defensive.

She didn't understand why, if he hadn't been around for years, he was suddenly turning up just when she had moved back home and her world had disintegrated. It was all too easy, all too coincidental.

Ciara smelled a rat.

'So he just phoned up and invited himself to dinner, did he? And he'll be flying in from whatever part of the world he's accounting in now, will he?' she demanded peevishly and, even she would admit, a little too forcibly.

'Now, Ciara, there's absolutely no need to be rude!' Her mother's voice was sharp. Then, with a slight inclination of her head, it changed into a let-me-clarify-something-for-you tone. 'You should be glad he still has the interest. It's not as though we've seen any of your other "friends" of late, now is it?'

Ciara sat on the bed and glowered. Those words stung. She knew her mother was bothered that her next-in-line-to-be-married-daughter didn't have a steady boyfriend. This bothered Ciara as well but what really hurt was the suggestion that she was devoid of friends. That she, Ciara Bowe, the week before her twenty-eighth birthday had to rely on her mother to pull old boyfriends out of the woodwork to masquerade as people who cared.

Unfortunately, this wasn't very far off the truth but her

mother wasn't supposed to know that, and Ciara certainly didn't want an ex-boyfriend to know it! Satisfied that she wasn't going to meet more resistance, Mrs Bowe got back to the business in hand.

'That's all right then. John will be around at one o'clock.'

Mrs Bowe ate dinner in the middle of the day. She had no time for the meal rearranging (as she saw it) that her daughters had taken to as soon as they'd left home. Dinner was the main meal and therefore should be eaten in the middle of the day to aid digestion and provide proper sustenance.

And she still wasn't finished with the subject of John. Her voice moved from pragmatic to unusually wistful.

'His mother tells me he has his own business. And he's for buying a house. I don't know how he's not married yet . . .'

She let that statement loiter in the open door for a while, allowing it to pose there, thumbs stuck in the pockets of its jeans as it cheekily threw come-hither glances at the subject-sensitive Ciara.

She turned her attention to folding the shirt, ignoring this provocation.

Seeing that she was getting nowhere, Mrs Bowe changed the subject and in a quieter voice said, 'You'll be down for something to eat, won't you? You hardly touched your tea and it's another hour to supper. I've circled a couple of jobs in the paper you should have a look at. It's such a pity you never finished that secretarial course ...'

Her mother didn't finish the sentence but left it hanging, shrouded in tangible dissatisfaction, in the cluttered room.

'I'll see you presently then.'

Mrs Bowe slid away like a ghost returning to the shadows, leaving Ciara to unclench her teeth slowly. What she didn't need just then were comments like that from her mother. Another thing she didn't need was a visit from somebody she hadn't seen for years who would immediately and, no doubt, triumphantly recognise what a shambles her life was in. After listening for her mother's step on the stairs Ciara threw herself back on to the bed. She had dropped the half-folded clothes to the floor and slid gently back into the little pond of poor-mes in which she had been wallowing before the interruption.

Only now the pond was deeper; it was filled to overflowing with images of Little-Mr-Successful, Little-Mr-Doing-So-Well accountant, John.

Was there really anything worse, Ciara wondered, than meeting people you'd known in school but hadn't seen for years? In school it had been all right, everybody was on an equal footing more or less. True, some people's parents might have been richer than others' but that didn't matter so much because you could always say that you would be rich when you grew up. And if somebody got really good results it didn't mean the end of the world for old Joe-average because everybody had heard of people who did really well without being academically brilliant. So back then it had been OK. The whole world was before you, a great big cream cake to be indulged in and enjoyed as soon as you were free from parental and school constraints.

And you *knew* it was going to be great. You would be rich, famous, successful, witty, talented, benevolent and sought after, and eventually at the ripe old age of about twenty-five or so you would fall madly in love with an equally rich, famous, successful, witty, talented, benevolent and sought-after mate with whom you would live happily ever after.

You weren't supposed to reach nearly twenty-eight and be unemployed, unloved, unmated and uneverythinged.

And then, to confirm your worst fears, one of the people who was in school with you turns up with cream and cake all over their cheeks from having indulged so freely in the good life. It's perfectly obvious they've achieved a good proportion of what you'd always dreamed of achieving. Worse than that, at nearly twenty-eight not only have you not achieved it, there isn't any hope left of your ever doing so.

Your towering ambitions have been reduced to one myopic desire: to move out of your mother's house as soon as you can ... again!

Ciara didn't want to see John Murphy. She didn't want to have to admit that the great love she'd been so preoccupied with three years ago had come to nothing. Didn't want to have to acknowledge that dreams are just that, dreams, and life often beats them up so badly they become barely recognisable. She didn't want to have to reveal her list of failures.

Ultimately and singularly, Ciara didn't want to be Ciara anymore.

Chapter Two

'Ciara, are you really going to drape yourself like that when we have a guest to dinner?'

Her mother's voice was shrill with criticism as she fussed around the table refolding the paper napkins and moving knives millimetres from their original position. John was due to arrive in fifteen minutes.

'What's wrong with the way I'm dressed?' Ciara retorted sharply, glancing down at her tracksuit bottoms and fleecy top.

'Well, I suppose they're suitable if you're going jogging but I really think you should smarten yourself up. After all, no matter how bad things are the Lord has seen fit to give you your health and a roof over your head. Something a little more fitting to entertaining a guest might be in order.

You don't want John to think you're letting yourself go, now do you?'

She looked at her daughter expectantly. Ciara knew that look. It stated loudly and in no uncertain terms that her mother had more to say on this subject. It was evident she was just waiting for a word from her daughter to open the floodgates of a major parental taking down which would inevitably focus on Ciara's various failings – ones that nobody but her mother ever seemed to notice. On the other hand maybe people did notice them but hadn't felt the necessity to say anything. Compassion is a great saver of friendship.

Ciara looked back at her and briefly considered her choices: change her clothes or face the derision of her potentially highly derisive mother.

Easy.

She sighed heavily so that her mother would be fully aware what a great burden she was and dragged herself slowly upstairs towards her chaotic bedroom.

It wasn't that she wanted to appear to be 'letting herself go', as her mother put it, it was more that she didn't want John to think she was making an effort for him. She also didn't want to appear as though she was trying to disguise the mess her life was in. By dressing down Ciara had hoped to work a sort of double negative.

She suspected, however, that as he'd known her for so

long John would be bound to figure out there was more to this than just unemployment. It wasn't that he was very perceptive, it was just that he would inevitably wonder why she was living with her mother. It could mean only one thing after all: her personal life had fallen apart. Of course he wouldn't have heard anything about it from Mrs Bowe because she refused to mention the existence of Gary to anybody, including Ciara.

Gary was Ciara's latest ex-boyfriend.

Ciara's married ex-boyfriend.

It was Gary with whom she'd been in love the last time she'd spoken to John.

As far as Mrs Bowe was concerned Gary didn't exist.

It hadn't always been like that. It had been fine when they first started seeing each other. Her mother just thought that the reason she hadn't been introduced to Gary was because he and Ciara were spending time 'getting to know one another'. When Ciara declared she was moving house, getting a place of her own, her mother suspected she was moving in with Gary. Not being a woman to leave a stone unturned, she had proceeded to excavate.

'Eat up those potatoes, I don't want them going to waste. Will you be living in your new flat on your own, Ciara?' she had broached the subject, one Sunday dinner soon after Ciara had moved.

'Yes, Mum,' Ciara answered shortly, bad-tempered and

intolerant from a hangover and the vision she'd been nursing all day, indeed all weekend and every weekend since she had started seeing Gary, of the cosy little family Sundays he must have with his wife and child.

Her mother looked doubtful.

Ciara hated it when her mother looked doubtful because it was usually the first indication of the establishment of an inquisition. Her mother would torture and persecute, pry and investigate, until she unearthed the truth.

'Don't you think you should be putting a little bit aside for a place of your own instead of spending a fortune on rent? I don't know why you ever left home ... here, put a bit more gravy on that meat, it'll help you finish it.'

Ciara gritted her teeth. Her mother was right, of course, she couldn't afford a high rent but the truth was that Gary was paying over half of it. He had complained bitterly and continuously about Ciara's housemates always being around so they had no time alone together. He didn't like to go out much with Ciara in case he was seen by somebody who knew his wife. Ciara understood this, so when Gary arrived one day saying he'd taken a lease on a lovely little apartment for the two of them, she was delighted and by the end of the week had moved everything she owned into her new home.

It was a dream come true, she and Gary with their own little love nest.

There was one drawback. He was only there a couple of times a week. Still, although Gary-access was limited, at least when they were together they could be together, alone.

'It's very reasonable really, Mum, the rent,' Ciara lied.

But her mother wasn't to be thrown off the scent so easily.

'Are you still going out with that Gary?'

'Yeah.'

'And do you see much of him?' Ciara's mother had gone into terrier mode, refusing to let go of the subject, doggedly tugging away at the blanket of secrecy in which Ciara had shrouded Gary.

'A bit.'

A bit! Even Ciara knew this was a weak one. How could you be seeing 'a bit' of someone?

Then, like the lull before the next wave, there was a pause in the interrogation as Ciara's mother worked herself up to the ultimate question. It crashed and roared into the conversation.

'Tell me the truth now, Ciara, are you and Gary ... well, are you and Gary living together?' She spat out the last few words as though they were foul-tasting. She also had a sob in her voice as if it would be the greatest betrayal, the disappointment of a lifetime, were one of her daughters to live with a man. She waited for an answer, an air of tragedy hanging over the half-eaten lunch.

Ciara now moved from evasion to intolerance. She stared at her hand-wringing mother and mentally tapped her foot with annoyance.

What could her mother possibly know about love, about passion, about finding the man of your dreams and doing everything necessary to keep that precious love alive? Her mother's life had always worked by the rules. She had found a man, married him, had children, and then when her husband had died of a heart attack, she had dressed herself in widow's black, drawn her small pension, put a tenant in the basement and continued life as though there had never been a Mr Bowe. She had obviously never experienced real passion and had no idea how the world had changed. It just wasn't so simple anymore, not that straightforward. It was time, Ciara fumed, her mother learned the truth, found out there was more to life than her own safe little world.

'I would live with him, Mum, if I had the chance. As it is I can't because he's married.'

There. She'd said it!

And she immediately wished she hadn't.

Mrs Bowe didn't take kindly to her daughters not doing what she wanted. Having an affair with a married man was definitely not what she wanted for her second daughter, or indeed any of her daughters. Still sitting, she straightened herself to her tallest, black-clad, tightly covered bosom jutting into the world assertively. The grief she had suggested at the idea of her daughter's living with a boyfriend was cast aside in the face of Ciara's shameless declaration of adultery, or at any rate adulterous collusion.

'A married man! Are you away with the fairies? How can you possibly be going out with a married man?'

To Ciara this seemed to be a rhetorical question so she didn't answer it. Instead she shrugged. Her mother's eyes narrowed as she broke into a lilting chant: '"I have seen also in the prophets of Jerusalem a horrible thing: they commit adultery and walk in lies, they strengthen also the hands of evil doers that none doth return from his wickedness".' Mrs Bowe did a good line in fire and brimstone morality. Ciara hadn't had a dose of it for a while, not since her mother found a condom in the pocket of her jeans and had given her a lecture on the evils of pre-marital sex. She'd been twenty then, still a child in her mother's eyes.

With a lifetime of experience Ciara was adept at getting the point of her mother's lengthy quotes. This one was about adultery.

'I'm not married so it can't be adultery,' she quipped. But her mother wasn't to be swayed by quippings.

'How dare you address your own mother like that ...
Jezebel! Have you no shame? You may call it whatever
you please, it's no more than fornication.'

They had moved into the third person and on to a
bit of name calling. There was now no hope of a normal
conversation, no hope of reconciliation.

'Until you learn some respect I think you'd better leave.
And don't come into this house again until you remember
how to treat your mother!'

It was always the same when things reached crisis point
with her family. If they weren't doing what she wanted
Mrs Bowe would banish them. On and off over the years
Ciara had been banished and unbanished while Ruth, the
youngest, had been banished years before for suggesting
that abortion should be left to the individual's conscience,
not dictated by the government.

There had been no discussion, no questions. Instead
in her quiet lilting voice Mrs Bowe had quoted: '"Their
feet run to evil, and they make haste to shed innocent
blood; their thoughts are thoughts of iniquity; waste and
destruction are in their paths. Cursed be he who hath
taken reward to slay an innocent."'

There was obviously going to be no agreement on the
issue so Ruth left. She took her mother at her word and
had not returned since even though some months later
Mrs Bowe, while never actually mentioning it, withdrew

her edict of banishment. Now, as a compromise, they spoke on the phone quite regularly.

Karen, the eldest, had never been banished. She had always done what she was told and now lived in a comfortable suburb with her consultant husband and two children.

Despite her staunch views Mrs Bowe would always come round within a month or so. Then she would behave as though there had never been a disagreement. Her way of dealing with the matter was never to mention the topic that had caused the confrontation, or anything related to it, again.

She had no tolerance for married men and their affairs; nevertheless Ciara's visitation ban was lifted within two months. But Gary was never mentioned again nor was the fact that there might or might not be a significant other in Ciara's life. She knew her mother must be fully aware that if she was back living at home her personal life had fallen apart. However, true to family tradition, the relationship with the 'married man' never came up in conversation.

When Ciara reached her room she stood in the doorway, still fuming at her mother. The floor was a mess of clothes, a clutter of tangled legs and sleeves. Those that weren't strewn on the floor were crammed under the bed and in the wardrobe. Ciara sighed and bent down to unravel the nearest mass, a faint desire stirring in her to reinvent herself as the well-dressed sophisticate she had been in her former life of two weeks before.

The idea of feeling good about herself started to take hold and her resentment of her mother faded. It came back again as soon as she put on her favourite wraparound fitted top. It didn't fit anymore. And the reason it didn't fit was a very simple one. Since she'd moved back home she'd put on a stone in weight. And it was all her mother's fault! Mrs Bowe pursued Ciara about the house with food. She served four meals a day with snacks in between and cooked something with extra butter as a treat if Ciara tried to skip a meal. 'If you don't eat, I'll have to talk to Dr Lynch about you,' was a constant threat.

The problem was Ciara liked food and with no work or indeed life to distract her she found eating very comforting. As a result she went to bed every night filled with self-loathing at her own lack of self-discipline, vowing that the next day would be different.

It never was.

Ciara, who had always prided herself on her slim waist, had now lost it somewhere in the layer of home cooking that sat just above her hips. She hastily replaced the fitted top with a baggy pink one that made her look like she was pregnant. Her mother would probably have a problem with that as well but Ciara didn't care, at least the colour suited her.

Having gone to the trouble of dressing she decided while having a closer look in the mirror that she might as well complete the picture. She gathered her dark bobbed hair on top of her head and put on some makeup. At least she hadn't put on any weight on her face! She was just adding the final touches to her lipstick when the doorbell rang. She squinted glumly at herself in the mirror. The moment she had been dreading was here, but she consoled herself that all she had to do was smile politely for an hour or so and it would be over.

As she came downstairs she heard her mother's voice in the sitting room.

'Ciara should be down in a minute, I can't imagine what she's doing up there. Your mother's been telling me you're starting a company.'

Typical! She'd hit on exactly the topic Ciara didn't want mentioned!

Now she'd have to walk into the room just as John revealed how many thousands of pounds he was worth, how many companies he owned, how many wives he had ... well, maybe not how many, but certainly how wonderful and beautiful the one he had was, or rather would be because they'd probably just got engaged.

Great!

Outside the living-room door Ciara inhaled, closed

the top button of her jeans and did a final hair pat, hastily pulling selected tendrils about her face in what she hoped looked like casual disarray. Taking a deep breath, she pushed open the door.

'About time! Come and say hello to John, Ciara, he's just telling me all about his business and how well he's doing.'

Her mother, having barely glanced at her as she came into the room, was smiling benevolently at the man by her side. Ciara nodded and opened her mouth to greet him but nothing came out. She stared. The man standing beside her mother was John but he looked odd. Yes, he had the same straight brown hair and fair skin as John, was the same height and wore glasses, but there was something different. This man was fat. Well, maybe not so much fat as filled out. It was John all right but he seemed to have become a caricature of himself. He was like those cartoon pictures they put in the paper of a politician who has a narrow head or a big nose, accentuating that feature so that it is undeniably the person but at the same time isn't them at all. That was what John looked like. It was as though somebody had taken all his features and stretched them – or rather expanded all the space around them so that you only knew it was him by picking out particular features and putting them back together without the flesh that had been superimposed between them. It wasn't that he was huge, just bigger. A lot bigger. And he was smiling warmly at her.

'Hi, how are you John?' she asked, hoping that he hadn't noticed her double take.

'Just fine, Ciara, how are you? You look great.'

His voice was enthusiastic as he moved towards her and awkwardly kissed her cheek. Living abroad for so long had obviously taught him that there were more ways of saying hello than just nodding your head in the direction of the person you've met and grunting, 'How's it going?'

Not that John had ever been like that. He came from a large working-class family that aspired to gentility and insisted that its children should become civil servants and teachers or, if they really came good, go into the more highly paid professions. John being the youngest by many years was the only one of his family to achieve the latter and had more than likely done so because of the massed ranks of civil servant and teacher siblings to urge him on.

John had always been more the handshake greeting type of guy. Nothing too enthusiastic, just a nod and a handshake. But now he'd graduated to the awkward kiss on the cheek. Before Ciara could fully recover from this radical change in social etiquette and appearance her mother moved in to take control of the situation.

'John, you must be famished. Ciara, would you take John into the kitchen? I have to check the oven. I'm sure you two have a lot of catching up to do.'

Mrs Bowe smiled understandingly and left the room. The Bowe house had been built at a time before fitted kitchens when it seemed the understanding was that kitchen equipment ought not to be seen. So the cooker and sink were isolated in a little lean-to at the back of the house, euphemistically referred to as the 'kitchenette' when there was a stranger in the house but more commonly known as 'the scullery'.

Throughout her childhood Ciara had never known anybody else with a 'scullery' and had decided that it was probably a legacy from the remote Scottish Island of Eigg where her mother had grown up. (Eigg had accounted for any number of idiosyncratic proclivities in Ciara's childhood.)

She was left alone with John.

She led him into the kitchen, feeling herself becoming tense as she tried to think of something to ask him that wouldn't involve career, money, marriage or any topic that would give him the opportunity to ask what she was up to. There was no chance of John jumping in with a question first. If she remembered correctly he was one of those people who played the 'if I don't speak first I can't be responsible for the conversation' game.

Ciara didn't understand this. Silences embarrassed her. She just had to say something.

'So, how's your mother?'

She knew this was a safe topic.

'Quite good really, considering her age.' John seemed relieved that he'd been asked an easy question.

His mother had been in her late-forties when the unexpected but much longed for son had arrived. Ciara had often wondered if having an older mother was what made him so steady and dependable. Well, actually, it was Mrs Bowe who regarded him as steady and dependable, Ciara saw him more as plodding and dogged. To her way of thinking, although he had no qualms about going to and living in different countries, John seemed to stomp his way through life oblivious to the world and its wonders. At least his very predictability meant there should be no surprising turns to their conversation.

'I think she's quite glad I'm back,' he continued conversationally.

Ciara had as good as forgotten what question she'd asked but as long as they were talking about anything but her miserable life and his successful one she didn't care.

'I mean, she has the girls but they have kids now and for so many years it was only the two of us in the house. It's just like it used to be.'

Mammy's Boy!

Mammy's Boy!

The words flashed, red-tinged and fluorescent, across Ciara's mind. She had forgotten about this little light show. It always used to happen when John spoke about his mother but it had been so long since she'd seen him now that she had forgotten. She was surprised the lights hadn't worn out or faded. But no, there they were, as bright as ever and such a shock she nearly repeated the words out loud. She nearly said, 'Mammy's Boy!'

Ciara curled her tongue in an attempt to stop the words leaping off it on to the table in an anti-social Samba frenzy, contorting themselves and swaying, back-stepping and wriggling, pelvic-thrusting indelicately around the condiments. No, that outburst was definitely not on the menu for lunch.

John shifted uneasily, not quite sure if he'd missed something in the conversation or if he was expected to say more. Ciara smiled, keeping her mouth shut for as long as possible to prevent a verbal disaster. Eventually she spoke.

'She must be happy to have you back then?'

'Oh, yes, she didn't like me working abroad at all. Too many risks,' he went on as though there had never been a Samba threat. 'She won't have me for long, of course, only until the new house is ready.'

Damn!

Despite all Ciara's efforts he'd succeeded in getting on to the topic of his life and how well he was doing. He had bought a house and just managed to work it smoothly into their casual chit-chat.

She had no idea how to react to this twist in the conversation without spitting. Well, snarling was another option but both were unacceptable. Instead she bit her lip. Fortunately at that moment, evidently believing that enough time had been spent 'catching up', Mrs Bowe swept into the room carrying the soup.

'I thought you'd have poured the wine, Ciara. John, you'd like a wee drop, wouldn't you?'

Ciara reached for the bottle as her mother moved straight on to her next question. 'The pie's nearly ready, now eat your soup. John, did your mother tell me at the weekend that you've bought a house?'

There was going to be no end to it!

Even if John had been reticent about bringing up the subject of his own success, which he wasn't, Ciara's mother would just get right in there and do it for him!

Chapter Three

'So, John, does that mean you'll be moving soon? You're such a short time back in the country it must be very disruptive for you.'

They had only just touched their soup with Mrs Bowe's stainless steel multipurpose spoons when she dragged the conversation straight back to John and his grating success. He pushed his glasses higher on to his nose and assumed an I'm-so-brave-I-can-move-out-of-my-mother's-house-at-thirty-years-of-age-and-bear-the-disruption expression and settled into the slow steady speech that epitomised his dependability.

'Well, it is, I suppose, especially as I'm also getting the new business off the ground but I have no intention of moving for a while. As I was telling Ciara, the house isn't nearly ready.'

'Oh, you have a business started here already?' Her voice was full of admiration.

Ciara cringed. Her mother was in her element now, spreading layers of flattery all over the conversation. Why didn't she just get under the table and lick his boots? This fawning was just too sickening. If somebody, anybody, had massaged Ciara's ego that much she would have had to pay them to do it.

Pay them a lot.

She watched John lap it up; he was obviously used to it, used to people fussing over his ability to make money. He didn't even have the modesty to look shy or embarrassed. He swallowed what was in his mouth and, laying down his spoon, threw Ciara a sideways grin that said, 'Let's just humour your mother, shall we?' This little intimacy was wasted on a resentful Ciara who decided he was checking to see if he had her full attention.

'I've just launched a new mobile phone company, Mrs Bowe. Gives me an excuse to get back to Ireland! That's always been my intention.'

He gave Ciara a meaningful glance. She didn't appreciate this look either and decided that life couldn't be so smooth and easy for anybody. She figured there had to be a hitch, some sharp bend that hadn't been so easily negotiated. She was annoyed by what she saw as John's smugness and wasn't prepared to admit that it might be jealousy on her part.

She wanted to shake his confidence. And she'd just figured out how!

'But what about that girl you were supposed to marry, the one in America?' Ciara burst out before she knew she was going to speak.

Her mother gasped involuntarily and a slow blush crept over John's face. He readjusted his glasses on the bridge of his nose and threw such a hurt look at Ciara that she almost regretted saying anything. Then he turned towards Mrs Bowe.

'Well, I ... ah ... em ... That didn't quite work out.'

He turned back to Ciara, quickly recovering himself.

'She was a bit too Italian-American for me. She was a wonderful woman, high-powered lawyer with a great career, but there was all this family thing. Big Sunday lunches every weekend ... stuff. She wanted to have loads of kids and adopt a few as well; it just didn't feel right for me. And I didn't really want to stay in the States and she couldn't have survived anywhere else, certainly not in Ireland. It was difficult but it was for the best.'

This was the longest sentence John had uttered since arriving and when he finished he presented the table with another I'm-so-brave face and gave Mrs Bowe a reassuring glance, absolving her from her daughter's rudeness.

Ciara had no idea what to say next.

John had fielded her question so well that she felt guilty and ashamed for having brought the subject up. She was sorry now that she'd said anything; she just wanted to disappear in a slow dissolve, but there was no chance of that.

Her mother, noting no doubt that her daughter had lost the power of speech as well as the capacity to be civil in company, picked up the conversation.

'I wouldn't worry about that, John, it happens to everybody at your age. It's better to find it out before rather than after you get wed. At least you were involved in a relationship that would have had a future, had it worked out.'

She didn't even glance towards Ciara as she said this but shook her head sorrowfully and reached for the bottle of wine.

'Another wee drop, John?'

Ciara sat frozen, her spoon poised in mid-air, unwilling to stomach her mother's sideways jab but unable to do anything about it without causing a scene and revealing the true extent of her misfortune to John.

In her mind's eye she saw herself naked, running screaming from the room, her hair streaming behind her in a mad tangle. She suspected she had seen something like this in a magazine or on a postcard once. It was a picture by somebody famous and dead like Picasso. But when she thought about it she was almost sure that the woman in the picture had been outdoors, jubilant, happy, and not tormented by the razor-sharp tongue of her mother. Maybe she came from some lucky tribe who just didn't have mothers and who, as a result, were constantly ecstatic.

Ciara stared at the table, mentally cowering from fear that her mother would step up her guerrilla activities.

'No, thank you, Mrs Bowe, I'm driving, but it is a very nice wine. Where do you get it from?'

John and she started to talk about the wine as though her mother's little relationship comment hadn't just dragged Ciara's life through the butter, rubbed it around the empty soup bowls, topped it up with a smear of mustard and thrown it in the corner where it crouched, whimpering inconsolably, gasping for breath between sobs.

Ciara suddenly realised that she was being talked about. Her mother's voice penetrated her resentful thoughts.

'As you know I don't usually drink so there was quite a bit of wine here that people had bought for Christmas. Though it seems to have decreased a wheen since Ciara came back ...'

Ah, she was on to the topic of Her Daughter the Alcoholic!

Ciara knew quite well that her mother had been watching how much she drank in the two weeks she'd been in the house. However, she could see no reason why this had to be made public. Her mother simply didn't understand that a girl in Ciara's situation had very few comforts in life, and she didn't think that 'nearly' a bottle of wine a day was an awful lot in the circumstances. Fortunately John didn't take the bait on Ciara's drinking and the conversation moved on.

She listened with reluctant admiration as he and her mother passed banter to and fro across the table like expert ping-pong players. Their smooth game was awe-inspiring, it appeared so simple. Ciara, after her last unsuccessful foray into the conversation, had no inclination to join in again. Instead she stared at her food and sullenly recalled other occasions when her mother had reduced her to a mortified midget, a tiny, shrivelled version of herself like plastic after it has been exposed to too much heat.

She remembered bitterly a visit the family had made to Blackpool when she was just fourteen. Auntie Pauline, her father's first cousin, lived there and even though Mr Bowe was dead her mother saw it as her duty to torment his few relatives with his offspring. She and her three girls would pack themselves into the old Volkswagen on a Sunday and drive to the home of a selected relative. The children would then be released from the car and while the adults sat chatting politely the three girls would run and tumble about their house, wreaking havoc and corrupting their children if they had any.

Ciara always figured that it was a form of threat by her mother, a means of preventing her father's relatives from having embarrassingly charitable thoughts about the Bowe children. It was a sort of don't-say-you-don't-see-enough-of-us-or-we-will-come-and-do-this-to-you-every-Sunday threat. Ciara based this belief on the expression of relief on the relatives' faces when it was time for her family to go home.

The visit to Blackpool had been a one off. Auntie Pauline complained each year in her Christmas card that the cousins never met. That year she had offered to pay half the cost of their visit. Mrs Bowe, incensed at this hint of charity, determined to take the trip and scrimped and saved for six months to make it possible.

This journey was resented all the more because, as a staunch Scot, she believed that anywhere south of Carlisle was a foreign place full of vice and skulduggery. Ireland was classified for some obviously non-geographical reason as being north of Carlisle. It was decided they should stay in Blackpool for two nights. At the time Auntie Pauline had four children in a three-bedroomed house. With the addition of the Bowe family the place became a zoo as the two women cajoled and corralled the gaggle of excited teenagers. Ruth, who was a bad traveller, had been sick on the boat and continued being sick throughout Saturday night so on Sunday morning Ciara and her mother went into Blackpool to find a chemist's.

The shop when they found it was enormous, Ciara had never seen anything that big in Dublin. Being on the younger side of fourteen (and probably not the most mature), she was still fascinated by brightly packaged products. It helped if they contained makeup or perfume but her attention was initially drawn by their attractive colours.

She was at a perfume counter when she noticed some small, slim, gaily coloured sachets in a basket. Ciara had an idea that they might be individually wrapped scented tissues. Each of them was a different colour so she assumed they must have different scents. She picked a green one and sniffed to see if it smelled green. She could smell nothing so she picked up a yellow one; this didn't seem to have any scent either.

At this point she noticed the shop assistant looking at her closely and moving a little nearer. Ciara straightened her shoulders, set herself into what she hoped was a nonchalant and confident pose and picked up another sachet.

No shopkeeper was going to frighten *her* off.

This next one was pink: when all else fails pick the pink, there's no scent as strong as the smell of pink. She was wrong; there was no smell from this either. Baffled, she took one last deep inhalation just as her mother spoke from behind her.

'Ciara, why are you sniffing those condoms?'

Condoms! What were they doing putting condoms in such gaily coloured packaging! And besides, at fourteen Ciara barely knew what condoms were, never mind how they were packaged.

She dropped the coloured sachet as though it was burning her fingers and stared about her to see if anybody had heard. Directly in front of her, arms folded with a so-what-do-you-think-you-are-up-to expression on her face, stood the shop assistant.

She had crept up while Ciara was sniffing and had no doubt been the reason that her mother had noticed what was happening. Ciara's colour rose with a mixture of fury and mortification.

'Really, Ciara, you won't be needing those until you're married and if you do decide to use them, I hope you won't be the one doing the purchasing.'

Besides living strictly by the word of the Bible, her mother had clarified a few of its teachings to make the path of virtue that much clearer or, as Ruth would later put it, that much narrower! One of these guidelines was 'No pre-marital sex'. Mrs Bowe liked a start and a finish point to everything. Not for her the fuzziness of modern theology. Therefore sex commenced with marriage.

Ciara, at the time of the condom-sniffing incident, had no intention of trying to work out why she shouldn't be the one buying the condoms. Neither was she interested in assessing her mother's or indeed anybody else's attitude to contraception. She didn't care if a condom was ever used again so long as she could get away from the critical gaze of the shop assistant and her mother's ever-disparaging tongue.

But there was no route of escape.

There seemed to be only one option. Ciara swung around and ran from the shop – actually it was a sort of half-jog, half-striding lope, resembling something Quasimodo might have done when he was in a hurry. All the shoppers turned to stare.

As she reached the door her mother's voice, Scottish accent more pronounced in her disapproval, drifted after her.

'Teenagers, really, they can be so changeable!'

'Ciara? Ciara . . .'

John's voice broke into her embarrassed recollections.

'Eh, what?' She hadn't heard what John had said, even

though she knew that he had spoken to her. She turned to face him as he sat quizzically assessing her frozen position, shoulders hunched in misery over her barely touched soup. Her mother was missing, obviously gone to the scullery to fetch whatever calorie-laden dish she had conjured up.

'I was just asking what you're up to now, you know, work-wise?' John said with what had to be assumed innocence considering it was a loaded question.

Oh, no. It had happened! Ciara had dropped her guard for a moment, and John had managed to slip in an enquiry about her career.

Her at the moment non-existent career.

What was she going to say?

Ciara took a deep breath to quell the emotions that were surfing in on the rising wave of panic that engulfed her every time she had to confront that subject.

'I, ah, I . . . well, actually, I'm looking around at the moment. Bit of a career break, you know. I was in PR until recently but I think it's time to move on now, maybe get more into advertising or the business side of things. Broaden my horizons. It's not so difficult with contract work.'

John looked at her, an expression of intense interest on his face. Ciara smiled and nodded and became preoccupied with her cold soup so as not to have to speak. She swilled her spoon in the green sludge wondering what on earth her mother was up to. She'd been gone long enough to hunt and kill the main course!

Ciara was on her own.

She decided that probably the best form of defence was attack. Well, if not exactly attack, at least a change of subject.

'So, John, how come you're in mobile phones? I thought that accounts was your thing.'

He smiled his smug accountant's smile and shook his head.

'It's all figures, Ciara. I don't know a thing about mobile phones but it works on paper!'

She nodded, racking her internal 'questions list' for the next relevant one, but before she could select it her mother bustled into the room and fussily placed a meat pie on the table.

'John, you must tell me more about your house. Ciara, you might just go and get the potatoes and vegetables. And give them a wee stir, the butter should be melted by now.'

As she moved towards the scullery Ciara had the distinct feeling that before this meal was over there might be more than the butter stirred and melted!

* * *

The main course was almost over and the conversation had lost some of its edge. Ciara was beginning to think it hadn't gone too badly after all.

'So, John, what stage is your business at now?' Mrs Bowe's thirst for John-knowledge seemed insatiable.

'We've launched our sales campaign, and everything's going according to plan. We're thinking of increasing our staff. It's looking good.'

Ciara felt a great surge of renewed hatred for him; for his success, his confidence in his own ability, his faith in his achievements. She hated him because she didn't have any success, confidence, faith or indeed achievements. But she wanted some — some of that ease, that confidence. She was almost knee-deep in self-pity when her mother cut in.

'If you're doing so well, maybe you would have a job for Ciara. She's looking for work, aren't you?'

Mrs Bowe turned and smiled into her daughter's stricken face. She froze and her voice disappeared, carried off by a band of scantily clad warriors from Sheer Indignation. They also absconded with her last smattering of pride, snatching it away without leaving even the comfort of a ransom note.

Ciara nodded.

John looked at her sympathetically. Ciara assumed the look was one of pity. She'd lost the lunch battle! John knew that she was not just taking a little break between contracts to reshape her career but that she was actually unemployed, jobless, a failure!

'By all means. I just wasn't sure you were looking for a job. You'd be working with our advertising team. It's not exactly highly paid but as good as you'll get with any other company. And, you know, if you just want to do it for a little while until something better comes along, I could probably arrange that it doesn't go through the books. You wouldn't have to pay any tax.'

Her mother, who had been looking at Ciara with an appealing expression on her face, diverted her gaze to John.

'"A little that a righteous man hath is better than the riches of many wicked."'

Mrs Bowe didn't want to be part of what she obviously saw as a tax-evasion conspiracy. She prided herself on her high moral scruples, particularly when it came to public displays of them. John looked startled. Evidently he had forgotten her liking for Biblical texts, but before he could respond she continued, 'But tax status aside, Ciara, you'd be well advised to take it.'

When all was said and done Mrs Bowe's morality was fairly flexible if it meant getting a job for her wayward daughter.

Attention focused on Ciara who sat open-mouthed, visualising a huge cartoon hammer landing repeatedly and with great force on her mother's head until she was driven through the floor like a nail.

This didn't happen.

None of the tortures she'd conjured up for her mother over a lifetime ever came to fruition. Ciara had discovered years ago that her mother was immune to any of her desires or curses. She still liked to think that it was possible to put curses on people. To date she had no positive proof of this but she wasn't prepared to give up . . . yet.

'I . . . I mean, that sounds . . . um . . .'

John, seeing she felt trapped, interjected quickly, 'Hey, you don't have to make up your mind now. Give me a ring later. I can start you tomorrow if you're interested. Or the next day. Think about it. It's not a problem whatever you decide. It mightn't be your field but it's pretty easy money.'

He smiled at her and nodded, a warmth in his eyes that suggested more than a job on offer. Ciara didn't notice this nor did she notice John tactfully turn back to her mother with the smooth change of subject that his slow speech pattern and 'trust me' appearance facilitated.

'Mrs Bowe, my mother was saying that you wanted to ask something about pensions? They're not my field but I might be able to help you . . .'

Their voices faded into the background as Ciara mentally retreated, silently licking her wounds after that brief but painful skirmish. She had to get away from this house; it wasn't so much the place itself as living with her mother. It was fine for an hour or so but anything more than that she couldn't do without prescription drugs. Well, actually, as she had never tried them she didn't even know if *they'd* help.

What Ciara needed was money. That was the only reason she was staying at her mother's. She simply couldn't afford a place of her own. She hadn't enough money for the rent, never mind a deposit. She was just coming to the end of her last pay cheque. When that was gone she'd have nothing.

She didn't know how things had come to this. Well, she did really, she'd been living beyond her means for far too long and now it had caught up with her. She'd counted on having the job she'd just lost for another three months so there had been no need to save ... yet.

Now she had no credit rating anywhere so she couldn't get a loan and her credit cards, all three of them (times used to be better), were dangerously close to being repossessed. If that's what happened to credit cards.

Her mother was no good for a loan. Her meagre pension and the rent from the basement didn't leave anything over for spendthrift daughters. Besides, being dependent on a parent over the age of twenty-five was a 'Thou shalt not' in her belief system. Even had it not been, it would be too degrading to have to ask your mother for money to live on at the age of nearly twenty-eight.

There was just one option open to Ciara and that was to take the job John was offering. It was the only one she'd been offered since she'd become unemployed. Besides, it was a job in advertising and it couldn't be any worse than sitting about the house blocking out her mother's comments, waiting for some miracle to change her life into the fairy tale it was supposed to be. Yes, Ciara would take the job. She was a friend of the boss and that was bound to make things easier. She would get paid, save the money and then find someplace to live far away from her mother. She could use her earnings to buy freedom!

At the table conversation had drifted on to house prices, government attitudes, and how well Mrs Bowe's eldest daughter's husband, the consultant, was doing.

Ciara wasn't mentioned again.

This was another of her mother's guerrilla tactics. She would launch a violent attack, stunning more for its unexpectedness than its force, and then she would disappear into the hills, metaphorically speaking, and allow the landscape to return to normal, as though nothing had happened; as though she would never do anything to humiliate a child of hers.

As soon as they got up from the table she moved out of the room, mumbling something about having to turn off the cooker. Ciara was left to see John out. They moved into the hall.

'It was great to see you again, John, thanks for coming by.' Ciara reached for the door handle.

'I meant what I said about the job. It's not in the least bit glamorous or anything but it's fairly hassle-free. You know, you'd be doing me a favour if you took it. It would be great to know that there's at least one competent person on the team.'

Oh, flattery, surely the way to any girl's heart. Or in this case ego!

Ciara nodded. She had made up her mind to take the job so now she was just looking for the easiest way of saying yes. John didn't know this, though, and proceeded to encourage her.

'You know what I think would be best? How about I take you out for a drink tonight and we can have a little chat about it? I mean, it's not like we've had a proper chance to catch up or anything, is it?'

'Yeah, OK,' Ciara accepted easily. She was relieved that even though John now knew all about her unsuccessful life he'd still asked her out for a drink. There was something comforting in the easy familiarity she felt with him. After all, they'd known each other since they were fourteen. There was lot to be said for that.

A drink together would be fine.

'See you at O'Grady's then, nine-ish.'

He smiled his slow pedantic smile.

Chapter Four

'So how come I didn't hear from you for years?' Ciara asked, vivaciously talkative after a few drinks. She spoke loudly so that she could be heard above the bustle of O'Grady's pub. If she'd been fully sober she would have remembered not to ask that question.

If she'd been fully sober she wouldn't have cared.

It's amazing the things that matter after a couple of drinks.

John blinked and looked hesitant. Drink didn't seem to make him more talkative. His cheeks had a slightly higher colour but that was the only indication that he had spent the last hour and a half in a pub. And he didn't have the appearance of a man who was about to present a ready answer.

Instead he sighed.

It had been so long since Ciara had seen him that she had forgotten about this habit. John was one of the world's sighers. If he was presented with a question he didn't readily want to answer (usually anything in the emotional field), he would sigh. First he would take a little break as though to distance himself from the question, then he would sigh. Ciara felt a warm wave of familiarity wash over her, though actually it wasn't so much warm as tepid. Along with this familiarity but partially screened by a veil of alcohol she caught sight of Annoyance. He was doing a little moonlit dance in his grass skirt, earlobes weighed down with the bones of previous victims as in the distance rhythmic drumbeats echoed through the forest.

Ciara shook the image aside and instinctively made up answers for John. She couldn't bear these long silences. She presented him with a tick-the-appropriate-box selection.

'Were you busy getting on with your career? Or did you decide that it wasn't worth the bother? Or did we just grow out of one another? Was that it?' She waited for a nod or a headshake, mental Biro poised to tick.

John didn't say anything. He just sighed again. The tempo of the Annoyance drums increased almost to frenzy but Ciara ignored them. The man was obviously thinking deeply and with feeling. She waited, forcing herself not to make up more multiple-choice options. Eventually he responded.

'You told me you were in love with somebody else, do you not remember?'

Ciara looked at him blankly. She had no memory of telling him that she was in love. She'd told him that she was seeing somebody but she'd never said she was in love, had she? John must have assumed, quite rightly as it happened, that she had been in love with Gary. And John wasn't finished; he'd obviously taken what she had said at the time very seriously indeed. And seemingly still did.

'You don't think I'd have stopped contacting you if it hadn't been for that, do you?'

Ciara was taken aback by the earnestness of his last remark. It hadn't bothered her either way when he didn't contact her anymore. All friendships change and move on, no matter what their origin.

'I mean, I thought you were going to marry that guy.'

Ciara laughed to cover up her unease.

'Marry him? Are you joking? He was a nice guy but not the one for me. You know, sometimes you have to hang around with someone for a while to find that out. It would never have worked.' Ciara finished with more emphasis than she'd intended, to disguise her feelings. She'd had every intention of marrying 'the guy'. Would have at the drop of a hat, only Gary was already married!

But she wasn't going to tell John that.

She reasoned that strictly speaking she wasn't lying. She had, after all, said that it would never have worked and now she knew this was true.

'So that's all over now then, is it?'

Ciara jerked back from Gary-land to the present. She'd almost lost track of what John was saying but he was looking at her intently, obviously expecting an answer.

'Yeah. Well finished,' she said with conviction, secretly wondering how they had suddenly got on to all this personal stuff. But by now she was drawn into it and couldn't resist continuing. 'Why?'

She hadn't wanted to ask that, it just sort of slipped out and she couldn't take it back now. John paused and sighed. The Annoyance drums sounded again in the distance. Ciara wished she could take her 'why' and his sigh, stuff them in a sack and throw them off Killiney Hill so that they drowned in the Irish Sea – lost forever in its watery embrace.

Fat chance of that!

She watched and waited as John pensively ran his fingers up and down his glass, making little avenues in the condensation.

Ciara stared at his hands. Another thing she'd forgotten was how short his fingers were. He had the soft indoor hands you would expect of an accountant but John's hands were not remarkable for that. What they were remarkable for was their size: they were very small. They were also oddly shaped as his fingers were noticeably shorter than his palms. His hands were odd little things, strangely out of place on his bulky body. Ciara had always noticed that they were somewhat small but when John was slimmer it hadn't been as obvious.

Now, taking the glass firmly in his hand, he glanced up at her with a tortured expression in his eyes. Ciara, taking this as an indication that he was about to speak, tore her gaze away from his hands.

'I always felt that we'd never really finished, you know, never really sorted out if we could have made something of our relationship . . .'

'Made something? How do you mean? In what way?' Ciara had a strong suspicion that she knew what he was talking about but decided to let him spell it out more clearly.

John seemed unsure how to continue or indeed whether he should. Uncertainty flickered in his hazel-green eyes. He took a deep breath and hit a neutral note.

'All I'm saying is that if you're not seeing anyone, there might be no harm in you and me spending some time together, like we used to.'

Ciara sensed there was more to come because now there was no doubt about it: John Murphy was asking her to go out with him! He, warming to his subject now, continued in a stronger vein.

'I mean, it's not like we don't know each other quite well and we've always got on, haven't we?'

Ciara knew that if she didn't stop him he was just going to keep on rationalising until they both became embarrassed. Talk about taking a pragmatic approach to asking someone out! All the same it did strike her that at nearly twenty-eight maybe it was time to accept the pragmatic approach. Maybe the romance did go out of things a bit and it was time to be more realistic.

'Yes, of course John, I mean, you're back in Dublin now and I live here as well so we're bound to see each other, especially if I take this job,' she answered quickly, eager to change the subject now so that she could have a little time to think about this new development. John, relief in his voice, followed her lead.

'So you will take it then?' A new light came into his eyes.

Ciara nodded and smiled, deciding that maybe there would be no harm in opening up to him a little. It might make him feel less resentful about her not having jumped immediately at the chance of going out with him.

'To be honest, if I don't find a way of getting out of living with my mother there will be a homicide on the Southside.'

He laughed and nodded sympathetically.

'I know exactly how you feel, it's the same for me. I'm staying with my mother until my house is ready and I'm already on the verge of putting her in a home. I feel like I'm fifteen again. When I'm out I even find myself looking at my watch at about ten o' clock, thinking that I should be heading home or I'll get given out to. Some things never change!'

Ciara chuckled.

'But your mother was never like that. I mean, you were always home on time and did your study and all that, you were a goodie-goodie,' she teased him, glad that the pressure was off. It was as though they had never grown up, as though they were back in the days of being teenagers together when the most consuming worry was achieving as much freedom as possible without being found out by their parents.

'Yeah, OK, so she wasn't quite as bad as yours but she was still pretty strict. I just didn't admit it because it wouldn't have been cool.' John sounded to be in deadly earnest, determined to be perceived, even at this late stage, as a normal teenager.

Ciara went into hysterics at this and he beamed, flattered that she should find what he'd said so funny.

What she was really laughing at, though for once she had the tact not to share it, was the idea that John had ever been cool when they were teenagers. He had been too sensible and stable for that. He'd never smoked cigarettes (never mind shown an interest in anything stronger) or worn a tatty leather jacket. If Ciara's memory served her correctly he never even wore jeans, and back then there was no street cred without jeans!

And he always got As in his exams.

And he knew that when he grew up he was going to be an accountant.

And she had never once heard him curse.

Ciara was ashamed to admit that at school, although she'd loved John's stability and the fact that he obviously adored her, she'd sometimes had qualms about his being 'uncool'. As a result of this and her constant need for 'drama', their going out was always 'off' or 'just back on'. This emotional yo-yoing became the main excitement of the relationship.

Now of course that wasn't an issue. John was a successful thirty year old who dressed expensively and wasn't an embarrassment in public. What more could any girl ask?

She stopped laughing and as soon as she did John became serious. Ciara was afraid that he was going to harp back to the practical arrangements for their going out. But this wasn't the case. Instead he said, 'I think I know a way for you to get out of home. I'd ask you to stay with me except it would be hell with my mother. A friend of mine knows a two-bedroomed place with only one person living in it, if you don't mind sharing?'

Mind sharing? What did he think she was doing at the moment if not 'sharing'!

'No, I wouldn't mind at all, that sounds great! It would be just until I get things together for my own place.'

'Of course. And it's probably rent-free, this guy owes me a favour.' John smiled. Raising his glass, he swallowed the last of his drink. 'Can I give you a lift home?'

'Sure,' Ciara answered gratefully, trying to disguise her delight at the prospect of a rent-free place to live and a lift home as well. She'd walked to the pub as it was only a short distance from her mother's house. However while they were there it had started to rain and for the last hour people had been pushing in at the door shaking themselves like dogs after a swim and standing about with moisture rising from them. Those unfortunate enough to have forgotten their raincoats stood in abject misery, their wet hair dripping on to their shoulders until a couple of drinks made them forget their dampness.

When they got to the door John turned to Ciara and said, 'Look, why don't you stay here and I'll bring the car around?'

He had always been thoughtful like that: opening doors, never allowing a girl to walk home on her own, always at the ready to hold a coat at the end of an evening, and he had always remembered her birthday. Every year without fail he would send her a flowery sentiment in his neat handwriting. Well, that is, he'd sent her a birthday card until he had decided to boycott her because she had said she was seeing somebody else.

Ciara hadn't missed the cards when he stopped sending them because by then her life was full of Gary.

While she waited in the draughty porch for John to fetch the car she allowed herself to think about going out with him again.

She was surprised to discover that she quite liked the idea.

She did not, however, feel as she usually would at the beginning of an affair. Ciara called them 'affairs' because that's what all relationships were at the beginning until they become recognisable in the eyes of the world as 'relationships'.

Usually at the beginning she would be consumed by a huge, almost frighteningly huge, physical desire which would scrape at the walls of her sanity until she let it in. Then, like the monster that it was, it would take over all rationality and drive her into compromising situations which might or might not work out to her advantage.

In this instance, though, she was calmly weighing the pros and cons. Perhaps this was what happened when you reached the last straight stretch to thirty. Or maybe she'd realised that at a certain age it was time to avoid that roller-coaster of emotions that usually led up to her relationships. Maybe she didn't want any more broken promises, any more living in panicked expectation, any more dreaming that Mr Right, Mr Perfect, would just sail into her life accompanied by heart palpitations and breathlessness.

It struck Ciara that maybe compromise was the way forward, and maybe what she was experiencing now was her first step towards that.

Maybe her mother was right; perhaps John was The One.

By the time he dropped her off at her house it had stopped raining.

'Thanks, John.' Ciara turned to smile at him in the yellow light from the street lamps. 'I'll see you tomorrow then.'

Instead of answering he reached out and caught her hand. Ciara was surprised by this move as John had never being very tactile. She looked from her hand to his face just as he leaned towards her and kissed her on the lips.

Now Ciara really was surprised. She was even more surprised by her own reaction. She hadn't considered this scenario but she didn't move away or scream or anything. Neither did she kiss him back. That would have required more decisiveness than she was capable of at that time of night. Eventually John sat back, pushing his glasses on to the bridge of his nose and looking at her stunned expression.

'That was nice,' he said as though he had just eaten a portion of a cake baked by Ciara and was complimenting her on it. She nodded.

'Thanks.'

Ciara couldn't believe she'd said that. It was as though she *had* baked a cake! No brownie points for situation-handling skills!

There was a big silence gathering around her little expression of gratitude. It jostled for space with any conversation that might even have thought of getting a look in. Ciara was afraid that John was going to get into a sighing tirade as punishment for her not returning his kiss.

'I'd better go in, my mother will be getting worried about who's outside with the engine running. I'll see you tomorrow, OK?'

She got out quickly, closing the door and turning to wave briefly as his car pulled away. She let herself quietly into the house.

'Did you have a nice evening, Ciara?'

She started. Mrs Bowe had come out of the front room as Ciara was closing the front door behind her. She eyed her mother suspiciously; she never went into the front room in the evening. Ciara concluded there could be only one reason for her having done so tonight: she had been spying!

'Well, you tell me, Mum, you've just watched the end of it through the window,' Ciara burst out defiantly, finally releasing the emotion generated by that kiss.

Indignation and anger battled for dominance on her mother's face.

'Excuse me, Ciara, I dinnae think that's any way to talk to me. I'll go into whatever room I like in my own house, with no comment from you.'

Mrs Bowe's accent became very pronounced as she moved up a gear to outright anger.

'Not that it's any of your business but I was getting my knitting. I promised your sister I'd have that hat finished for wee Joseph's birthday.'

She waved a mass of wool and needles at Ciara as irrefutable proof of her own innocence. Then, with a quick intake of breath, moved on to biblical self-justification.

'"How could you address me in such a manner? Do you not take heed? Honour thy father and mother as the Lord God hath commanded thee."'

This was her mother's favourite chorus when it came to keeping her daughters in line. Ciara, having vented her anger with her original outburst, reasoned that she had no proof that her mother had been looking out the window and stepped in to appease her.

'Sorry, Mum, really I am. I'm just nervous about starting this job tomorrow, you know?'

She knew her mother wouldn't be able to resist that one. She couldn't stay in a huff once she knew Ciara was going to do what she wanted.

Ciara was right. Mrs Bowe's face cleared instantly.

'Really? Oh, that's wonderful.'

While they were on the subject of moving on Ciara decided that this might be the best time to slip in the fact that she'd be doing a bit of physical moving on as well.

'Um – John's also told me about a flat a friend of his has that I can probably move into.'

Her mother looked taken aback, but Ciara could tell that because John was offering it she wouldn't make a fuss. Ciara continued on to the excuse for leaving she'd rehearsed.

'It will be so much nearer work, Mum. I mean, you know, advertising. I'll probably be working all hours so it'll be handier if I'm in town.'

She wondered why a nearly twenty-eight-year-old adult was making excuses to her mother because she wanted to move out of home. It was absurd!

Still, those were the rules. The last time she'd moved out it had been the same except then she'd been much younger.

In the end Mrs Bowe gave in quite easily – surprisingly easily for a woman who was giving up her only remaining child. Again. Ciara supposed that it was perfectly natural for a parent always to view their offspring as being in some way dependent, still controllable.

Well, actually, she was just thinking about her parent, as she had no experience of being anybody else's child.

'So I suppose you'll be going next week then?' Her mother no doubt planned on doing a lot of baking to send with her and needed to calculate when to start.

This was the hard bit.

'Actually, no, Mum. I'll be moving tomorrow. I mean, I'm starting work then, and it'll just be easier if I don't have to travel too far.'

Mrs Bowe looked stunned, then resigned. 'Well, I suppose that if John says . . .'

'Yeah, he does, it's fine. Look, I have to get up really early to pack the car and stuff, so goodnight.' She had moved towards the stairs.

'You know, you could do worse than John, especially at your age . . .'

Ciara swung around on the bottom step and stared speechlessly at her. Mothers were supposed to support you in your hour of crisis, not present you with mating ultimatums. And she wasn't yet finished. Assured of Ciara's attention her mother continued, 'He's doing very well for himself, always has done. And whatever happened when you were younger . . . you know, you cannae be a dreamer all your life.'

Ciara opened her mouth to say something, anything, but her mother raised a hand to prevent her.

'Now I know you'll tell me it's none of my business, but it is really. And it's obvious he likes you which is quite decent of him under the circumstances . . .'

'What?' Ciara was at a loss for further words.

'Well, your behaviour. Cohabiting with that man when you knew nothing could come of such an abomination. And as if that wasnae bad enough, he was a married man too. He got what he wanted and now . . . well, it makes you nae more than a harlot. I ne'er told Mrs Murphy about it but now that he's back John's bound to find out. What will he think?'

'Mum!' Ciara was indignant but still having difficulty being more than monosyllabic. She wasn't astonished by such sentiments as she knew all of them by heart. What she was astounded at was her mother's sudden willingness to mention the unmentionable, to speak about her actually having lived with Gary!

All the near-Victorian morality of her childhood reached out of its dark vault to take hold of her, slimy and stinking, its grasping bony fingers trying to choke out of her all the progress she'd made since leaving home.

Ciara took a deep breath. 'Let's just leave it, Mum, shall we?'

Her mother shook her head in the gesture of a doctor to a dying patient and moved towards the kitchen. She was aware that at some point soon her daughter would become more articulate and she wanted to be out of the way.

'You may just leave it too long. There willnae always be men lining up to kiss you goodnight or indulge in whatever fornication was going on in that car just now, you know.'

With that she gently but deftly closed the kitchen door.

Ciara clutched the banister in rage.

Her mother *had* been watching out the window!

She *had* been spying, gleefully rubbing her hands together at the intimacy she'd seen in John's car.

Ciara wanted to run into the kitchen and try to cast a spell on her mother. She would turn her into a toad or a cormorant, anything that would live in cold watery places for the rest of its days and never come indoors to bother its daughter again.

Ciara didn't go into the kitchen.

And she didn't cast a spell.

Instead she bit her tongue and went upstairs to her room.

* * *

Dressed as a rabbit, her foot trapped under a piece of building equipment, afraid to call out in case she was the victim of a murder attempt, did nothing to calm Ciara.

Furious at her predicament, she renewed her efforts to release the rabbit's paw from under the generator.

However, even though she used all her strength, nothing moved because the machine was wedged tightly against the wall. In her struggle Ciara lost her balance and toppled backwards, landing on her fluffy and none-too-comfortable-to-sit-on tail.

She lost her view of the world as the peephole in the neck of the costume was dislodged. For a moment she sat in darkness, considering whether or not she should take the head off. However, as it was bitterly cold and pouring with rain, she decided it would be much better simply to be a wet rabbit rather than, when she put the head back on, a wet person inside a wet rabbit.

Ciara pulled off her paws and readjusted her head. Now she could see the world again and there was still nobody about to help release her. There was no sound from the building site, either. There had never been any sound from the building site; it was as though the generator had just fallen from the sky. Things were so quiet that she was beginning to suspect that maybe it hadn't been a murder attempt after all. On the other hand she could think of no reasonable explanation for the generator having fallen off the scaffolding just when she was standing underneath.

Fate wasn't a consideration for Ciara. Nor was bad luck. There could be only one explanation: somebody *was* trying to kill her!

Chapter Five

'I'm bleedin' telling you, the genny's down there. Look at it.'

'It can't be fuckin' down there, we left it up here before we went for breakfast.'

'Yeah? Well, Mr We-Don't-Need-Security-Mary-Street's-Very-Quiet, take a look.'

'Jesus, Anto, you're right! How'd it get down there? Hey, hang on, there's a fuckin' rabbit havin' a go at it. See him? See him? He's fuckin' stealin' it. Where's the fuckin' ladder ...'

Large lumps of dried cement were falling on Ciara's paws as she struggled panic-stricken with the generator. The deluge increased as the two men on the scaffolding shuffled about to get a better view of what was going on below them.

Ciara needed to get out of there. Even if whoever it was who had tried to kill her hadn't succeeded in dropping the generator on her, these two might well lynch her for theft or vandalism or something. She turned back to the machine and started to push again. This time it moved but not because she'd pushed it. The force was coming from the other side. She hurriedly pulled her foot free and swung around to see what was happening at the far side of the machine.

Standing three paces away from her, allowing the generator to crash back on to the pavement, was another rabbit. He was identical in every way to Ciara except that he was wearing a pink bow. He was breathing heavily from the struggle and gesturing to attract her attention. As soon as he was sure she had noticed him he started to run down the street, beckoning furiously to her to follow.

Ciara hesitated for a moment.

Her inclination was to obey but at the same time she felt very foolish about this *Alice in Wonderland* situation. Why on earth should she follow a complete stranger, especially one whose face she couldn't even see?

Suddenly just above her she heard a loud shout. Looking up, she saw the sturdy, mud-splattered boots of a construction worker scrambling down the last few rungs of a hastily placed ladder.

'Stay where you are 'til I bust you, you bleedin' vandal, you!'

Ciara, forgetting her hesitation, picked up her large saggy stomach and, turning her feet well out so that she wouldn't fall over the giant paws, shambled off down the street after the pink-bowed rabbit. She followed him the length of three streets until she was unable to run anymore. A combination of not having exercised for two weeks and the well-insulated suit guaranteed that within seconds she was breathless and badly overheated. As they rounded on to the quays she stopped to remove the head of her costume. She had to practically put her own head between her legs to heave it off. When it finally gave way she stood upright. The other rabbit, having stopped while she was doing this, suddenly turned and sprinted down the street.

And this time he wasn't looking back to check that she was following. It was as though when he saw who she was, he had run away.

'Hey, hang on, where're you going? Come back.' Ciara raised her voice and shouted again: 'Come back!'

But the pink-bowed rabbit didn't stop. Instead it disappeared around the end of the street in a flurry of tail and paws and was gone.

She leaned back against the wall, panting, her rabbit's head clutched by her side. Those passers-by not cut off from the world by their umbrellas smiled at the spectacle: a red-faced woman, her head crowned by a neat but very flat dark bob protruding out of a shuddering rabbit costume, panting and gasping for air.

Ciara, had she noticed, wouldn't have seen the humour.

She had started this job an hour before and had already lost count of the number of times she'd wished she hadn't! Distributing little cardboard cut-outs of mobile phones to promote a new phone company did not live up to the job in 'advertising' that she had imagined. In fact Ciara wouldn't have described what she was doing as a 'job'. It was more a performance, pantomime, a circus act requiring no skill or training.

And she was identityless, cocooned in layers of fur and padding inside a costume which added a foot to her height and made her walk as though she had giant cardboard boxes on her feet.

As if that wasn't bad enough she just knew the rabbit head was ruining her hair!

This morning when she'd turned up for work she had thought she was coming to a place where she would be an integral part of a team marketing a new and innovative telephone idea, the Easi-tel T2.

The T2 was a very small and discreet mobile phone. It was three inches high and its face contained only a small rectangular display screen and one large round fluorescent button. At any rate the promotional models had the fluorescent button. The publicity declared that the product also came in executive colours which Ciara presumed to mean no colours at all like grey or dark blue.

Easi-tel's T2 had one large button on the front because it only took incoming calls. This phone was being promoted as 'the ultimate toy for the busy-on-the-move executive'. The way to 'always be available for those important calls'. The 'quality line for quality time!'

It promised massive improvements in your business because with the T2 you could confidently say, 'I'm always here for you'.

By facilitating incoming calls only this phone would free up the owner's usual phone and ensure that a special client need not be put on hold or greeted by an answering machine. It was advertised as being a private number given only to the 'special' people in your life who might need to make urgent contact with you.

Ciara figured that the T2 had endless possibilities. For example, a guy goes on a date with another woman and hasn't told his girlfriend. However as he knows she might ring, he has provided her with his T2 number. She is the only person with this number so when the phone does ring he can excuse himself, go and stand in the noisy street pleading his car has broken down and that he's having difficulty getting a taxi but he'll be home soon . . . honest, dear.

The T2 could also be the ideal device for companies who wanted to be able to contact an employee. They needn't issue the phone number to anyone, including said employee. This way there would be no prolonged incoming gossip calls.

This employee-employer arrangement had its advantages for the employee as well. For instance the woman who's taken the afternoon off to get her hair done for a hot date that evening but has told the boss she's gone to visit her oh-so-sick mother in hospital. If the T2 rings she knows it's work so gets the hair salon to turn off everything except the gently humming overhead dryer. Switching this on and off rhythmically throughout the call she can explain to the employer that it is the sound of her mother's respirator, poor aged, sick woman.

Ciara of course had no such use for the T2 that was in her front pouch. In fact she had no use for it at all. What was the point in carrying about a telecommunications gadget if she couldn't use it to communicate?

Easi-tel's T2 was supposed to appeal because the only cost incurred was a basic unit fee. It was a no-commitment, no-long-term-devotion relationship. The perfect pitch for a decade with so many zeros in it.

And, of course, Easi-tel had a slogan. It went: 'If you want to rabbit on, go EASI.'

Hence the rabbit costume advertising!

They had even put the slogan to music for their radio and television campaign. It was the *Ghost Busters* theme with different lyrics, the refrain of which was 'GO EASI' instead of 'GHOST BUSTERS'. The animated TV commercial had the white rabbit from *Alice in Wonderland* as its central character, pulling a T2 out of his pocket instead of a watch.

Ciara was now dressed as that white rabbit. Inside the furry pouch of her costume, along with her T2 phone and now her paws, were the advertising flyers she was supposed to hand to passers-by on their way to work.

So far, for obvious reasons, she hadn't handed out any.

And she didn't want to hand out any . . . ever.

All the same, now that she was on the street in costume and unfettered by any construction equipment it seemed only reasonable she should do her job. Besides she was on early lunch so she had another hour to go before she could legitimately take a break. Maybe when she got back to the shop she'd find out who the other rabbit was. After all he must be working nearby to have passed her and come to the rescue.

Ciara shook some of the rain from her hair and, pulling on her head, set off back to Mary Street. The rain had eased now and there were more people about. She fished her fur paws out of her front pouch and, slipping her cold hands into their snug warmth, proceeded to distribute the flyers.

'You're in very early.'

Gráinne looked at her watch and spoke sharply to Ciara who was trying to slip unnoticed into the back of the shop to take her lunch break.

'Am I?'

Ciara knew that she was nearly four minutes early but didn't expect to be reprimanded for it. Besides 'early' was a bit of an exaggeration!

She felt like a teenager who'd been caught coming back late to class after a forbidden cigarette at the back of the playing pitch. Of course at school the teacher had a good chance of being about twenty years older than her while the girl who had just spoken to Ciara didn't look a day over twenty-one.

And she was plain.

Ciara hated thinking this about anybody but with Gráinne she didn't just want to think it, she wanted to shout it loudly to everyone. From the moment Ciara had arrived that morning Gráinne had been cutting and critical, sarcastic and superior. Her thin lips were set in a hard line and her short hair and stocky body gave her a masculine, implacable air. Even before she opened her mouth her stance was that of a bully and she had already demonstrated all the qualities Ciara hated in a boss.

Gráinne managed the Easi-tel shop. She also managed the rabbits or 'promoters' as they were officially called. She ruled with a clinical efficiency and sharpness that prompted all her workers to do exactly what they were told, when they were told.

As soon as Gráinne confronted her everybody behind the counter who wasn't dealing with a customer stared at Ciara. Within seconds those dealing with customers and the customers themselves were also staring at her. Ciara shifted uneasily on her giant feet.

Gráinne, arms folded, raised an eyebrow in a 'Well, what have you got to say for yourself?' way. Ciara pretended to peep at her watch by struggling with the sleeve of her costume. Hoping that she could confirm her innocence by appearing oblivious to the time, she gasped and opened her eyes wide with surprise.

'Oh, so I am,' she said with a short laugh to cover her discomfiture. Gráinne continued to stare at her, as did everybody else in the shop. They were all waiting for the showdown.

'I'll go back five minutes early. Start at twenty-five past.' Ciara made her tone contrite. She was frantic now to stop everyone staring.

Gráinne let that little offering hang in the air for a

moment then inhaled loudly, shaking her head slowly like a stern parent.

'I suppose as it is your first day ... But I don't want it to happen again. I mean, if everybody just waltzed in and out of here whenever they liked we wouldn't have any sort of business, would we?'

She looked around the shop for the right response and was rewarded with a chorus of mumbles. Even the customers appeared to join in, adding their right-eous agreement with that of the staff. Ciara wished the marble-effect lino tiling would swallow her up. She screwed her mouth into a weak smile and attempted to finish her journey to the staffroom, haven for scolded rabbits.

She'd nearly reached the promised land when Gráinne's voice came loudly from behind her. 'Excuse me.' Ciara, assuming Gráinne was talking to her, decided nevertheless that as she was so near the door she could probably safely ignore the note of command. This was a miscalculation. Gráinne's voice grew louder.

'Excuse me – *you*. I'm speaking to you!'

Ciara turned around slowly.

'Me?'

'Yes, you, what's your name? I can't seem to remember it.'

'Ciara Bowe.'

'Yes, that's right, Ciara. Well, what are you doing in a blue-bowed costume?'

Ciara stared at her blankly, thinking, this must be a trick question.

'I ... uh ... I ...'

The whole shop waited for her reply.

'It's the one I was given this morning.'

Gráinne tilted her head sideways and spoke even more loudly.

'Oh, I don't think so, Ciara. I gave out the costumes and I most certainly did not give you a head with a blue bow.'

Ciara knew this statement begged a response but she wasn't going to answer. She remembered now she had been given a different head but it had smelled so badly that she'd swapped it for another on the way out. She hadn't known that their bows were colour-coded but didn't want to have to explain.

She shrugged.

Gráinne sighed.

'The ones with the blue bows are for the guys, the pink are for the girls. They're different sizes.'

Ciara, having always had an unreasonably large head, thought this system lacked logic but it didn't seem like a good time to bring that up.

Gráinne wasn't finished.

'I had to give a pink one to Dimitri this morning. Neither of us was very pleased about it. He's in the same area as you, have you seen him?'

Ciara shook her head.

She didn't feel inclined to share her fears about the attempted murder with Gráinne nor about the strange rabbit who had disappeared into the distance as soon as she'd taken off her head. At least now she could assume the strange rabbit was Dimitri.

'What, you didn't see him?' Gráinne moved closer. Even her short hair seemed to be standing up in little question marks. The onlookers started to lose interest as soon as the attention moved away from Ciara. They could sense the danger had passed, there would be no killing now.

Ciara shook her head again.

'Right. We'll see about that! You're always supposed to be within a street of each other so that the girls are never completely on their own in case of trouble. He should have been within sight of you all morning. You're sure you didn't see him?'

'No, I didn't see anyone else giving out leaflets this morning.' Ciara evaded the truth.

'Well, I can guarantee you there will be someone different on with you this afternoon. Now go and have your break, I'll sort out your head before you go back on the street.'

If only!

Ciara trailed her feet glumly into the staffroom.

She felt bad about getting the pink-bowed rabbit into trouble. After all, if it hadn't been for him she would probably be hanging upside down from a piece of scaffolding now with large boot marks all over her fur. He *had* looked after her; he just hadn't stayed around afterwards. It was the rescue equivalent of a one-night stand: one close intimate moment and then without so much as a backward glance he was gone forever.

Ciara turned on the kettle and rummaged in her bag for her lunch. When she found it the smell and feel of the heavy little package reminded her of the lunch her mother used to give her for school. All the other girls had small trim sandwiches made with sliced pan and a piece of cake or a packet of crisps. Ciara's clumsy home-sliced wedges on the other hand were a constant embarrassment to her so she used to pretend she had no lunch. The food would lie squashed at the bottom of her schoolbag, festering into soft pungent repulsiveness until she would take it out on the way home and throw it in the bin.

That morning, before she'd left her mother's house, she had found a package on the kitchen table beside a note which read, 'Better take this in case no dinner'.

Her mother seemed to be under the impression that she was heading off into a wasteland with no shops instead of going to work in the middle of town. The fact was, however, that now Ciara was very relieved to have food with her as it saved her from having to go back through the shop to buy something.

Relieved, that is, until she opened it. She might have known! It was as though she had reverted twenty years to those school lunches. Gone straight back to opening her mother's doorstep sandwiches. Only to Ciara the adult it wasn't the way they looked so much as the fact that she knew these creations were a composite of all that is most fattening in the world. Great big chunks of white bread lolled on the greaseproof wrapping, exposing crispy crusts in a wanton fashion, convinced of their irresistible allure.

Ciara cringed. Bread was a big no-no, she never ate it if at all possible. Its very presence even in a bread shop window screamed, 'You'll get so fat if you even think about me!'

If she needed a bread 'thing' she ate diet crispbreads or rice cakes. Her mother knew that! But it wasn't just the bread. Inside all her mother's sandwiches lay at least a quarter inch of butter on *each* slice of bread. On top of this she would liberally smear most of a jar of mayonnaise. This and all other creamy dressings were also a no-no in Ciara's lite-figure maintenance.

In between all those calories her mother had put egg. Hard-boiled egg. She always put hard-boiled egg in her sandwiches. As a child Ciara had assumed she did this because she was from Eigg. But then she'd also assumed that the Island of Eigg rose from the sea, a white slippery dome filled with the sulphurous smell of cold hard-boiled eggs. The same smell that was now gleefully permeating the staffroom, oozing into cupboards and under chairs, determined to disgrace its liberator.

Ciara stepped back and looked hungrily but guiltily at the proposed meal. It was always the same with her mother. No matter how many times you told her you didn't eat butter she would still pile it on to and into everything.

Ciara grimaced and bit hungrily into one of the egg sandwiches. Everything in her revolted against the fat content while her tastebuds went into a riot of jubilation at the flavour. She carefully rewrapped the rest and threw the package in the bin. She reasoned that if she left it on the table, chances were she would eventually break into it and quadruple her fat consumption. If it was in the bin it was unlikely she would lose her resolve and scramble about after it. Slowly she took another bite of her permitted portion of egg sandwich.

Just then another rabbit came into the room, struggling to remove its head. Ciara stared and held her breath because around its neck the rabbit wore a pink bow! What if this was Dimitri? She wouldn't of course recognise him but if she was to go by what Gráinne had said he should be the only man wearing pink that day.

But it wasn't him. When the head finally came off a tousle-haired young woman was revealed. At first she didn't notice Ciara as she busily loosened the fur around her neck.

'Hiya.' Ciara spoke through a mouthful of sandwich.

The woman jumped in surprise and turned fearfully towards her.

'Hallo,' she said, a rich foreign accent curling the word around her tongue. Her dark eyes lost their fear and hardened into suspicion. She didn't smile, and as soon as she had made eye contact looked away and busied herself putting water in the kettle.

Ciara, a little put off by her unfriendliness, decided that she was probably just shy. She couldn't be blamed for being rude. If her morning had been half as bad as Ciara's own she was entitled to be bad-tempered.

'Pissy day to be out on the street, isn't it?' Ciara spoke conversationally as though the other had been open and friendly.

The dark-eyed woman half-turned and looked at her blankly. Ciara thought that she might not have heard her over the noise of the kettle.

'I said, pissy day to be out on the street, isn't it?' Ciara raised her voice to what she thought was an appropriate level. The young woman frowned and shrugged and turned back to the kettle. Ciara stared at her back, trying to work out why she was getting no answer. It couldn't be the volume so it must be that she didn't understand Ciara's colloquial expression.

'I'm just saying that it is very wet today, you know, the weather.' Ciara spoke very slowly and loudly, enunciating each word perfectly.

For a moment the woman didn't respond. She stood still, her back rigid in its costume, her head bowed. Ciara was just about to repeat the sentence again when the woman swung around and with what appeared to be a cross between an indignant and a dismissive jerk of her head issued a mid-length sentence of aggressively guttural foreign speech. Then she paused and with another jerk of her head, this time for emphasis, she repeated the last three words and turned away.

Ciara was dismayed.

She had no idea what the woman had said but had no doubt that it was unfriendly. From a misspent youth passed watching Bond movies Ciara guessed that the woman was speaking Russian, although she was well aware that what she called Russian could be any one of tens of Eastern European languages.

She had a distinct feeling that she wasn't about to find out which one this woman had just spoken. Ciara put the last piece of her sandwich into her mouth and wondered if everybody on this job was downright unfriendly. In mid-thought the door burst open and Gráinne strode in. The foreign woman turned around but as soon as she saw Gráinne she lowered her eyes and became motionless.

'Right, so ... ah ... Ciara, we'd better sort you out,' Gráinne barked.

Ciara looked at her blankly, wondering how she intended to do that. Gráinne however was in no doubt.

'The best thing would be if you take Anna's head,' she nodded in the direction of the silent unfriendly woman, 'and when more of the promoters come in at quarter to twelve we'll be able to sort it out. OK?'

Gráinne snatched the rabbit's head from the counter beside Anna and presented it to Ciara. Anna, meanwhile, remained motionless, her eyes downturned. Gráinne didn't seem in the least disturbed by her behaviour.

'Your next break is at three-thirty and here are some more flyers. How many do you have left from this morning?'

Ciara shrugged. She didn't want to have to admit to not knowing or indeed caring. All the same she knew she had a lot left. She reached into her pouch, selecting about half of the flyers, and showed them to Gráinne.

'Hmmm, you'll have to do better than that, you know,

you should really be getting rid of all the flyers I give you. Dense coverage is the name of the game here.'

Ciara nodded as it seemed the appropriate thing to do and thought that some gutter would be getting very 'dense coverage' as soon as she was out of sight of the shop.

'Have you any questions?' Gráinne's flow of speech never stopped.

'No.' Ciara shook her head.

'Right, well, somebody will be in the same area as you by midday but I don't want any gossiping going on. You're covering separate streets so you should never meet unless there's some sort of emergency, OK?'

Ciara nodded, took the head from Gráinne's out-stretched hands, mumbled ''Bye' and moved towards the door. When she got there she glanced back into the room and, raising her voice, said, ''Bye, Anna.' Anna jerked her head up for a moment but on catching Gráinne's eye immediately lowered it again.

Ciara pulled on her new head, passed through the shop and back on to the street.

Chapter Six

'Ciara ... Ciara! Hey, Ciara!'

John's voice carried to where she was handing out flyers on the crowded early-afternoon street.

'Ciara, hey!'

She swung herself from side to side in an attempt to see through the peephole in her costume. She couldn't locate the speaker.

'Ciara, over here.'

Eventually she spotted him; he was at the end of the street, one foot on the road, the other in his car as he leaned over its roof, waving furiously in her direction. As soon as he was sure she'd noticed him he beckoned to her to come over. Stuffing the remaining flyers into her pouch, she shambled down the street towards him.

John, parked mostly on the kerb, was eager to move.

'Come on, quick, into the car. I'll take you to that flat now and fix you up with a key and things.'

Ciara could think of nothing she would like better than to jump into John's big shiny car and drive away from her job. She was, however, sure that it would be a different story if Gráinne found out.

Shortly after she'd come back from lunch another distributor had started working on the next block. She could see him there, working away, any time she faced that direction. He hadn't gestured or waved when he arrived so Ciara had decided that, like Anna the unfriendly foreigner, he was low on communication skills.

Perhaps this was a requirement for a job in the 'communications' business.

Ciara glanced uneasily at Mr I-never-waved-or-came-to-say-hello blue-bowed rabbit who was taking a pause from his work to stare towards her. He would probably instantly alert Gráinne if she tried to play truant!

'But, John, I can't,' she said through her costume. 'I can't just walk away!'

'Of course you can, what time is your next break?'

'Three-thirty.'

'There, see, it's only one now. You'll be back before anybody even knows you're gone!'

'But if Gráinne ...'

'If Gráinne what? Don't you worry, I'll sort her out for you. Who owns this company anyway?'

Ciara heaved a sigh of relief and proceeded to pull off her exceedingly tight head. She emerged, flat-haired and red-faced, eyes squeezed tightly shut from the effort. John didn't comment on her appearance but the ghost of a smile played on his lips.

'How did you know it was me?' Ciara asked as she opened her eyes.

He laughed. 'That was easy. I found out at the shop what street you were on and you're the only rabbit I could find here!'

'Ha, ha, very funny.'

Ciara eased herself into John's leather-upholstered car. As she did so she looked across the road towards the next block. There, now standing in the middle of the pavement, hands on his hips, was the other rabbit.

There was no doubt he was watching her.

A little stab of Gráinne-panic ran screaming through Ciara's mind. It knocked over the furniture and left all the doors wide open, not caring what it disturbed in its frenzy. She froze for a moment then, with a defiant toss of her head, slammed the car door in the face of her fear.

'Nice car, John!' Ciara squirmed her furry bottom on the leather seat as the car swept away from the kerb. She'd known the night before that it was a nice car but in the dark she hadn't realised just how nice.

'Do you think so?' He smiled. 'I quite like it myself. Of course, it's on the company. I have to confess it wasn't the most economical but then *I'm* the company and I certainly won't be asking any questions.' He chuckled smugly. 'I just really like this S-class Mercedes, and besides there's a certain amount of image at stake here!'

'Has your mother seen it?' Ciara wanted to avoid serious conversations like 'What do you think of the job?' or 'What did you think of that kiss last night?'

Mrs Murphy seemed like a surefire decoy. Besides Ciara knew that her pride in her son was something John loved talking about. There's nothing like The Mammy as a topic of conversation to keep things going with a Mammy's Boy!

His smile spread even wider.

'Oh, yeah. When I'm at home she keeps looking out of the window to watch people noticing the car as they pass. She's even made me promise to park it right in front of the house so that everybody on the estate will see it.'

Mrs Murphy was convinced that both she and her children were far better than the other inhabitants of the working-class housing estate in which she lived, and put a lot of time and energy into proving this.

John's mother lived in the not-so-well-off part of the

Southside suburb in which Ciara's own mother lived. She held Mrs Bowe in high regard because she lived on a prestigious old square. It didn't seem to matter that the Bowe house was a much later addition, tucked humbly away in the corner. Or that it had been inherited, not bought and was now, after years of neglect on a widow's income, very rundown.

'We drove to the shops on Saturday,' John continued. 'She complained that since her hip operation getting in and out of a car this low is difficult. I just told her that this model was even more expensive than the others so she decided to suffer in silence. But enough of that, how did this morning go for you?'

It was unlike John to change topic in the middle of talking about his mother. Ciara was caught unawares.

She'd forgotten just how intense John's interest could be at times and felt an unfamiliar, grateful warmth spread through her. The urge to blurt out that the job was horrible and her life wretched nearly broke free from its have-you-no-self-respect prison. However, following a brief struggle involving some mental violence, she managed to restrain it.

'Yeah, great, it's very interesting meeting all those people,' she said lamely. And then to avoid any further care-about-Ciara questions she launched into the story of the murder attempt.

'Something really strange happened first thing ...'

John looked at her with mild curiosity.

'I think somebody tried to kill me.'

The mild curiosity changed to amused disbelief.

Ciara didn't notice this and went on to recount the events of the morning. John nodded, concentrating on the road as she talked. He only interrupted once and that was towards the end after she had introduced the pink-bowed rabbit.

'And what did this guy say? What did he look like?'

Ciara had, of course, to reveal that she knew nothing about the man who'd run away before she could find anything out.

She hadn't finished when John stopped the car in front of a block of flats. Turning the engine off, and seemingly forgetting what they had been talking about, he announced, 'Here we are, not the prettiest but inside's much better. Come on, I'll show you.'

He closed the car door and moved towards the building. 'There are about ten blocks here. This one, the one you're in, is called McDonagh House.'

Ciara stared in astonishment. The buildings were set in a wasteland of concrete and rubble interspersed with clusters of thriving weeds. In the damp day the whole landscape took on a grey colour, one shade running into the next. Whatever colour these blocks of flats had been painted was long gone and every reachable surface was now covered in graffiti, including the walls of the outdoor walkways that ran along in front of each storey.

Ciara watched a woman with a pushchair work her way down from the third floor. She lugged and carried, pushed and bullied the buggy, a nearly walking child and a three year old. She came into view at the end of each walkway to take the stairs and struggle around the corner on to the next flight.

Ciara got out of the car and threw her paws and mask on to the seat. John glanced at the building and shrugged apologetically.

'Sorry, no lift, and you'll have to excuse some of the neighbours. It's these stairs over here.'

He pulled his coat closed against the cold and ran towards the shelter of the building. Ciara shuffled after him, much to the joy of the three year old.

'Mammy, it's a bunny, it's a bunny!' It was just beginning to dawn on him that the 'bunny' had a woman's head when his mother dragged him away bodily.

Ciara followed John up four flights of stairs on to a walkway which had a number of boarded-up doors and windows. They stopped in front of a faded pink door some yards from the stairwell. He inserted a key in the lock and walked in, yelling, 'Hello.'

As Ciara moved into the hallway behind him a door opened on one side of it and a young woman emerged.

'Ah, you're here!' John spoke to the girl who stood quietly, looking young, startled and extremely pregnant.

'Elena, this is Ciara. Ciara, Elena. Elena, Ciara is going to be staying here for a bit, OK? I'll just show her the other room.'

He walked past the girl who stepped back into her room, looking curiously at Ciara.

'Hi, Elena,' she said, reaching out to shake hands with the now almost cowering girl. Elena didn't say anything but shook her hand in return and nodded her head.

'Come on, Ciara, I'll just show you around quickly and then we'll head back.'

Ciara smiled at Elena and did an eyes-to-the-ceiling, here-we-go-isn't-he-an-awful-man routine before following John into the next room. It was a bedroom. Crammed inside were a double bed and wardrobe, both of them far too big and obviously second hand. Despite this, the room was clean, the walls had been freshly painted and the curtains on the window, though cheap, were new. The floor was made of some sort of polished tiling and as Ciara examined it, John explained, 'These flats have underfloor heating so there's no carpeting but you won't have to worry about getting cold feet!'

He was right. Despite the place being somewhat dated

and unglamorous it was beautifully warm, so warm in fact that Ciara was starting to sweat in her padded costume.

John very quickly showed her the bathroom and the living-room-kitchen area and then guided her towards the door again.

'Oh, and there's no phone.' He sounded apologetic as though he was responsible for its non-connection.

Ciara shrugged. 'One less bill to pay.'

John laughed and nodded, evidently thinking she was joking. Elena was nowhere to be seen as they left the flat.

'Shouldn't we say goodbye?' Ciara asked as they closed the door.

'Oh, don't worry about that. I think she's quite shy. Anyway you'll be seeing her again later when you move your gear in, you can chat then. I wouldn't pay much attention, though, from what my friend says she talks complete nonsense, lies mostly.'

Ciara, wondering if she was about to move in with a weirdo, followed John towards the stairwell.

She remembered the last time she'd moved into a new place to live. It had been the apartment with Gary. Even though he hadn't lived there full-time it had been their place, just the two of them. All that week Ciara had been ecstatic. Not only had she met the man of her dreams but he loved her and was proving this by giving her the nearest thing they could have to marriage: a love nest just for the two of them.

It was a brand new apartment so they were the first people to live in it. This made it even more special.

'I'm afraid it's unfurnished,' Gary had said as he threw open the door. 'But unfurnished or not it's ours and ours alone, no more interruptions from interfering Susans or Marys. Oh, and by the way, there's one other thing . . .'

He turned around and picking Ciara up in his arms carried her ceremoniously across the threshold. And then, and this had been the best bit, while she ran joyfully around the apartment he'd gone to the fridge and taken out a bottle of champagne. Taking a fluted glass from each pocket, he had led Ciara into the empty sitting room and poured the champagne, declaring with a seductive wiggle of his eyebrows, 'And here's a little something I prepared earlier!'

The late-afternoon sun poured in at the window as they sipped champagne and made love on the newly carpeted floor. They were still there as the red-streaked evening sky grew dark behind a city view full of magic.

The next day Ciara bought a bed and moved in. Over the next few weeks she had furnished the apartment, snatching quick late-afternoon shopping rendezvous with Gary when she could get off work early.

Weekend shopping together was out as he spent the

weekends with his family. That was unless he was working somewhere exotic.

In those instances Ciara would fly to wherever he was and snatch whatever time she could with him in his hotel room. This way they'd seen the inside of hotel rooms four times in London, three times in New York, one glorious weekend in Barcelona, another very cold weekend in Paris and a rather dark weekend in Copenhagen.

Even though the flight was the longest, Ciara had preferred New York. No matter how dark it was the city was always bright. No matter how cold it was the city was always warm. And the shops! Ciara could account for most of her credit card bills by checking the number of times Macy's appeared on the debit listing.

Her dream had been to run away with Gary and live in New York in one of those old mid-town apartments, bringing her groceries home in paper bags and buying flowers on street corners. As that was a bit unrealistic she had wished she and Gary could live in their apartment in Dublin without his marriage being an issue. This couldn't happen either. Gary had a wife and a daughter. He'd said all that was holding the marriage together was their child. She was ten when Ciara and he had met.

'I wish you could meet her, Ciara. She's so trusting, so happy. If I left now she'd think I didn't love her anymore. I just couldn't do that to her.'

Ciara thought she could see tears in his eyes and reached out a comforting hand.

'But you'd still see her. You've got rights, you know. You'd be allowed to see her.' Ciara, totally unfamiliar with this type of scenario, was speaking from information gathered from watching American television courtroom dramas.

She'd really thought he was going to cry when she'd said this. When he spoke Gary's voice held a hint of bitterness.

'I couldn't be reduced to seeing her just at weekends, or worse still every second weekend. Besides everything else it's just the wrong age for a little girl to be without a father figure.'

He was in an awful dilemma. Ciara understood and loved him all the more for his attachment to his daughter. Sympathised with him too, for having to stay in a loveless marriage. She would be patient and supportive. After all, he constantly told her how much he loved her.

She had been patient and supportive for three years.

During that time she had lost most of her old friends. They had grown tired of watching Ciara being traumatised and upset at Christmas and other special occasions because her lover couldn't be with her. They had become exhausted from going out with her to party furiously on the nights Gary was at home with his wife.

They had listened to Ciara justifying her half relationship with a man they rarely met but who seemed to have gobbled up their friend, emotionally and psychologically.

Eventually they had criticised the situation so Ciara stopped calling them. She claimed that they'd drifted away because they were envious that she had found the love of her life while they floundered from one unsuccessful monogamous relationship or one-night stand to the next.

Besides she now had the singles gang from work. They went to all the 'in' places and concentrated on having a good time. Anybody who wanted to do the same was welcome to go along. So on nights when Ciara was Garyless she would drown her loneliness in the midst of her gregarious clubbing workmates.

Until recently it seemed Ciara had lots of friends. Or at any rate lots of people with whom she could go out for a good night's partying.

Until two weeks ago to be exact.

Two weeks ago her well-structured, relatively predictable life had come apart. Actually 'come apart' suggested it had become overcooked and gently fallen off the bone like so much slowly simmered meat. Which wasn't the case.

It was more that her whole world had exploded, detonated, erupted; like an egg in a microwave it had popped into a thousand pieces and splattered itself all over everything within reach. It had made such a mess that rather than clean it up, Ciara had chosen to avoid as much of her former life as possible.

'Ciara, it has central locking, you know! Ciara?'

John was laughing across at her, standing on the other side of his car, hand on the door handle, eyes fixed on the shiny paintwork.

'Sorry.' Ciara smiled and climbed in. She cradled her paws and head on her lap as they left the carpark.

'There's a set of keys in the glove compartment that you can keep for as long as you need them, OK?'

John spoke softly, then he reached out and put his small hand on top of hers.

'OK?' he asked again.

Ciara nodded and remained motionless. She remembered his kiss the night before and the little speech he'd made in the pub.

Maybe going out with John might be the best thing for her. He was kind, attentive, considerate and intelligent, and there was a lot to be said for a man who could maintain his passion for over ten years with little or no encouragement.

Maybe what she craved for and needed was a steady, stable, predictable, high-earning man who would love, honour and obey her for the rest of her life. Or at least as long as she could stand it.

Maybe her mother was right after all!

'How about we go for something to eat later?'

John squeezed his hand more tightly around Ciara's, taking his gaze off the road for a second to look at her.

'Oh, I'd love to, John, but I've got to move in. I can't leave my stuff in a carpark all night.'

For a split second Ciara had considered doing just that!

'We can eat later, after you've moved your gear. I'd offer to help but I know I'll be going straight through till eight. What time do you finish?'

'Half-six.'

'Plenty of time. We can meet up at about half-eight. Is that OK with you?'

Ciara nodded gratefully. They were already back on Marlborough Street.

'Now, see, it's half-past two and you're back, I'll bet you weren't even missed.'

'Yeah,' she replied glumly, thinking only of the horror of getting back into her stuffy furry head.

'You got one of the T2s, didn't you?' John yelled as she closed the car door. Ciara paused and thought for a moment. Then, reaching into her pouch and groping about amongst the flyers, she fished out the tiny phone.

'*Voila!*' She waved it towards him.

'I'll give you a ring on it later when I know where we're going, OK? I've got the number. 'Bye.'

John's car purred away and with it heat and sanctuary.

Ciara prepared to put on her head and get back to work but before she did so took a quick glance around. At the far side of the junction, a little way down the street, stood the blue-bowed rabbit. He was in exactly the same position as he had been the last time she'd seen him. He was still watching her. He didn't beckon, didn't gesture, just watched.

Spy! she thought as she pulled on her head.

He'd probably just checked his watch to find out how long she'd been gone! As if it wasn't bad enough having to do a job like this without having to put up with informants as well!

Ciara turned and bad-temperedly stomped her way up the street towards the shops. Things had become even busier since she'd left and most of the crowd seemed to be teenagers in school uniform. They also seemed to be at that particular age when all teenagers are boys, always eating chips and spotty.

And, as Ciara was to discover, they also liked to torment people dressed as rabbits.

It started with a few jokes.

'Hey, Mister!' Their voices were singsong, taunting.

'Hey, Mister, how do you know carrots are good for your eyes?'

A boy with his teeth imprisoned in braces stood defiantly in front of Ciara, hands in his pockets. Behind, egging him on, were his friends, laughing and shoving each other. She turned and faced the other way, shoving flyers into the hands of passers-by, hoping to form a barrier between herself and the gang. Suddenly the boy appeared in front of her again.

'Well, Mister, did you hear me? How do you know carrots are good for your eyes?' Without waiting for an answer he went on, 'Because you never see a rabbit wearing glasses.'

He fell about laughing as though he had just said the funniest thing in the world and behind her Ciara could hear the laughter of his friends. Suddenly she was being pulled backwards and had no choice but to move with the pressure. She could hear even more laughter from behind and guessed that one of the boys had grabbed her tail and was pulling her across the street.

There was nothing she could do.

The costume was so cumbersome she couldn't turn around and didn't have enough balance to resist the pressure. If he kept this up he was going to knock her over.

'Stop, for God's sake. Stop, you little eejit!'

Her muffled voice coming from the suit made the boys laugh even more. Now that he knew she was female, Joke-Boy came up with another one.

'Why are girl rabbits like calculators?' he yelled above the noise. And again without waiting for a response answered himself. 'They multiply really fast!'

There was another outburst of guffaws.

A small crowd had gathered, some of them shaking their heads in disapproval, others laughing at the spectacle.

Nobody stepped in to the rescue.

Just when Ciara thought that she should give up and allow herself to fall over, the pulling stopped. She swung around and saw the boys run away.

Before she realised what was happening a pair of hands grabbed her shoulder.

'Are you all right?' a male voice demanded.

Ciara knew she'd been rescued but she couldn't see by whom! She pulled her head off and in the welcome stream of cold March air came face to face with a man who stopped her breath.

He was very handsome.

Not drop-dead-gorgeous-supermodel handsome, he was more cute in a handsome sort of way. He had dark hair that seemed to force itself to the front of his head, hanging over his forehead in springy curls. Underneath his candid eyes shone blue, almost violet, his dark lashes making the shade seem even deeper.

When Ciara tore her eyes away from his she noticed his mouth. This was set in a half smile and was one of those versatile mouths that with one little movement could express as much as a short sentence.

Ciara knew this because already she could see it saying, 'Well, come on, of course you were in a bit of a tight spot but what do you expect if you will go around dressed as a rabbit?'

And she could accept this from him!

Because from the neck down he was dressed in exactly the same way as Ciara and in his hand he carried a head with a blue bow. He was the rabbit who had been watching her every move all afternoon!

'Better now?' The handsome rabbit spoke softly, eyes full of violet sympathy.

She nodded and smiled.

Maybe being watched wasn't such a bad thing!

Maybe this wasn't such a dead end job!

And maybe, just maybe, there was life in Bunny Land after all!

Chapter Seven

'So, how did you get on this afternoon?'

It was 3.35. Gráinne was standing in the doorway of the staffroom, arms folded, seemingly addressing no one in particular.

Ciara was sitting at the table having a cup of tea. For five minutes now she'd been eyeing an open packet of Jaffa Cakes that screamed if-you-eat-one-you'll-finish-the-pack. Ciara, though hungry, was hesitant to take on that sort of calorie-guilt. She dragged her attention away from the biscuits and looked at her boss.

'Fine, no problem, yeah, grand.'

She looked closely at Gráinne to see if there was any hint she might know that Ciara had been off getting on with life for an hour an a half in the middle of her shift.

Gráinne seemed unaware.

She also seemed unaware that Ciara had taken a fifteen-minute break for a quick but satisfying chat with the handsome rabbit after his timely rescue of her. Ciara figured it did no good for a girl to be offhand with her knight in shining armour. Even if that armour was made of fur!

'Hi, I'm Ken.' The handsome rabbit had taken off one of his paws and extended his hand towards Ciara. He'd smiled warmly and probably decided to introduce himself because she was gaping at him dumbly, her mouth open in what she liked to think was post-traumatic reaction. She started out of her my-god-he's-so-cute reverie and, pulling off one of her own paws, extended her hand.

'Ciara. Hi. Thanks for that, I thought I was going to topple over any second.'

The idea obviously amused him but he kept a straight face.

'The thing to do if kids come at you, which they always do between about twelve-thirty and two, is to get your back to the wall, and if that doesn't work just take off your head. Once they see your eyes they'll back off.'

'Thanks.'

She would probably just have gone on saying thanks forever if he hadn't started a conversation.

'I haven't seen you on the job before. New today?'

She nodded. 'Just started this morning. You been on this job long?'

'Two weeks. Well, nearly, it will be by the end of the week. They'd been up and running about a week when I came on board.'

'And how has it been?'

'OK. Like being back at school,' he laughed, eyes sparkling with merriment, his soft out-of-town accent only adding to his charm. 'The fact is that seeing those boys off just now is the most exciting thing that's happened to me so far.'

Ciara was dying to ask Ken why it was he'd taken this job. She couldn't imagine that anybody would *want* to work as a rabbit. But she didn't dare ask because she was afraid that he would ask the same question back and she just didn't want to get into that. She didn't want to have to confess to having taken the job because she was a close personal friend of the owner of the company!

Of course Ken had seen her going off in John's car. Still Ciara didn't think that there was any reason why he should know who John was. After all, Gráinne ran the shop and it was obvious John kept a low profile. All the same, she didn't want to take any risks.

'Well, I guess I'd better get back to work . . . Thanks again.'

'Don't mention it. I consider it my duty to rescue reversing rabbits!'

Once more his eyes sparkled with mirth and Ciara found herself laughing more heartily than his joke warranted.

Evidently not being the sort of man to leave on a one-liner he continued, 'On a more serious note, what time do you finish?'

She looked at her watch. 'I finish at six-thirty but I have a break at three-thirty. I don't know if I'll be working on this street after that.'

'Oh, you will, there's hardly ever a change of location in the middle. You'll be coming right back here. My break isn't until three-fifty but I finish at six-thirty as well. I'll pop down to you then and we can walk back together, all right?'

It seemed to Ciara that it was much more than 'all right'!

When she left the street for her three-thirty break Ken waved cheerily to her from over on the next block.

'Are you listening to me?' Gráinne's voice sounded more irritated now and over-loud in the small staffroom. Ciara nodded. She hadn't heard a word the stocky girl had said. 'Have you handed out all the flyers I gave you?'

Ciara knew this question had no 'no' option so once again she nodded her head. She hoped there wasn't a frisk-on-departure policy. She could just imagine curious and accusing hands unearthing scores of undistributed flyers from her stuffed pouch. She folded her arms across her chest as best she could and changed the subject.

'Um . . . that guy this morning. Did he get a blue-bowed head in the end?'

It wasn't that she wanted to raise the subject of her having taken the wrong head, more that it was the only thing she could think of to say to Gráinne.

The other girl gave her a look that stated plainly it was none of her business but answered her anyway.

'Dimitri? Oh, yeah, by the time he came in we had a blue one for him. He ended up having to do the dual-carriageway shift.'

'What's the dual-carriageway shift?'

Gráinne looked at Ciara disparagingly and exhaled impatiently.

'We cover two dual-carriageways a day, one in the morning and one in the afternoon, so that we get the incoming and outgoing traffic. The promoters give out flyers to the drivers same as you do to pedestrians in town.' Gráinne paused and then as an afterthought added, 'We'll let you try it later in the week once you're a bit more used to the job.'

Ciara made a mental note to mention to John that she didn't think that the dual-carriageway shift would suit her at all.

'Isn't it time you were getting back?' Gráinne presented her with another 'no-isn't-an-option' question. Ciara looked at her watch. It was only three-forty; she was entitled to another five minutes.

'Yeah.' She pushed herself wearily from her seat.

'Here are your flyers, come back at six-thirty.'

Ciara nodded and pushed the next batch of little cardboard cutouts into her pouch. As she left the staffroom she grabbed three Jaffa Cakes from the packet and stuffed them into her mouth.

Outside the cold March breeze poked its freezing fingers down the neck of her costume as she pulled on her head. She slipped her hands into her giant paw-gloves, bitterly contemplating how her life had changed. She used to have a good job, a boyfriend, a nice apartment, friends, a future! Now she was part of a circus with a boss who was a cross between a kindergarten teacher and a member of the SS. Somebody had tried to kill her. She'd been brutalised by children. And she was about to move into what appeared to be some sort of Corporation housing development.

Her life wasn't supposed to be like this!

Maybe if she'd never met Gary things would have

turned out better. Life might have been different; it might have gone in a straight line instead of boomeranging back at her as it had just done.

Yes, perhaps everything would have been better if she and Gary hadn't got together.

Ciara had met him three years before; or rather Gary had met her. It had been one of those meetings that had, through social dexterity on his part, been bound to happen. They had met in a carpark and though at the time it had seemed like fate, he later confessed that he'd followed her there to give himself an opportunity to speak to her.

Ciara of course had been oblivious to this though with hindsight was almost sure that her life would have been better without it!

Just before she'd met Gary, Ciara had started a new job. It had been the job of her dreams, if working had anything at all to do with dreams. Ciara didn't believe in work. She saw it as torture designed to eat away at leisure, its only use to provide the money for leisure-pleasure. She didn't see why anybody should have to work. She was addicted to buying lottery tickets. Believed with a mixture of superstition, stoicism and a smattering of religious hocus-pocus that she was in line for a big win . . . one of these days.

Ciara bought lottery tickets twice a week on lottery-draw days.

In a world where she had no choice but to work, the job of her dreams was with a PR agency which contracted her out to different PR companies. Although she was by no means an ambitious person, after dropping her secretarial course because of boredom she had studied 'Media'. She had done this because if she had to work she wanted a 'cool' job. A job with a high-profile firm that did 'cool' things. Any job that made people say 'Really? How interesting!' when she told them where she worked.

Her very first contract had been all that; it was with the PR firm BIG (Big Irish Gigs!) that promoted all the most famous names in the music business. Over the next few years she had worked frequently for this company, often doing her damnedest to give the impression she had a permanent job with them.

She loved the fact that famous people, or even the agents of famous people, continually roamed the corridors. Ciara felt she had finally come into contact with the real world. It didn't matter that her job was to see that transport, toilets and food were constantly available for whoever needed them or that she spent all her time on the phone to unglamorous contractors and PAs. Her job gave her the right image! When she was with people who didn't work with her and didn't know her exact status she would mention the names of the more famous clients as though she spoke to them regularly.

To celebrate her new job she'd bought a car. Of course she already had one but now she bought a special car, one that was older even than she was. It was a Volkswagen Karman Ghia in a stunning baby blue colour. It gave her that feeling of being individual, special, different, she'd never had before. It also gave her a lot of mechanics' bills but she figured it was worth the cost. Her sister Ruth on the other hand declared that the car was nothing more than a liability and anytime it was mentioned would break into a Culture Club tune.

Tunelessly but with no self-consciousness she would chant, 'Karman, Karman, Karman, Karman, Karman Karman Ghe-ia, you never go, you never go-oh-ho-ho.'

Fortunately Ruth lived in Wexford so Ciara didn't have to plot violent and permanent ways of silencing her.

She chose simply to call her car by its brand name, Karman Ghia. She thought it sounded like a temperamental and melodramatic Italian opera singer and she liked that.

Ciara had been in her new job three weeks when she'd met Gary. It was Friday evening and she had gone for the end-of-week drink with her new workmates. When she left the bar and went across the road to the company carpark her car wouldn't start. This, even though she'd only had it a week, wasn't unusual but what was odd was the promptness with which a cheerful and attractive man came to her assistance.

'Well, I must say, the view from here is very pleasant.'

The carpark did have a stunning view of the sea but the speaker was looking directly at Ciara when she turned around from the car.

'Pardon?'

'The view,' he'd said, waving his hand sideways at the sea and smiling knowingly. 'Having a problem? Let me have a look. They say I have the . . . touch!'

From anybody else this would have sounded completely sleazy but not from this man. Ciara had seen him at work. She'd watched from a distance as the rest of the staff treated him with a respect and deference she wished she could command. She'd never thought she would get to speak to him.

Now to her astonishment he was rolling up his sleeves as he stepped around her to the car. She was quite unsure what to say to this slim, enthusiastic, denim-clad man bending over the engine. Then, as though to acknowledge her delight, he looked up and flashed a smile at her as confident, warm and white-toothed as Tony Blair on the election trail.

Ciara was instantly enamoured.

She soon found out that his name was Gary. He was thirty-seven, thirteen years older than Ciara, but hadn't yet lost his youthful bounce and enthusiasm. He was narrow-faced and sallow-skinned with hazel eyes that would appear to become lighter in the summer as his tan deepened. His smile was a burst of eager white teeth that seemed to Ciara to light up the world around him. She never tired of admiring his narrow waist and tight bottom that looked so great in jeans. He was a cameraman so always had gadgets hanging from his waist. These gave the eye an excuse to drift in that direction without feeling guilty about being found out. He worked freelance but shot most of the promos for BIG and was renowned for his innovative style and ability to interpret what a director wanted.

In the 'cool' hierarchy of the PR company he ranked highly, his visits there during pre-production being seen as the visitation of a sort of artistic demigod who miraculously blended the technical and the creative to make beautiful images.

That evening in the carpark Gary had charmed Ciara. He'd charmed her even more when he came around the following Saturday to have a 'proper look' at her car. And he'd continued to charm her over the next few weeks and then, as things moved up a gear to being more serious, months. Until finally when he'd told her he was married there didn't seem any way back.

Ciara was so hooked by then that she believed her

life would be unbearable without him. She knew he would eventually leave his wife, it was only a matter of time.

And time was something Ciara considered she had plenty of.

A persistent electronic ringing noise brought her back to the street. She looked about to see if anybody close by had a phone ringing.

There was nobody nearby because, although they were initially interested in the rabbit, most people took an elaborate detour to the edge of the pavement as soon as they realised she was giving out flyers. After a puzzled moment Ciara realised that the ringing was coming from inside her pouch.

Ripping off a paw, she rummaged about among the clutter of flyers and unearthed the little T2. There was no number on the call register screen. She pressed the large fluorescent button.

'Hello?'

'Hi, Ciara. It's John.'

'Oh, hi, John, what's up?'

'I just wanted to sort out tonight.'

'Oh, right.'

'Of course I'm still a bit out of touch, but I thought

we might try The Harnden, it sounds interesting. What do you think?'

What did she think? The Harnden was only the trendiest place to be at the moment. She and her friends from work used to drink there at weekends, when they had the money. She'd never eaten there, though.

What a scoop!

Here she was, unemployed – well, as good as – and eating at The Harnden! Ciara did a quick mental check on the day to ensure she wouldn't meet anybody from work. Ex-work rather! No, it was Wednesday, they wouldn't be there.

Naturally she'd love it if they could just see her going into the restaurant. It would be wonderful after all the humiliation she'd been through. However, when she thought it through, she felt that under the circumstances it might be best if she met nobody from work for a while.

'Ciara?'

'That would be great, John, yeah, I'd really like that.'

'OK, I'll meet you there at nine. 'Bye.'

Ciara put the phone back into her pocket, excitement spreading through her like an intravenous drug. She couldn't believe that she, Ciara Bowe, no hoper of the month, was actually going to dinner in The Harnden!

Better still, going to dinner in The Harnden with a man!

It had been some time since she'd had that feeling. She'd had it for more than two years with Gary whenever she was going to meet him. It had only been in the last six months that it had disappeared. And when eventually they had broken up, Ciara, much to her surprise, after some initial feelings of regret, had felt only relief.

She couldn't remember the exact day that things started to change, but it had been some time in late August after they had been together two and a half years. She had always taken an interest in what Gary's daughter Leah was doing though he rarely spoke about her unless Ciara asked. She knew that Leah had been to sailing school in Cork and asked when she would be back.

'Next week,' he said shortly, discouraging the conversation.

'And when does she go back to St Mary's?' Ciara was used to his reticence in talking about his family, assuming it was from guilt. Nevertheless she tried to find out as much as she could about the child, feeling the knowledge would bring her nearer to Gary.

'She's not going back, she's finished sixth class and has to go to secondary school now.'

Ciara's heart leaped. Leah was almost grown up! That meant that soon she and Gary could be together all the time.

'But won't she just continue on in the senior section of St Mary's?'

Ciara had quizzed one of the girls at work who'd gone to St Mary's as soon as she had found out that Leah went to school there.

Gary shook his head. It seemed as though he wasn't going to continue speaking but then, probably remembering Ciara's persistent and consuming curiosity in his child, he decided to give her some information.

'She's going to Kylemore.'

'Kylemore! But Kylemore's in ...' Ciara searched the geography section of her mind '... in Connemara!' she finished, surprised and confused. Connemara was a four-hour drive away. Hardly suitable for commuting!

Gary nodded and changed the subject. Ciara knew not to pursue it further but it was quite obvious Leah was to go to boarding school. By Ciara's calculation this meant she wouldn't be living at home. Gary had always said the reason he stayed in his marriage was because of his daughter. Now that she would no longer be living at home, he could leave his wife.

But he hadn't said anything about that, in fact hadn't mentioned it at all, and Ciara didn't have the courage to. By October she'd begun to find stray doubts in her mind that suggested her relationship with Gary was not based on anything she understood or even cared to understand.

She was in her late-twenties and had the distinct feeling she'd just wasted almost three precious years on a man who may have been less than truthful; less than sincere. Over the next few months she waited for Gary to name the date he would be leaving his wife. He never did. Things just went on as they always had.

Little armies of dissent formed in Ciara's mind. They grumbled and shuffled their heavily shod feet, each group ready for action but also unsure what sort of support they would get if they were to fire the first shot.

Because all Ciara's energy was going into keeping down the coup that rumbled continually about her brain she lost the cutting edge she used to have for her work. She'd been offhand with a couple of clients at a corporate evening and the company she was working for at the time complained to the agency.

They issued a warning and didn't employ her for two months. Nevertheless at the end of January she was given another contract with BIG. Gary was also working on the project so she was seeing more of him than usual. Which only fuelled her discontent.

Eventually the armies of dissent erupted.

It was the end of February. Gary's birthday. Ciara had never celebrated with him, he'd always said Leah got almost as excited about it as she did about her own so he had to spend it at home.

But this year there was no Leah.

'It's your birthday next week, Gary.' Ciara was almost holding her breath with the tension she felt at bringing up the subject.

'Is that so?' He looked up from the meal Ciara had cooked for them. It was a Monday night. Gary was supposed to be at a pre-production meeting in Belfast but instead had made the trip there and back in one day so that he could spend the evening with Ciara.

'I was wondering ...' She took a deep breath to still the tremor in her voice. 'I was wondering what you'd like to do? You know, for your birthday?' Her voice trailed off as she saw the expression on his face.

Or rather the lack of expression.

It was a complete blank. Ciara's heart sank; she hated it when he looked at her like that. It was the look that preceded the what-can-you-be-thinking-you-know-I-can't-possibly-do-that statement. And here it came.

'Ciara, I can't possibly be with you on my birthday. Besides everything else Leah will be phoning us at home on the speakerphone, I can't let her down. She'd think I'd forgotten her just because she has gone away to school. No, it's out of the question, you know that.'

And that's when it happened.

Somewhere in the back of her mind the first shot was fired and a shout of camaraderie went up drawing the dissenting armies together. The revolution was on. It was time for action! But what action? The armies arranged themselves in formation and waited for orders.

Ciara brooded for three whole days during which, even though she wasn't seeing Gary, she didn't go out drinking with her friends. On the third day she had a brainstorm. The solution became clear to her. She would let Gary's wife know that he had a lover and when she questioned him about it he would have to admit it and move out. It would take the responsibility of making the first move away from him and eventually, when they were happily living together, he would thank her for it.

So she parcelled up some of Gary's more colourful underpants and mailed them to:

Mrs Maeve Sullivan,
Floral Lodge,
Howth Road,
Sutton,
Co. Dublin,

She had no idea why she did that but she didn't regret it.

The worm had turned.

She spent that evening with Gary trapped between misery and excitement, jubilant that finally things were going to change. She so wanted to tell him what she'd done, the decision that she'd made for both of them so that they could celebrate, but some store of reserve held her back.

She didn't sleep that night.

At 3.45 the next day, unannounced and unexpected, Gary walked into the office accompanied by a heavily pregnant woman.

As usual when at work, Ciara glanced in his direction hoping to catch his eye. This eye contact would be the only indication they knew each other. He didn't look at her. Instead Gary walked straight to her desk, his downturned face darker than she had ever known it could become.

The whole office followed his rapid measured step. Most of them knew that there was something between Ciara Bowe and Gary Sullivan but they really weren't that interested. In their business relationships came and went like Irish sunshine.

The pregnant woman followed Gary step for step. A feeling of foreboding closed around Ciara as they drew nearer.

This wasn't good.

At the last moment she saw that Gary was carrying a crumpled package. It was the parcel she had sent to his wife!

Ciara froze. Her army of dissidents gathered up their

weapons and supplies, ripped their half-dried clothes from about the fire, and dropping boots and socks in their hurry, scampered to the hills and safety, leaving Ciara alone on the battlefield.

Gary stood in front of her. He dropped the torn parcel on her desk, allowing the underwear to flop on to her keyboard. He spoke in a low but disconcertingly audible voice.

'Ciara, I would like to introduce you to my wife Maeve.' He indicated the pregnant woman beside him.

Ciara gasped. The pen she'd been clutching as a safety anchor dropped out of her hand.

His wife!

How could this be Gary's wife? She was pregnant and they didn't have sex, he'd always assured Ciara of that.

Maybe she was pregnant by somebody else? That must be it!

Gary had been staying with her to be supportive, not daring to tell her he was in love with somebody else in case it would be too much for her in her condition. Now that his wife knew there was somebody else in his life it was time for all three of them to sit down and discuss the future. That afternoon probably wasn't the best choice but at least it was a start!

After a brief pause Gary continued speaking.

'Maeve and I are expecting a baby next month and

we ...' he paused again, reaching out to take his wife's hand, looking at her reassuringly '... we would like it if you had nothing more to do with our lives. Mine or any other member of my family. I would appreciate it if you had your things out of the apartment by Sunday.'

He took a deep breath. Raising his voice, as if the whole room hadn't heard him already, he said, 'And I'd rather we weren't in the situation of ever working together again.'

With that Gary and Maeve must have walked away but Ciara didn't see them. She was blinded with shock and embarrassment. She hid behind her computer, willing the red colour to fade from her face.

How could this happen to her?

In public!

It was bad enough that her worst fear had been confirmed, Gary didn't love her, but to declare it all around the office!

The other women in the room threw her sympathetic looks as the men smiled at one another. Nobody came to speak to her because none of them wanted to be seen fraternising with a PR person on the wane, especially a temp!

Ciara kept her head down and tried to work out a strategy for dealing with work on Monday. She needn't have bothered.

At the end of the day she was told she wasn't to come

in again. The agency had warned BIG about her recent record and in the light of what had just occurred they were terminating her contract.

Later, very drunk at a club, Ciara discovered it was Friday the twenty-ninth of February and a leap year, or rather had been. By then it was the early hours of Saturday morning. It would have been her one chance to propose to Gary if everything hadn't gone pear-shaped. She now knew her misfortune could be blamed on the constellations!

At the time it seemed to explain a lot.

Chapter Eight

'Ciara.'

'What?' She swung around.

Ken was standing beside her, bare-headed, laughing.

'You'll never get rid of those flyers if you just stand there with them in your paw. I think the idea is that you actively pursue the punter and press one into their hand. I thought you'd frozen to death.'

Ciara laughed with him. She'd lost concentration ages ago but hadn't realised she'd become completely motionless.

'Is it half-six already?' she asked as she pulled off her rabbit's head.

'No, it's only six-fifteen but there's hardly anyone on the streets, it's not worth our while standing about. I thought if we headed off now and walked really slowly we'd get back to the shop at about the half-six mark. Walking slowly has to be more interesting than standing around here, what do you think?'

Ciara agreed totally. Her legs ached and she was starving. The prospect of finishing work was very appealing.

Also very appealing were the warm eyes and friendly smile of Ken.

'Great, can't wait to get out of this suit.' She returned his smile.

They turned and walked slowly down the street.

'What if somebody spots us?' Ciara asked by way of making conversation.

With a raised eyebrow and in one deft movement Ken plucked the remaining flyers from her hand and, bundling them with his own, dropped them into a nearby bin.

'Well, fancy that, we've run out of flyers! We'll just have to go back to the shop for more. Darn, I do wish we'd brought enough with us!'

He shouted this as though he was announcing a circus was coming to town or a fantastic unbeatable sale. Ciara laughed appreciatively and they fell into step with one another.

'So,' Ken said, looking sideways at her, 'what's a nice girl like you doing in a costume like that?'

Ciara grimaced. It hadn't taken long for him to get on

to the one question she didn't want to answer. Time for a little glossing over of the truth.

'Between jobs. You know, needed a change. Wondered if I should move into telecommunications so I thought I'd check this out.' Then with a half smile she added, 'I didn't realise it would be so intellectually challenging!'

Ken matched her half smile and nodded, seemingly accepting her explanation.

'And you – what made you decide to do this?' Ciara resorted to her usual strategy of getting the other person to talk about themselves. It meant less chance of awkward questions being directed at her!

Ken answered easily, 'Oh, I was moving from Waterford to Dublin and needed a job straight away for the rent and things, so I'm doing this while I look around for a "real" job.'

Ciara laughed. She liked the way he insulted their job as she had done without thinking for one moment that it might upset her. His seemingly easy outlook on life made her curious to know what sort of job he called a 'real' job.

'And what sort of job are you looking for?'

Ken paused as though he didn't have a ready answer for that.

'Ah ... I was working in printing, newspapers and the like, and I want to stay in that, get into it in a bigger way. Maybe I . . .' He stopped in mid-sentence, narrowing his eyes as he looked down the street. As Ciara followed his gaze he exclaimed, 'Hey, look, is there some sort of commotion going on outside the shop or is my eyesight really bad?'

Ciara peered closely into the dusk. Sure enough there seemed to be quite a crowd outside the Easi-tel shop.

Without a word the two quickened their pace. In the shop doorway, still in their rabbit costumes, a number of promoters were milling about. Behind them on the pavement a few passers-by had stopped to see what was going on.

Before Ciara and Ken had time to say anything Gráinne stepped into the shop doorway. She looked about at the crowd, then raised her hands for silence.

'If I can have your attention, please. Thank you. It is with great sadness and regret that I have to tell you this. One of your co-workers, Dimitri Slavinsky, was killed in an accident on the Naas dual-carriageway this afternoon . . . I'm sorry.'

A shocked and disconcerted mumbling spread through the assembled group. Gráinne held her hand up again.

'Because of this there will be no late shift tonight. You can all go home, schedule as usual tomorrow. Check your times with me before you go.'

Ciara turned to share her reaction with Ken but he was

already talking to a young promoter who'd been with the crowd when they had arrived. She stood alone in the mumbling group, stunned. The only thought that kept going through her mind was, what if it had been her turn to do the dual-carriageway? What if Gráinne had decided she had enough experience and sent her out that afternoon?

She would be dead now!

Inside her head came a loud clanking and whirring as her deductive machinery started up. It echoed through the passages of Ciara's brain. Soot-encrusted workers struggled to feed fuel into the burner to get the deduction locomotive up to speed. Meanwhile, disoriented from being called into action at such short notice, the driver manhandled the controls, trying to find the right track.

Surely Gráinne had said something about sending whoever was on with her this morning to the dual-carriageway? What if that was the same guy? What if the murder attempt that morning and the death of this Dimitri were connected?

The clanking and whirring grew steadily more powerful.

What if whoever had tried to kill her that morning hadn't given up but had followed the wrong person? They had mixed up the promoters and killed him instead!

There was a screech of brakes; having reached a conclusion the locomotive ground to a halt.

Somebody *was* trying to kill her!

'Penny for them, Ciara?' Ken's voice came from somewhere beside her, close and intimate.

She started, still engrossed but nervous now because of her conclusion.

'Oh, I was just ... just ...' Ciara searched frantically for a reasonable end to her sentence '... thinking that I don't know anybody here,' she finished lamely.

But he wasn't listening.

'Bit of a shock about Dimitri.' Ken eyed her closely. 'Did you know him?'

His voice had an unfamiliar edge. Ciara reckoned he'd had a shock. After all, he probably knew the dead man. She shuddered at the idea, and shook her head.

'One of the lads just said you were on the same area as Dimitri this morning.' Ken, still staring at her intently, nodded in the direction of the other promoters.

Ciara glanced uneasily at the group. Did they guess it was her fault that Dimitri was dead? That he had been killed instead of her?

She had a feeling that now wasn't the time to raise the subject.

'No, I didn't meet him. Didn't see him at all actually.'

She wondered if Ken would sense the lie in her voice.

'Really?' Everything about the way he said this suggested to Ciara that he didn't believe her. As she could think of no reason for him not to do so, she decided that she was just being paranoid. Suddenly Ken snapped out of whatever thought he'd been following and the familiar twinkle came back into his eye.

'Well, at least nobody noticed we were back a bit early!' He switched to a jovial tone and Ciara laughed because she was so relieved he was behaving normally once again. 'Let's get out of these costumes, will we? No point in spending any more time in them than we have to!'

Ciara followed him past the last group of people who lingered outside, through the crowded shop and into the staffroom. This gave the impression of being positively overflowing as there were five other workers there in various stages of undress. They all looked about eighteen and Ken knew each of them by name.

'Stephen, this is Ciara. Jen, Ciara. Ciara, Mary. And those two over there are Sally and Damien. They're all taking time off lectures for the glory of being bunnies!'

The students smiled and nodded as Ciara wondered how she was ever going to remember all their names. She felt really thrilled that it was Ken who was introducing her as everybody in the room seemed to like and respect him. She could see the young student girls thought he was the best thing since their first alco-pop.

After the introductions the room fell silent. The only sound was the rustle of bags and clothes changing. Nobody mentioned the accident. It was as though they could pretend it hadn't happened if they didn't talk about it.

As they left in ones and twos they mumbled goodbye, quietly and tonelessly.

'Come on, let's get out of here,' Ken said as soon as Ciara had put on her coat and picked up her bag.

They moved out of the staffroom and into the shop. This was now far less crowded and Gráinne, standing behind the desk, looked up as they passed through.

'I hope you're not leaving without your starting times for tomorrow? Unfortunate as the events of today have been, the show must go on.'

She made it sound as if the circus tent had fallen down rather than that one of the team had been killed. Ken and Ciara stopped in mid-departure.

'OK, right.' Gráinne poked at a tiny laptop computer on the counter in front of her. 'Ken, you're on a half-eight. And, Ciara, you're on a half-nine. Ken, you'll be working the late shift – Thursday, you know!' She made this last statement to Ken as though it was in some way his responsibility. Ciara and he nodded and, mumbling goodbye, headed for the door.

Outside, standing in the alley beside the Easi-tel shop, was a huddle of people in rabbit costumes. Little clouds of smoke from their cigarettes drifted into the evening. Their hushed voices carried along the quiet street. They spoke in staccato sentences, throwing words at one another as though playing a bizarre game of pass the verbal parcel. Ciara couldn't understand what they were saying but the tone seemed puzzled and fearful.

As soon as they saw Ken and Ciara they stopped talking and stared in their direction. Ciara could make out four figures now, one of whom she recognised as Anna, the unfriendly woman she'd met earlier in the staffroom. Ciara nodded in her direction but Anna didn't seem to notice.

'I'll be back in a minute.'

Ken caught Ciara's eye for a split second and then moved towards the cluster of promoters. Ciara stayed where she was. She watched as Ken shook hands with one of the men, had a quick word with the others and then returned to her side. He must have seen the question in her face because he nodded towards the group and said, 'That guy is Dimitri's cousin. The group are all from Russia. Dimitri was only in the country three weeks.'

Ciara didn't know what to say. Situations of death and mourning weren't her strong point.

'God, how awful,' she muttered, hoping Ken would change the subject really fast. But he seemed determined not to.

'Yeah,' he said gloomily, 'I hope they at least give us some time off to go to the funeral!'

Ciara didn't react to this statement as she could think of nothing more horrifying than going to a funeral, particularly that of somebody she didn't know.

Would she be expected to go? She just didn't want to think about it, never mind talk. There had to be some way out of this conversation. She looked at her watch.

'Oh, wow, look at the time! If I don't get my car out of the carpark before seven they'll charge me for another hour.' She knew it was a feeble interruption but it was all she could think of without seeming completely uncaring.

She did need to get her car out but as it had been in there all day it was probably just going to cost her the flat day rate no matter what time she picked it up.

Ken looked taken aback.

'Oh, I was going to suggest going for a drink, but OK, maybe some other time. See you tomorrow then, Ciara.'

'Yeah ... 'bye, Ken.'

Ciara could have kicked herself as she watched him walk away. She knew she had to move house and go on a date with John but surely she could have fitted in a little drink with Ken? If only she had guessed she would never have mentioned her car.

Too late now!

She continued to watch as he moved down the street.

This was her first opportunity to assess if his body lived up to his head. She knew when she first met him that he was a nice height but until he removed his rabbit costume she'd had no way of checking out the rest of him. It wouldn't have done to look him up and down in the crowded staffroom!

Now, as he walked away dressed in his short Puffa jacket and fitted combats, Ciara could find nothing to complain about. He carried himself like somebody who was fit. She cringed as she detected the distant, rhythmic thud of the Lust-army boots as they shuffled into mobilisation.

This was not what she'd intended!

After all she'd made the decision to go out with John and now here she was lasciviously assessing another man!

This couldn't go on!

She tore her eyes away from Ken's receding figure, mentally shaking a reproachful finger at herself. But even as she did so the image of his smiling eyes and ready grin floated up in front of her.

Ciara sighed. Surely, she thought, there was no harm in just looking? No harm at all. And if that was the case there might be no harm in having a drink some other day! Simply because she was going out with John didn't mean she couldn't have men friends, did it?

Happy with her conclusion, Ciara swung around in the direction of the carpark. Immediately she noticed that the group of Russians had been watching her in silence as she'd studied Ken's finer features.

Caught in the act of lustful imaginings!

Ciara frowned and blushed, then with a nod in their direction, walked away.

'Hello, anybody home? Hello.'

Ciara let herself into her new flat and stood in the hall, waiting for a response. Everything was quiet even though all the lights were on. Then, slowly and carefully, the door to Elena's room opened and a timid face peeped out.

'Hello, Elena,' Ciara said. 'I just wanted to let you know that I was here ... in case you thought I was a burglar or something.' She laughed at her own little joke.

Elena remained frozen on the threshold of her room, an expression of trepidation on her face.

Ciara stopped laughing.

'That is, I didn't want to just barge in, you know, as you live here.'

Elena still didn't react. It was as if she didn't understand. Ciara thought about it for a moment; chances were she *didn't* understand, her English might not be up to it. Ciara groaned inwardly. Here she was, home after a hard day at work, one which had included an attempt on her life and the death of a co-worker. And now Karman Ghia, full of her life's possessions, was parked in one of the dodgiest areas in Dublin. She didn't want to switch into United-Nations mode!

When she'd tried it that morning with Anna it had been pointedly rejected! However she couldn't just stand here and say nothing. Ciara took a deep breath and spoke very slowly, distinctly and loudly.

'I am going to move in now so I have to bring my stuff up from the car. It should take about ten minutes.'

She had packed only the essentials into the car, enough to keep her going for a couple of weeks until she was back on her feet and able to find a proper place to live.

'I will leave the door ajar so I will not have to be opening and closing it. OK?'

Ciara looked at Elena questioningly. A slow smile spread across her face, transforming it from merely pretty to that of an angel. She spoke.

'I would like to help you but I expect a baby and must not lift anything. Will I make you some coffee?'

Her accent was full of the rolling Rs that had been in Anna's voice that morning, but Elena's tone was gentle, warm and friendly.

Ciara smiled, relieved.

'Oh, yes, please. Coffee would be lovely. I'll just get the stuff and then ...' She left the sentence unfinished because Elena had nodded and was already moving towards the kitchen.

As she went down the stairs towards the car Ciara glanced over the railing into the yard below. There, even though she'd only left her car minutes before, was a group of teenagers peering in the windows at her collection of bags and boxes. Cursing under her breath, she scuttled quickly down the three flights of stairs, making as much noise as she could in the process.

The gang had dispersed by the time she got to the car. Staring fearfully about her into the dark wasteland, Ciara wondered yet again what had happened in her life that she'd ended up living in the north inner city in this block of flats, working in a dead end job where it appeared somebody was determined to kill her.

She threw one last frightened look into the darkness and quickly started to unload the car. It took four trips and by the time she'd completed the last run there was a glorious smell of coffee in the flat. Throwing the last bag into her room, she made her way to the kitchen. Two cups of steaming coffee were sitting on the counter and Elena was struggling to cut a lemon into large wedges with a very blunt knife. Then she deftly squeezed the lemon into the coffee and dunked the rind in after it. Hearing Ciara behind her, she swung around and presented her with a cup.

'I have already put in the sugar, I hope that it is OK?'

The idea of an unspecified amount of sugar having gone into something she was about to drink, never mind the fact that her coffee had been doused in lemon, bothered Ciara enormously but she didn't have the heart to say this to the gently smiling Elena.

'Thanks.' She smiled back, taking the cup in both hands and looking into it. The coffee was black and the peel of the lemon floated unenticingly on the surface. She held the cup to her lips and forced herself to take a sip. She knew now that this whole coffee thing had been a bad idea. She had thought it might perk her up before she got ready to go out with John but in fact it would probably just make her sick and unable to enjoy the expensive meal he had booked.

She took a sip. It certainly tasted odd but strangely it wasn't unpleasant. A little sweet perhaps but this helped the lemon and the coffee to blend. The best thing about it was that it was so strong she could already feel her heartbeat quicken. It might indeed give her just the boost she needed!

She nodded at Elena and smiled again, wondering how many of these strange little customs she would have to get used to while they shared a flat.

'So, Elena, where are you from?' Ciara decided that in

the light of the other girl's hospitality she ought to have a polite conversation during the coffee-drinking.

'Ukraine.' Elena responded with a great rolling of Rs and a sob in her voice, but said nothing more.

'Have you been here long?' Ciara hoped this question might provoke a more detailed response.

'Only some weeks, not long.' Elena smiled humbly as though being in Ireland only a short time made her in some way a lesser person. Then, searching for the words, she asked, 'And you? You work in town?'

'Yes,' Ciara said, speaking slowly, 'I started today, I work with John's company. The guy who was with me earlier?'

She had no idea whether or not Elena knew John's name as so little had been said when they had first come to the flat. Elena nodded, not indicating whether or not she fully understood. 'I would like also to work but it is too soon with the baby.'

She put her hand on her stomach and Ciara had a sudden panicky idea that the baby was going to be born there and then.

'When is it due?'

'Any weeks now, soon.' Elena bowed her head slightly and placed her hand on her stomach again, a beatific expression crossing her face. The hand movement drew Ciara's attention to her wristwatch.

It was 7.45!

She had no time at all to get ready to go out with John. She drained the rest of her coffee, paused to spit out a pip then exclaimed, 'I have to be in town in an hour, must dash.'

Elena looked momentarily puzzled but soon realised what Ciara meant when she ran to her room and started to empty her belongings into the middle of the floor.

Even being able to see all the clothes she had in one glance didn't solve Ciara's dilemma. What on earth was she going to wear to dinner at probably the trendiest restaurant in town?

She sat on the edge of the bed for a moment, her head in her hands, staring in dissatisfaction at the pile of clothes on the floor. She pulled out and slipped on a tight-fitting strappy top that she liked because it showed off the finely textured skin of her shoulders. But while it still looked great at the shoulders, it bulged out below the ribcage in a way this top was never meant to do. And it wasn't just the bulge. Her whole waist area looked like a tree trunk, as though there was nothing between her top and her hips except a thick band of stuffing.

Ciara ripped the top off and flung it on the floor.

There was nothing else for it. She couldn't wear any of her fitted clothes so it would have to be the loose man's shirt she wore on pre-menstrual days. That over her black baggy trousers and high heels would have to do. She knew she didn't look very trendy but right now she didn't feel very trendy either.

Bad-temperedly, she threw the clothes she intended to wear on the bed and, grabbing a towel, stormed out of the room towards the bathroom. She almost collided with Elena en-route. The startled expression on the other girl's face forced Ciara to slow down.

'There is trouble?' Elena's command of English seemed to desert her in her shock. Ciara shook her head, ashamed that her bad mood had frightened her timid flat-mate.

'No, no, nothing's the matter. Everything's fine. Do you think there's any hot water? I'd like to wash my hair.'

Having just spent two weeks in her mother's house where to get even a small amount of hot water required an application almost a week in advance and a lot of sighing about wasted resources, it wouldn't have surprised Ciara if the answer had been no. But Elena's face cleared and she nodded enthusiastically.

'Of course, there is much hot water, very hot. It is like the flat, always warm, it is wonderful.'

Her joy at having constant hot water seemed all-consuming and Ciara wondered what conditions were like where she came from that this everyday convenience was such a luxury. Perhaps, unknown to Ciara, she had been living with Mrs Bowe!

After washing her hair, she styled it so that it regained some of its body. She hadn't realised just how bad it must have looked all day until she got home. The idea that the same thing was going to happen again the next day once she put on the revolting rabbit's head made her feel physically ill. To take her mind off the idea she concentrated on her makeup, peering closely in the small mirror on the dressing table in her bedroom.

She was retrieving her bag from the kitchen when Elena appeared in the doorway. She held out one hand towards Ciara, palm facing downward. Ciara looked at her questioningly.

Elena smiled.

'It is a custom in my country when you make a new friend to give a little gift so I would like to give you this.' She indicated her outstretched hand. Having no choice in the matter, Ciara held out hers to accept the gift. Elena dropped a small oval object into her hand.

'It is a holy thing and will bring you blessings.'

Ciara didn't want a 'holy thing' but neither did she want to appear ungracious. She glanced at the object in her hand. It looked like a rather large locket. There was a hinge on one side and a clasp on the other. She undid the clasp and opened it; it was indeed a 'holy thing'! Inset inside each half was a religious picture. These two were done in a different style from the Irish 'holy' pictures she was used to but there was no doubting the fact that they were 'holy' too.

'Gosh, Elena, this is beautiful. Thank you,' she lied. Elena had that beatific expression on her face again.

'It is for the handbag so that it will always be with you.'

Ciara had the distinct feeling that by the time she was finished stuffing her handbag with cosmetics for the evening there would be no room for the holy thing. Nevertheless she nodded at Elena.

'Yes, of course, how sweet. Wonderful.' Then, pointing urgently at her watch, she said, 'Dead late, gotta go.'

With that she raced to her room, swept most of her makeup off the dressing table into her handbag, forced it shut, and with a final wave to Elena fled out the door.

By the time she realised she was still clutching the 'holy thing', she was sitting in the car. She stared at it for a second, wondering if she could throw it out the window.

Perhaps not.

She thought for a moment, then tore open the ashtray to stuff it inside. This was what she did with things she didn't want to lose. She didn't allow smoking in her car so it was a perfectly safe haven.

As she put the 'holy thing' inside she heard the sound of paper crumpling. Of course! She had stuffed her lottery ticket in there after buying it on the way to the flat! It was 8.40 now, the draw had been on TV at 8 p.m. and she had missed it. She would have to wait until the next day to find out if she was a millionaire or not! She folded the lottery ticket and put it inside the 'holy thing'. Maybe if Elena's gift did bring blessings it might shower them on the lottery ticket!

She stuffed the 'holy thing' into the ashtray. She didn't want to keep it but didn't feel that she could take the risk of throwing it away in case whatever God it represented punished her. Life was bad enough without having to fend off His wrath as well!

Chapter Nine

'Can I get you something to drink?'

John was sitting at the bar when Ciara walked in. He slid from his seat and moved ponderously towards her to give her a quick peck on the cheek.

He was looking very prosperous, wearing a different suit from the one he'd been wearing that morning. This one was a lighter colour and it struck Ciara, knowing his personality, that this was probably his 'fun suit'.

'Have we time?' she gasped, breathless from rushing to get to the hotel at the appointed time.

'Sure,' John answered confidently. 'Our table's not going anywhere, what would you like?'

He pulled up his stool and patted it, indicating for her to sit down. Before doing so she took off her coat and looked about the bar. It was as she had expected and remembered, full of the trendiest sorts. She did a quick check to assure herself that nobody from BIG was in the room, still torn between not wanting to meet them because of the shame while wanting to be seen, alive and trendy, in The Harnden.

She knew they would be mad with envy if they saw she was going to eat in the ultra-designered, golden-hued, slightly-oxygenated, feng-shuied dining room. Ciara sat in a position she hoped indicated she would be going to the dining room soon just in case one of her ex-colleagues walked into the bar.

'I'd like a Dry Martini with a twist.' She smiled at John. Well, she wasn't paying for it, was she? And she'd need a little something to get her through the evening.

Before he passed on the order he looked at her with a slight smile on his lips.

'Would you like that shaken or stirred?'

His voice was deadly serious but Ciara remembered this tone and, quickly catching his eye, laughed: 'Touché.' She'd forgotten his deadpan humour and wondered if she was going to have to be on the ball all evening. She was already under enough strain without that.

Maybe a few drinks would help.

What she really wanted, and what she had longed for all the way into town in the car, was some coke.

She hated to admit it but it was true.

It wasn't that she took a lot of drugs, she didn't even approve of their easy availability. She had always been completely in favour of hefty jail sentences for those found selling or possessing them. Ciara couldn't in fact justify her own attitude. She had the same confused reaction to coke as she had to drinking and driving: she was disgusted by anybody who drove while drunk and thought they should be banned from driving for life, yet she herself had on occasion driven while over the legal limit.

It was as though she was two different people, one a law-abiding, righteous citizen and the other a character of doubtful morality.

Jekyll and Hyde!

She'd always believed that she would never use a hard drug, a dangerous, addictive one that rotted your teeth and made your skin rough-textured and dull. But as her relationship with Gary became more unsettled and his unavailability more marked she found herself going out with her newfound friends from PR companies up to four times a week and the task of drinking enough to forget became more onerous.

Even though she tried as much as possible to drink shorts, it soon became apparent that she was putting on weight. Her trim waist started to bulge and fight against her standard size twelve outfits and she noticed a belly developing.

A belly!

She'd never had a belly! And the worst thing about it was that she suspected it was a beer belly. The idea made her shudder with revulsion.

How could Gary go on loving her if she let herself go like that?

It was a Thursday night about a year and a half after she'd started going out with him. She was yet again working on contract with BIG. A few drinks after work had turned into an impromptu let's-make-a-night-of-it-and-who-needs-to eat-anything-anyway evening. The no-really-I'm-just-having-one drinkers had gone long ago and Ciara as usual was left with the die-hards. She was in great form, wouldn't have minded something to eat but knew that nobody else was hungry. And besides, eating always ruined her alcohol high. At one point she'd gone to the bathroom because she'd realised that once more she was drinking much faster than everybody else. She'd noticed this happening a lot since she'd fallen in with her regular partying crowd. They drank much more slowly than she did but nevertheless seemed just as merry and talkative. And at the end of the evening they never drifted into incoherent slurring.

In the bathroom she met Melanie (or Melanoma as

Ciara liked to call her in the hope that it would make her seem less pretty and less successful). She worked in what Ciara referred to as the 'real' part of the company. She actually got to meet and talk to all the famous people. Melanie had worked with BIG since she'd left university and now managed all the photo and video shoots for the company.

Because of this her hours were much more irregular than Ciara's so she was rarely out with the gang. They were always making jokes about how she couldn't make it because she had to 'do' dinner with Bono or make sure that Andy (Lloyd Webber) had the proper seat at his Irish première of whatever musical he'd recently put his name to.

On this particular evening Melanie was out because she'd just started work on a video promo that wasn't taking up too much of her time yet. Everybody knew the promo was for a new boy band called 4U, pronounced of course For You. The official story was that they were in rehearsal but everybody in BIG knew that the problem was they didn't exist yet. All their publicity was in place but the four 'lucky' teenagers had not yet been selected. Nevertheless 4U would take the world by storm in the next twelve months and Melanie was managing their image.

Ciara rarely spoke to her because of their different status

and the envy and awe that overwhelmed her any time she saw 'Melanoma'.

That evening Melanie had smiled broadly when she saw Ciara coming into the bathroom.

'Hi, how are you? I haven't had a chance to talk to you all evening, you were right at the other end of the table. So you're back with us for another while? Isn't it great just to get out like this and forget all about work?'

Ciara nodded, not quite sure how to take this friendly outburst. She had, after all, been sitting three seats away from Melanie all evening without the girl even once looking in her direction. Occasionally, when she'd turned her head, Ciara had heard her mention all the names she wished she could drop so casually into her own conversation.

Melanie was part of another world, one that required her to jet here and there for meetings, a world that took her to all the best restaurants and where you didn't survive long without that cloak of confidence that billowed about her every time she moved. Melanie was what Ciara wanted to be.

Ciara had no idea how to become Melanie.

'Are you coming on to The Harnden with us?' Melanie asked conversationally as though Ciara was a stranger to the group and had to be invited to join them when they moved. Ciara felt a little resentful about this but as nobody had yet mentioned The Harnden to her it could only mean she wasn't part of the 'in' crowd that evening. She had no choice but to nod.

'Sure. Pointless paying for drink here when I can pay twice the price somewhere else!'

Melanie threw her a baffled look and smiled politely.

Ciara, seeing her joke had fallen flat, stuttered, 'That is, I mean, of course I'm going to The Harnden.' She smiled benignly. Melanie regained her good humour.

'Great. The more the merrier. Can't party without a crowd.' She moved towards the door then, pausing, took a quick glance at the cubicles to ensure they were empty before stepping back towards Ciara.

'I guess you could do with some of this then.'

She pressed a tiny piece of folded paper into Ciara's hand. Taking the puzzled expression on Ciara's face for hesitation, she added, 'There's only enough for one line, barely, but it'll keep you going for a while.'

She smiled an I'm-such-a-generous-person smile and disappeared through the self-closing door.

Ciara was left alone clutching the little piece of paper.

She knew what it was, she had been to enough parties to know how coke came. This piece of paper would be opened carefully and reverently tipped out on to a shiny surface. The contents would be diced with the edge of a credit card or blade and set into neat lines to be inhaled.

She'd frequently been invited to join in the ritual but had always refused. Eventually nobody offered it to her anymore. Melanie obviously hadn't been at all these parties or else hadn't been paying enough attention to Ciara to notice that she didn't take coke.

The bathroom door opened and another woman walked in. Watching her in the mirror to make sure she didn't notice, Ciara closed her hand about the little parcel and went into a cubicle. She placed the piece of paper on the cistern lid and slowly unfolded it. Caught in the folds inside was the white powder.

She stood back and stared at it for a moment.

It was time to make a decision. She didn't think there could be any real harm in having a go; her friends all did it and none of them was haggard or homeless. And it certainly went a long way towards projecting a cool image. It struck Ciara that using this drug was probably a passport into Melanie's confident world, the removal of all barriers to a life that was always exciting and fulfilling. Maybe if she took coke she would have some of that confidence. And this was her chance to try the drug in private!

Ciara needed her privacy because she had no idea how to take it. She'd watched people suck it up their noses but wasn't sure she could do that. After all she went into hysterics if she got water up her nose, never mind stuffing it full of what looked like icing sugar! She'd always been afraid she would blow all the powder back out again. She had often imagined the scenario: the room would be full of people, all of the coolest, best-dressed variety. She'd snort loudly, panicking as the powder suffocated her, and everybody would turn around to watch as Ciara, unable to help herself, exhaled through her nose, blowing away all the remaining lines of coke.

She would be left sitting in a very expensive cloud of white dust, the focus of attention. Naturally it didn't end there. Before she'd tried the coke she would have been talking to an extremely attractive man in a designer evening jacket. He would, up to this point, have been showing an interest in her in that my-aren't-you-an-attractive-cosmopolitan-woman way that men who were cool and wore designer evening jackets did to attractive cosmopolitan women who are just doing a quick line of coke. He would be so mortified at her display he would probably try to sue her for destroying his 'cool' credibility and peppering his priceless clothes in coke.

And even if she did succeed in inhaling it properly, the chances were that her system would be so shocked she'd have a heart attack or a seizure. She would keel over and, with a succession of ignominious jerks, unceremoniously depart this life.

For Ciara the taking of coke in public was so fraught with potential embarrassment that to date she'd resisted it.

Now, looking at her own little pile of white powder, she realised this was her perfect opportunity. She might still blow it back out or indeed keel over dead but at least she would be doing it on her own and with any luck would be found at closing time by a complete stranger. Besides, it was obvious that Melanie had just taken some and she was fine. In fact, she had been more than fine, she had been downright friendly!

If taking the coke would make her more like Melanie, she would take the coke!

Ciara fished out her mirror compact, opened it and tipped the powder on to its glossy surface. She took out her credit card and swept the coke into a rough line, then rolling up a twenty-pound note she lowered her head to the mirror. It wasn't that difficult. She inhaled then threw back her head, afraid the powder would fall out of her nose.

She stood in front of the toilet and waited for death.

Nothing happened.

Her nose was a little numb and her heart beat a little faster. But this and the fact that she had successfully taken the drug just made her feel exhilarated. She emerged from the cubicle feeling quietly triumphant.

Her heartbeat seemed to be returning to normal and she was overtaken by a feeling of excitement and energy. The evening was opening up with new possibilities and new potential. She was ready for all the Melanies of her world. In fact eager to go and talk to them!

She grabbed her bag and went back into the bar. She felt she had a new sparkle, an edge, that she hadn't had earlier. She even had a conversation with Melanie about her work, something she had never dared to do before. For the first time she felt she belonged, that she was really part of the group, part of the bigger picture. Now she was only interested in talking and dancing, she didn't want to drink anymore and she certainly wasn't hungry.

A whole new world had opened up to her.

After that Ciara took coke once or twice a week. It was expensive but it was worth it for how it made her feel. She was no longer boring old Ciara the party pooper: she was full of energy and ideas. And to her surprise she lost the weight she had put on. She had assumed it was because she was so happy with her new self.

Conversation was so much easier, more relaxed, and the world so much more fun with coke than sitting beside John in The Harnden, still drinkless. Ciara wished again that she had a little tonight, just to help her along.

But her coke contacts had gone with the job.

Besides this evening was the first time in over two weeks that she'd even thought about coke. Probably because what she'd needed at her mother's house were downers, not stimulants, tranquillisers to make her go slower and be unaware of her surroundings. Just thinking of her mother's house reminded her of the extra stone in weight that clung to her midriff like a life belt. Ciara shifted in her stool and straightened her back, inhaling sharply to reduce the size of her stomach. John hadn't noticed as he was watching the barman preparing her Martini.

When the drink arrived he turned to Ciara. Pushing his glasses up to the bridge of his nose with his forefinger, he said, 'So did you get settled in OK?'

Ciara nodded in mid-sip of the first shock of her Martini. She swallowed quickly.

'Oh, yeah, I didn't have much with me so it was no problem.'

She wanted to add, 'And I didn't get mugged or beaten up or anything,' but decided that this would make her appear decidedly ungrateful. She needed to store up favours if she was to get out of this rabbit job as soon as possible.

'Elena's very nice. She even said she'd help me with my gear only she was too pregnant which was really sweet of her. Do you know her well?'

Ciara was determined to turn the conversation away from herself.

John parted his lips in the way he always did before he spoke. Most people parted their lips and spoke at the same time. John let them part slowly as though he had to exhale through his mouth, then when he was sure his lips were in the right position, he spoke.

'I don't know her at all. I knew that there was a room in the flat because a friend of mine has some connection with the Corporation and he mentioned it. It's really a family flat, you know, but it's just that little bit too high up for small children.'

It crossed Ciara's mind that it was odd John had friends who knew so much about public housing. After all, he'd been away from the city a long time, and public housing was definitely not the sector he'd be choosing to live in now he'd returned. But the Martini was hitting her empty stomach and she wanted to talk about more interesting things. She wanted to have a conversation that matched the new cosmopolitan woman image she wished to present to him. She had some catching up to do as the last time he'd seen her she'd been dressed in that hideous rabbit outfit.

She took another gulp of the Martini.

'So how was work today?' Ciara took her voice down an octave to a more sophisticated key and looked at John with an expression she hoped matched her tone. His face clouded. For a moment she thought he was going to comment on her change of voice and tried to think up a reasonable excuse for the affectation.

Neither of them spoke. Her sentence hung between them like an inappropriately loud laugh, Ciara wished she could take it back. She sat through the silence, trying not to stammer out a follow-up that would only make the situation worse. Eventually John spoke in a sad voice.

'Well, there was all that business with the accident. Terrible.'

For a moment Ciara had no idea what he was talking about. What accident? Then it dawned on her. Of course, the accident on the dual-carriageway, how could she forget? It had completely slipped her mind in the hustle and bustle of this evening. She pursed her lips and nodded sympathetically.

'Did you know him well?'

John gave her an I-don't-think-so look.

'Know him? Of course not, he was a promoter, not my side of things at all. No, this just causes huge complications for the company. It's really unfortunate he was working for us when it happened!'

'Yeah,' Ciara was puzzled, 'but isn't it unfortunate whenever it happened?'

John looked at her, a hint of impatience in his face.

'Yes, of course, naturally. What I mean is ... well ... the man is ... was ... illegal and we shouldn't have been hiring him without papers. He was only in the country a few weeks. I suppose we'll just have to say he was on a trial day, that we hadn't actually employed him yet and he'd said his papers were on the way.' John paused, looked as though he might say more then decided against it. He changed tack.

'It's not the sort of thing that happens regularly, you know.' He smiled reassuringly and added as though on the same topic, 'We really ought to be heading in now. I've hardly eaten all day.'

He patted his paunch and laughed good-naturedly, easing himself off the stool as he buttoned his well-cut jacket across his girth.

Ciara quickly swallowed what remained in her glass and slid off her stool. The almost neat alcohol was having the desired effect and she now felt more comfortable in her surroundings. The restaurant was everything she had heard it was. The place was awash with golden light which bathed the diners in a rich glow. The room was laid out so that only three or four tables were visible when they walked in, giving an air of privacy. The atmosphere was hushed and reserved. Just looking about, Ciara wished she could eat here every day. In fact, she wished she could live here, just move right in and never have to leave this quiet golden heaven again.

It wasn't until they were being shown to their table that Ciara noticed Melanie. She was sitting in an almost private alcove with two men Ciara didn't recognise but who looked as though they wanted to be kept out of the public eye and would be much happier wearing dark glasses. However, even they must have guessed this would look silly indoors. Nevertheless they sat with their gaze cast down in case anybody attempted to make eye contact. Melanie was obviously on guard for any unwanted intrusion. At intervals her eyes darted about the room to check for approaching threats.

Warmed by her Martini, Ciara smiled towards the table.

'Hi, Melanie, long time no see.' She changed direction, veering slightly towards them.

Melanie turned her face suddenly in Ciara's direction, her expression of surprise immediately replaced by a cold stare from diamond-hard eyes. She formed her mouth into a shallow U, displaying just enough pearly teeth to appear like a smile.

'Hi, how are you?' she said smoothly and in a tone that would more easily have been associated with saying, 'Piss off, why don't you!'

She held eye contact with Ciara just long enough to reinforce that tone and then returned to her conversation.

Ciara felt the rebuff like a blast of air from a cold room when the door is suddenly opened. She just prevented herself from freezing on the spot by taking John's arm and following his progress across the room after the waiter. John was very pleased by this physical contact and covered her hand with his.

Ciara was so stung by Melanie's reaction that she didn't even notice John's. She did, however, through her angry hurt, have a feeling that with her arm through his she was safe and protected from the dismissive coldness of her ex-colleague.

But even this didn't stop Ciara's mind racing.

Melanie must have heard about the incident at work. She must know that Ciara had been fired. Ciara had thought that being seen eating in The Harnden would give her a certain amount of status but this obviously wasn't the case: when she had lost her job, she had lost all that. Ranks had closed at the first sign of trouble.

Ciara had no doubt that Gary, even though he had never been part of the 'partying' crowd, was still revered and respected, still inside the fold, cosseted and swaddled and being fed comforting I-told-you-sos and there-there-never-minds in the unlikely event that Ciara's name was ever mentioned. She felt a little halo of bitterness form about her head. Like the Colgate smile it 'bing'-ed into existence.

Of course now she was glad Gary was out of her life but it still galled her that, even though *he* was the one who was married, the one who'd cheated, lied and exploited, it was *she* who had lost her job and her life as she had known it.

Or maybe, just maybe, Melanie had found out that

Ciara now had a day job as a rabbit! That would certainly be cause for social annihilation.

'Ciara?'

She looked up from the menu at which she had been staring to hide her embarrassment since she'd sat down a few moments before. John was looking at her questioningly as was the waiter.

'I'm sorry, what?' Ciara knew that she had been asked something but she had no idea what.

'Something to drink before dinner?'

You bet!

After the way Melanie – Melanoma! – had just brushed her off, Ciara felt she could do with another strong drink.

'Dry Martini, please, with a twist.' Never mind 'with a twist'. After two of those she'd be twisted herself!

She was grateful to John for not mentioning the incident with Melanie even though she was sure he had noticed. Ciara focused on the menu in an attempt to forget her humiliation. It was a plain piece of card listing an incredible range of mouthwatering dishes some of which she had never even heard of.

After Melanie she'd thought she'd lost her appetite. However, the sight of all that promised food stirred her stomach into a little grumbling monster. Why, oh why, hadn't she been invited to this restaurant just over two weeks ago when she had been a stone lighter? When she could have eaten whatever she liked without guilt and in the knowledge that a big meal here or there wasn't going to make her feel like crying from sheer disgust at her own lack of will-power.

She glanced across the table at John who was carefully studying his menu. He held it in one hand while the other stroked his tie down across his stomach as though it was some sort of furry animal. As she looked at him Ciara realised that if she and John started seeing each other regularly she would be eating out all the time. She would be constantly faced with calorie-laden menus and if she didn't keep an eye out would just keep ballooning. She could kiss goodbye to even the memory of her youthful trim waist. She would be twenty-eight and shapeless.

Twenty-eight and mateless.

Because John probably wouldn't want to go out with her anymore if she got really fat. On due consideration Ciara figured that maybe it wouldn't have been such a bad thing if that murder attempt had succeeded, if that generator had fallen on her. Though maybe an injury would have been best. A small painless one that would have put her in hospital for a week or two.

She'd be bound to lose weight in hospital, wouldn't she? And she would get loads of sympathy. Her mother would be crying at her bedside, abject remorseful tears at having sent her daughter out to work as a rabbit. And John ... well, it would obviously have been his fault for giving her such a crummy job. Penitent, he would fill the room with flowers so that everyone would know just how loved she was.

Of course if that had happened she would never have met Ken.

Ken ...

Ciara checked herself. She really shouldn't be thinking about him if she was going out with John. John who was taking her to dinner at The Harnden.

John who was still devoted to her after all these years.

John who could give her the security she needed on the final stretch of the narrow, treacherous path to thirty.

John, an oasis, a haven.

John who must have been learning the menu off by heart, he'd been looking at it for so long.

'So what do you think you'll have?' Ciara asked brightly to break his seeming trance. John looked at her sheepishly.

'Everything, I think.'

Ciara laughed politely as he continued, 'I think I'll start with the calf's liver, with either the veal or the duck as a main course.'

'Will you be having the gooseberry thing in between?' Ciara assumed from its position on the menu that the unpronounceable dish between the starter and the main course was a sorbet. She did a quick mind check to see if she knew how many calories were in sorbet.

'The Grenache? But of course, a man has to clear his palate between meats, you know.'

He was teasing her again. This took Ciara by surprise but she didn't laugh, still unsure if he was serious. John must have noticed her reaction as he quickly asked her, 'And you? What would you like?'

Ciara bit her lip. Skipping all the tastier options on the menu, she concentrated on the salads and fish.

'Salad to start and then the marlin.' That would be served with something called 'samphire' which she hoped wasn't fattening.

As they ordered Ciara's drink arrived. She gulped it down in record time then moved on to the wine. Everything was starting to become nicely blurry. The restaurant had receded to a background haze and John's little stories took on a new interest.

Unfortunately the food was delicious. Ciara had been hoping simply to play with it in a sophisticated thin-woman sort of way but as soon as she tasted it she wanted to gobble it all up. She was just relieved the portions were fashionably small. She even managed to resist dessert and watched as John worked his way through his chocolate and cream pie.

By the time she had finished her own brandy coffee Ciara felt nicely removed from reality. She felt as though she was floating on a little cloud of affluent pampering. And she didn't even have to see the bill; it disappeared in a flurry of John's credit card. She felt warm and happy, feelings she hadn't experienced for some time. She felt that she could get used to this sensation, this cocooning, this easy life.

Maybe there was a lot in what her mother had said about finding a financially secure man, a steady dependable type who could ensure she would never want for anything. Ciara had read all the articles on marriage. They said that the 'love-glow' wore off after three to five years and all that was left were bills, bad breath and a lot of time to regret a commitment made in an irrational state of lust.

Lust!

It wasn't as though it had ever brought Ciara anything except heartache and disappointment. (Well, a number of hours of pleasure as well but where did that fit into the grand scheme of things?) Maybe the time had come to be practicable. Practical ... sensible.

Even though Ciara was only thinking her words were slurred! The alcohol was having its effect.

It wasn't until they got up to go and were passing Melanie's table that Ciara remembered her. She was still there, looking tired now, obviously sitting out whatever lengthy conversation was keeping her we-don't-have-to-get-up-early dinner-companions at the table.

Ciara didn't notice her expression. The only thing on her mind was that Melanie had cut her dead earlier and now it was time for a little payback. After all, she didn't know who Melanie's companions were and was most unlikely to see them again. Ciara walked unsteadily over to their table and, leaning her hands on it, spoke to her ex-co-worker in a loud voice.

'So, Melanoma, are these the assholes you said you had to have dinner with? Keeping them up a bit late, aren't you? But you did say they were the sort of boring farts who'd natter on all night, didn't you? That is the expression you used, wasn't it? Boring farts?' Ciara raised her voice to ensure she was being heard.

The whole restaurant had fallen into hushed silence and was watching the scene with interest. Melanie was speechless. After a quick surprised stare at Ciara the two men had lowered their eyes, unwilling to acknowledge her. They abandoned the blushing Melanie to Ciara's attack: after all, the girl obviously knew her.

From the corner of her eye Ciara caught the movement of the maître d', manoeuvring his way over to dispel the awkward situation. She, however, had anticipated this and was already moving away from the table towards the door and John.

Melanie's embarrassed, appeasing voice followed her across the restaurant and Ciara felt a glow of satisfaction.

'Somebody you know?' John inquired as he ushered her out of the door.

Ciara nodded. 'Somebody I used to know,' she said flippantly, closing her coat around her as she stepped into the damp March night.

Chapter Ten

'I'm sure I left it here, John!'

Ciara was shivering with cold and annoyance as she stood on the edge of the pavement where her car should have been.

'But this is a double yellow line, are you sure?'

It was the third time he had asked this question in one form or another. Ciara was growing impatient with the repetition. She wanted him to move on, to find a solution, rescue her from this impossible situation.

'Look, I was in a hurry, there was nowhere else to park that wouldn't have meant walking for miles, OK?'

Once again she justified her double-yellow-line parking. Once again John shook his head in incomprehension.

'So do you think it's been stolen?'

Maybe it was a necessary part of being an accountant to ask obvious questions but Ciara thought it just too pedantic in these circumstances.

'Yes, I think it's been stolen, why else would it not be here?'

She spoke slowly and clearly with more than a suggestion of sarcasm in her voice. She couldn't even remember if she had locked the car, she had been in such a hurry. She wasn't going to admit this, though.

He didn't react to her sarcasm.

Earlier, when they had left The Harnden, the conversation had turned to getting home.

'Can I give you a lift?' John had dangled his keys in the general direction of where his car was parked.

'Well, I've got my car.' Ciara had waved her arm towards where it was parked. She wished she didn't have it with her because she didn't feel like driving home. Besides the fact that she had drunk far too much, the altercation with Melanie had left her with no inclination to be on her own. She needed distracting from herself.

'I couldn't possibly leave Karman Ghia where it is overnight,' she'd protested.

John had laughed and, raising his hands in surrender, put his keys back in his pocket.

'Let me walk you to your car then.'

He slid his arm around Ciara's waist and guided her in

the direction she had indicated. It had been a long time since she had experienced a public display of affection like this. Gary would always pretend he wasn't with her if they were out together. She felt safe and secure with John's arm about her and was almost sorry when they neared her car.

But of course it wasn't there.

Ciara felt as though somebody had stolen her soul. She couldn't believe this had happened. She had thought her car was immune to theft. It was too old and slow to appeal to the go-faster joy rider and more often than not it wouldn't start. Trust it to do so on the one evening it was being stolen!

She sighed with relief that she had taken her various bags and boxes out of it earlier. All that had disappeared along with the car was her emergency lipstick and her Karman Ghia-teddy bear, curator of the car since she'd bought it and patient recipient of post-traumatic road rage. Anything else left in there had just been papers and debris from her former desk at work.

As she studied the empty patch of road where the car had been Ciara had a feeling John was going to mention the double yellow line again.

If he did she would scream.

'Shouldn't I tell the police or something?' she asked him aggressively as though all this were his fault.

John paused, unsure of her mood.

'I guess so. Do you want to use this?'

He took a mobile phone out of his pocket and held it out to her.

'Yeah, I suppose so. Thanks.'

She was contrite now, starting to accept that her car really was missing and that focusing on the spot where she'd last seen it wasn't going to bring it back.

'Will I go and get my car? It would be warmer. You could call from it.' John's suggestion was tentative.

'No, it's OK, I'll walk with you. Pointless staying here. Could you give me a lift home?'

Ciara's voice was sweet and cajoling now. She was ashamed of her earlier sarcasm. Had realised that she was being unfair to John; that he was being supportive and considerate and she was treating him as though he was responsible for her misfortune. She slipped her arm through his and smiled up at him. John smiled back, nodding his relief at the return of a more rational Ciara.

In the car on their way through town she phoned the police. Unfortunately she knew nothing about her car except the colour so they said that she should find her car registration details and let them know as soon as possible. When they arrived at the flats, John switched off the engine and turned to her.

'Are you OK?'

Ciara nodded, a sudden surge of emotion catching her throat. Why did her car have to be stolen? There were thousands of cars on the streets, why did it have to be her Karman Ghia?

Even in the semi-darkness John could see she was upset.

'Come on, let me take you up. The least I can do is see you to your door. You never know, when we get there you might find a couple of glasses for this?'

As he spoke he reached into the back seat and produced a bottle of brandy. Ciara looked at him incredulously and he smiled slowly.

'I figured you wouldn't have time to stock up the drinks cabinet. Look on it as a housewarming gift.'

Ciara felt her self-pity receding. It was so nice to have somebody on hand who cared. Somebody to comfort her and be there for her. John was certainly making all the right moves! And she'd really like another drink.

Another drink might make her forget.

She handed John his mobile phone. She missed not having her own though the fact was she did have her own mobile, it just wasn't connected. The agency had provided her with one when she had started working with them so that she had no choice but to be constantly on call. She'd loved having a mobile phone; had upgraded it every year at her own expense so that she always had the smallest, trendiest, most-functions model. When she'd been fired they'd disconnected her. So while she still had a lovely little phone, she had no number and simply couldn't justify or afford a reconnection.

It was the same with her e-mail. She had the address but no computer. She knew she could go to a cyber café but for what? Without her job she had nothing to say in her e-mail. Her job had provided her with the confidence to maintain her on-line friendships. She wasn't about to start e-mailing London and New York telling everybody about her 'career change'.

Her virtual life was finished.

But then, so was her real life.

'Thanks for the use of the phone, John. Come on then, let's do some housewarming!'

They left the car and made their way up three flights of urine-smelling stairs. Ciara felt a stab of shame that this was now what she called home. Even reminding herself that it was John who had suggested she live there didn't help.

As they rounded the corner from the stairs on to the fourth floor, Ciara noticed that the area in front of the flat door was brightly lit, rather too brightly lit considering the bulb above it didn't work. She moved quickly towards the flat and, sure enough, when she reached the front door it stood wide open. Light flooded from the naked bulb into the hall. Ciara stopped dead, staring into the glare.

'What's the matter?' John asked, catching up with her in a few strides.

'The door's open.'

'So,' he said good-humouredly, 'maybe it was just too hot and Elena decided to leave it open. She's probably overheating because she's pregnant.'

He stepped into the open doorway and called loudly, 'Elena ... Elena? Hello, Elena.'

There was no answer. His voice echoed in the hallway and out along the walkway in front of the other flats. It sounded uncannily loud in the silent building.

'She's probably asleep. Come on in and close the door.' John beckoned to Ciara where she stood, hesitant and apprehensive, framed by the darkness.

Because she couldn't think of a reason not to Ciara stepped into the hallway, gently closing the door behind her.

She felt sure the door hadn't just been left open accidentally. Elena hadn't struck her as the sort who would fall asleep with the door open in a neighbourhood like this. No matter how foreign she was, she'd be bound to know it would be a stupid and dangerous thing to do. Anybody could walk in. Besides Elena was so impressed by the heat in the flat that she would rather simmer at boiling point than waste it by letting it float off into the cold Dublin night.

'Nobody here, Ciara.' John emerged from the kitchen. He stood in the hallway looking bothered; he was about to say something when Ciara cut in.

'Maybe you're right, maybe she is asleep in her room,' she said, not for one moment thinking that Elena was. John looked at the closed door of her room.

'I suppose I should take a look ...' He reached out and flung the door open, clutching the brandy bottle like a weapon. As he moved into the room, Ciara stepped in behind him. Elena was not there, her room was very bare, and what was in it had been thrown about as though a hurricane had whirled through the place. The mattress was off the bed, the drawers were out of the chest of drawers, the wardrobe was toppled as though somebody had been looking behind it, and Elena's clothes were strewn about the floor.

Ciara inhaled sharply.

'It looks like it's been burgled.'

John gave her a worried glance.

'That's what I was about to say. The kitchen is the same. The whole place is like this – really trashed. Maybe you should check your room.'

Ciara moved quickly down the hall and threw her bedroom door open. It did seem odd to her that somebody would ransack the place and then carefully close all the doors. She thought wryly that they had probably been told in the health and safety section of their lectures in burglary school that keeping internal doors closed cut down on the chances of fire spreading if one should break out during the burglary!

In Ciara's room somebody had finished unpacking for her. The clothes she hadn't thrown on the floor were now out of their boxes and strewn untidily about. Even the remaining contents of her cosmetics bag had been tipped on to the bed. Some of the larger items were left open, their lids missing somewhere in the bedlam.

This was the last straw for Ciara. It really hadn't been a good couple of days. In fact, it hadn't been a good couple of months but the last two days had been too much. Her new job was a joke, somebody had tried to kill her, one of her co-workers *had* been killed – probably because of her – and she'd been snubbed in one of the trendiest restaurants in town. On top of all that Karman Ghia had been stolen and her new flat was in such a high-risk area that she'd barely had time to move in before she'd been burgled!

Life seemed to be going from bad to worse. She wanted to tell whoever was making the world go around in such a crazy fashion to stop the cycle, she wanted to get off.

And there was another thing. Where was Elena? Pregnant Ukrainians couldn't just vanish into the night! Well, maybe, for all Ciara knew, they could in the Ukraine and such places but not in Dublin, not when they were supposed to be sharing a flat with her.

The idea that something might have happened to Elena distracted Ciara from her my-life-is-such-a-mess thoughts.

'What do you think's happened to her?' she said more to herself than to John. He, however, answered.

'Oh, I wouldn't worry too much about Elena, she's probably just gone to stay with some friends. They all stick together these immigrants. I mean, you don't even know her.'

He spoke so dismissively that Ciara stared at him in surprise.

'How do you mean? Do you think she burgled her own flat and then went to stay with friends because she couldn't stand the chaos?'

Ciara bit her tongue and reminded herself that sarcasm wasn't going to achieve anything.

John laughed dryly.

'No, what I'm saying is that she was more than likely out when it happened and when she got back and saw it like this she was probably frightened and went off to her friends. I have no doubt they'll come by soon to sort things out. It doesn't look like anything's missing, does it?'

Ciara shook her head. It was difficult to tell in the chaos but what little she'd had when she'd arrived all seemed to be there. Somewhat more widespread, but there.

'See, nothing missing, no worries,' John said.

'But if nothing's stolen, what did they want?' Ciara wasn't letting go so easily. She'd moved on to petulance. John's voice was soothing and matter-of-fact.

'Drugs or money. It's probably some local checking the place over for drugs. In this neighbourhood that's the most likely thing, isn't it? New people, new faces, they were just checking you out. It's my fault really for suggesting you stay here. I should have known it wasn't suitable, but it was the only place I knew where you could stay rent-free ... if only my house was ready.'

Now Ciara felt guilty. John had gone to the bother of getting her somewhere to stay and it wasn't his fault if the neighbours weren't the best. The flat was clean and warm, and nothing had been taken. Elena was probably, even as they spoke, off drinking her coffee concoction in a friend's house, safe and comfortable.

Maybe Ciara was overreacting.

She turned to face John with a rueful smile.

'How about a drink then? I'll go dig out some glasses.'

She went to the kitchen. There wasn't much digging to be done; all the dishes were already out of the cupboards and sitting on the unit tops. The saucepans lay on the floor. The tea and sugar and other indefinable packaged goods had been poured down the sink, forming a powdery speckled mountain in the basin.

Ignoring the mess, Ciara picked up two cups. There didn't seem to be any glasses in the flat. She went into the living room where John was replacing the cushions on the sofa. He turned the small cane coffee table upright to hold the cups and brandy.

'Not exactly *Homes & Gardens*,' he commented.

Ciara nodded, throwing herself on to the sofa as she watched him carefully unseal the bottle with his small deft hands and pour a measure into each cup. He presented one to Ciara and held his in the air.

'To a better day tomorrow!' He swallowed the contents. Ciara nodded and did the same.

After John had refilled the cups he took off his jacket, lowered himself on to the sofa and, loosening his tie, turned to her.

'You haven't told me what you think of your new job?'

Feeling happier now as the brandy burned through her, she almost laughed into her drink. She'd been so careful all evening not to mention her part on the Easi-tel sales team. And John was the last person to whom she was going to talk about how humiliating the job was. She neutralised her voice and spoke cautiously.

'Well, it's certainly interesting.' She didn't feel she

could elaborate on that without giving away her true feelings.

'Anything else happen during the day?' His voice was politely enquiring.

Ciara had a sudden feeling of guilty panic. Did he know she'd struck up a friendship with Ken? That they'd finished work early and he'd proposed they should go for a drink together? Not that it should matter, nothing had happened.

'What do you mean?' Her tone was defensive, sharp. John looked taken aback.

'Nothing. It's just that you said this morning something had nearly fallen on you and you seemed to think it was more than just an accident.'

'Oh, that!' Ciara was relieved, she'd totally forgotten having told him about the murder attempt.

'No, nothing else. I'm sure that was nothing, just a coincidence.'

Ciara knew this wasn't true but didn't want to appear melodramatic. It seemed bad enough to have had her car stolen and her house broken into let alone trying to push for the recognition of a murder attempt as well.

'Everything is all right with the job then?' John's question was rhetorical now, as though he was wrapping the subject up.

'Oh, yeah.' Ciara nodded. Then, thinking quickly, she

added, 'The people in the shop ... you know, the sales assistants or whatever you call them ... how did they get those jobs? Did you have to find people with shop-floor experience?'

She made it sound as though this was simply a matter of curiosity, an innocent inquiry. In fact she needed to find out why she had to walk the streets dressed as a rabbit, being tormented by every passing child, when she could just as easily have an indoor job. One that allowed her to stand behind a counter dealing with grown-ups who had made up their minds that they wanted the T2.

John smiled slightly and pushed his glasses higher.

'Oh, that's Gráinne's domain. And she's in charge of the promotional workers. Anything to do with the shop is down to her.' John paused, the smile playing over his lips as though he was enjoying pleasant thoughts, then continued, 'Gráinne's great at that side of things. In fact, she runs the whole on-the-ground operation, don't know how she manages it.'

Ciara could feel a sarcastic comment bubbling to escape. It rose, fully formed, frantic to reach the surface and explode into the world. It would erupt in a splutter of, 'Fascism can be a powerful force with the right woman as a figurehead!' She swallowed hard, hoping the physical action would prevent the words from escaping.

During this pause she realised that she was furious.

On second thoughts, though, she wasn't so sure it was fury.

Taking a closer look, she started in surprise.

It couldn't be, could it?

Was the emotion she was feeling jealousy?

She could certainly see a green tinge around the edges of her anger. It wasn't that Ciara was unfamiliar with envy or jealousy. He entire life seemed to have been spent envying other people! It stretched back any number of years shrouded in a tell-tale green cloud.

For three years she'd been driven wild with jealousy any time she thought of Gary's wife. And, she had to admit, sometimes to her shame, she'd even envied his child because she had a legitimate place in his life.

She envied people like Melanie who managed to be beautiful and have successful careers. Yes, Ciara was well acquainted with jealousy but was surprised that John's mention of Gráinne and her good qualities had aroused the feeling.

She wasn't envious of Gráinne because of her job. What bothered Ciara was that John obviously thought his manageress was great. He thought she was so great that when he spoke about her a pleased smile played around his lips.

This wasn't the way it was supposed to be.

He was supposed to be devoted to her, to Ciara Bowe,

193

love of his life since she was fifteen. He'd said the night before that he was still interested in her and tonight he'd taken her out for an expensive, romantic meal. He wasn't supposed to take pleasure in the thought of other women, particularly plain, stocky, shopkeeper-type women!

'Well, if you think she's so great, maybe you should go out with her then!'

As soon as she said it Ciara knew it was the wrong thing to say, the wrong attitude to take. But she couldn't take it back now.

She silently vowed to give up drink.

John looked as though she had just given him an electric shock. The smile disappeared from his lips and he stared at her with an indescribable expression of hurt in his eyes. He opened his mouth as though to say something but instead sighed. Then his mouth opened and closed as if he really was going to say something this time but instead he sighed again.

Ciara's heart fell.

She did so hate Sighers.

People who think that sighing is actually a way of expressing emotion. In situations of anger, love or anxiety, instead of expressing the emotion they are feeling they sigh, usually quite heavily and with meaning.

Ciara hated Sighers because she could never figure out which emotion they were sighing about!

She had detected a hint of a sigh earlier in the evening during the double-yellow-line episode but had decided to overlook it. Now, however, she was being confronted with a whole shoal of sighs and couldn't very well ignore them.

She remembered John's sighs over the years. The most notable sighing session had been just before he'd gone to America when they were in a 'going out together' phase. On their last evening together, Ciara, upset that he was leaving, had looked for reassurance that she wouldn't be forgotten the moment he got on the plane.

'So, John, do you think we should call it a day now that you're emigrating?' she'd asked lightly, not wanting to sound too serious. Lots of their friends had relationships that continued quite well between countries, flights being accessible and cheap these days.

All John had to say was something along the lines of, 'Well, now you have somewhere to go at weekends!' Or, 'I'm going to buy you a magic carpet so we'll never be apart!' Or, 'You know that being away from you won't lessen my feelings for you!' OK so that one was a bit soppy but he could have said, 'I'll be home so often you won't even know I'm gone, and anyway wouldn't you like Christmas in New York?'

He could have said anything but instead he said nothing. He just looked at her with that same all-consuming hurt expression and sighed. Then, moving his lips as though about to speak, he sighed again. It was obviously meant to convey a huge depth of emotion and sensitivity but to Ciara it was simply an insulting silence. That evening, as so many times before, she got up and stormed away, determined not to stay involved with a man who became a deflating airbag in times of emotion.

This hadn't been the only notable sighing incident.

Years before, just after she'd left school, John had invited her to Paris for the weekend to attend an accountants' ball. Ciara thought this very grown up and even bought a long dress for the occasion. Unfortunately the airline lost John's bag en-route, leaving him without a dress suit. The airport staff in Paris just shrugged and said it might turn up later and they should wait in their hotel. Instead of ringing the airline in Ireland and trying to trace the luggage, John had sat in his hotel room and sighed as though fate was determined to destroy his evening and there was absolutely nothing he could do about it.

It had taken all Ciara's energy not to shake him. Eventually *she* had phoned and his bag was traced in Dublin, put on the next flight and reached Paris in the nick of time. It constantly amazed her that a man who was so successful at managing other people's lives, or at any rate their money, could be so inert, so inactive in his personal life.

But it was no good thinking about that now, she reasoned, it was all in the past. She'd been very young then and full of all sorts of expectations. What was a sigh or two in the grand scheme of things? Everybody had faults and if she went about looking for Mr Perfect, Mr Faultless, she'd be spending a lot of time on her own.

In fact, now that she thought about it she'd already been spending a lot of time on her own. Too much time.

No, she had to be mature and accepting because if she could just overlook the little things that annoyed her, she and John were perfectly compatible.

'Because I'd rather be with you.'

John had spoken. He had worked himself through a storm of sighing and had reached a whole sentence.

Ciara couldn't remember what she'd asked him but she was interested to discover that if she didn't stalk out in the middle of his sighing he would eventually say something.

'Pardon?'

'I said that I don't go out with Gráinne because I'd rather be with you, Ciara.'

This was exactly the answer she had been looking for!

Maybe time away had changed John. Maybe he was now able to deal with emotional situations. Maybe, a bit of sighing aside, John had become Mr Perfect. Or at any rate Mr Nearly Perfect! Maybe all she needed was a bit of patience and everything would work out fine.

Maybe steady, dependable John could also be romantic, passionate John.

Ciara remembered that he had been very romantic when they had first started going out together.

He used to write verses to her. For ages Ciara thought he'd written them himself but it later transpired they were taken from the sleeves of his CD collection. He collected CDs and tapes when other boys were devoting their time to mitching class. And he wasn't collecting contemporary music; he was collecting the earlier works of Bob Dylan and Leonard Cohen.

When he and Ciara would break up, which was every month or so, he would send her a little mournful verse that always finished on a poignant note like:

But let's not talk of love and chains and things we can't untie,
Your eyes are soft with sorrow,
Hey, that's no way to say goodbye.

She had no idea why she remembered those lines. Maybe when she thought he'd written them she'd been so impressed she'd learned them off by heart.

Besides they rhymed!

Ciara had thought this verse-writing was the ultimate in romantic passion. That is until they'd read *Wuthering Heights* in school. As soon as she discovered the relationship between Cathy and Heathcliff she knew what she was missing in her life: passion.

She wanted what she saw in *Wuthering Heights*, a love that even death couldn't divide. She wanted a Heathcliff who would dig up her grave twenty years after her death, just to kiss her lips once more.

She wanted to be obsessed and haunted, torn and destroyed for that one great love.

She wanted a man who would torment her in life and after death.

Ciara decided John Murphy would never be anything more than the 'other man' in the book, an Edgar Linton: a sweet but ineffectual man who couldn't understand the depths of her soul. One who would never love her with the wild abandoned passion she dreamed of. John would always be like some faithful dog, instead of the savage beast that would devour rather than let its love go.

Ciara had decided then that what she needed in life was a dark-eyed stranger who would take her in his arms, sweep her off her feet and fill her life with tortured love until their very kisses were enough to keep winter away and the tempest of their touch drowned the storm on the moors . . .

She now knew that it could all be blamed on raging teenage hormones.

She *hadn't* known this at the time.

Now at nearly twenty-eight Ciara still needed passion but the years in between had taught her that life was just not up to fiction. That faceless, nameless, tortured dark stranger she held in her imagination would, if she ever met him, probably be just another one-night stand. Maybe what she needed *was* an Edgar Linton, a safe and stable man who would love and take care of her.

She reached across the table for a refill and swallowed the brandy immediately. John watched her silently. He was looking for some sign that what he had just said meant something to her. She met his eye.

'That's a really nice thing to say, John.'

He sighed and, half smiling, reached out to take her hand in his. After a pause he spoke.

'I have a lot of nice things I could say, given the opportunity. There is one thing I'd like to say first, though. I don't think you should stay here on your own tonight in the circumstances, and besides I'm a bit over the limit . . .'

Ciara nodded. 'You're right, you're in no condition to drive.' Her voice was calm but her mind was racing.

Now what?

John edged closer and just like the night before in his car, leaned over and kissed her. Whether it was the brandy or nervousness, Ciara couldn't help herself and burst into giggles. He drew back, scowling and hurt.

'What?' he demanded shortly.

She had absolutely no way of telling the truth without hurting him further so prattled the first thought that came into her head.

'I was just thinking of those songs you used to write to me.'

John's face softened. He liked to think she remembered that. He used to keep a special pen just to write those verses for her. 'Yeah,' he said with a short laugh. 'Do you remember how your mother thought Dylan's "Lay, lady, lay" was about his pet hen?'

Ciara had forgotten this but the memory of it sent her into more helpless giggles. When she stopped John was looking at her seriously again and in a quiet voice said, 'And do you remember the lines that went:

> '…"I love you in the morning,
> Your kisses soft and warm,
> Your hair upon the pillow …"'

Ciara nodded. It had been a long time since anybody had looked at her like that and spoken soft poetry to her.

This time when their lips met she didn't giggle.

Chapter Eleven

'Can I give you a lift to work?' John lay in Ciara's bed, his hands behind his head, a satisfied expression on his face.

'Er ... OK, thanks,' she mumbled from somewhere on the floor where she was hunting for clean clothes. She didn't look up, couldn't bring herself to. She just didn't know how to react.

She and John Murphy had made love the night before.

She wished she could set the clock back and rearrange the night so that she hadn't made love with John. She knew this was impossible and now she had to get through the morning-after moments as though the night before had been the manifestation of everything she had ever dreamed of.

When in fact it had been a disaster.

Ciara now knew that whoever had said size didn't matter was lying.

Size mattered!

Size mattered greatly!

On a scale of one to ten of mattering Ciara figured that size came in at an even ten. She had never known this before. Somewhere at the back of her mind it bothered her that at the age of nearly twenty-eight she hadn't known this.

She felt so naive, so unworldly.

And now, as a consequence, so disappointed.

She could accept that John wasn't very well-versed in foreplay. However, she found it difficult to accept the fact that sex had been a slight sensation, a lot of panting from John and no orgasm for her.

She felt bewildered.

She felt betrayed.

Nevertheless, and despite having a hangover, she knew that she was only disappointed because of her great expectations. She had decided that maybe, just maybe, John was The One and now she felt let down.

Her newly discovered instinct for compromise told her the sex thing was just another situation that required mature handling. Unfortunately this morning she just didn't feel up to mature handling.

'What time do you have to be in, Ciara?'

John, a little neglected alone in the bed, propped himself up on his elbows and looked in Ciara's direction. He wasn't wearing his glasses so she wasn't sure if he could see her.

'Nine-thirty. I should just make it if I get a move on.' She threw a reassuring smile in his direction just in case he could see that far and stood up, pulling her T-shirt as far down over her thighs as possible. She suddenly felt very shy and vulnerable. She clutched her chosen clothes to her chest and scuttled from the room.

'I should be out of the bathroom in about ten minutes, OK?' she called over her shoulder as she went. 'Help yourself to whatever ... sorry, I don't have any food in.'

She ran into the bathroom, shut the door, dropped the pile of clothes on the floor and stared in the mirror.

Panic stared back at her, daring her to look away. Daring her to admit that she might have made a mistake. To distract herself from that stare she grabbed her cleanser and started to remove last night's streaked makeup.

Panic frowned.

'Sex isn't everything, you know,' Ciara whispered at the intruder, challenging Panic to contradict her.

'So what if he isn't the handsomest or the most shapely of men? Gary was handsome and shapely and look where that got you! We can work on the bed thing. It'll be all right.'

Panic gave in and fled, leaving in its wake a trace of Concern.

A big trace of Concern.

What would happen if she married John?

Marriage hadn't been mentioned recently but she knew that John thought about it. When they were young he used to talk to her about their getting married. Together they had made great romantic plans for the future. Somewhere between then and now those plans had been lost but it was only logical that as they were together again things would get around to that.

In a couple of years she'd be thirty and couldn't deny that she'd always thought she'd be happily married by that time.

And John was the obvious choice.

They would have a proper sort of wedding, attended by lots of professionals in morning coats and inappropriately large hats. People with big mortgages, good prospects and trophy cars. Life after marriage would be a spin of dinner parties with the occasional day at the races or on a friend's boat. Conversation would be about property prices and the best schools to send the children.

The children!

Ciara's concerned reflection swallowed hard and fought an unsuccessful skirmish with the newly returned Panic.

What about the children?

Before she could stop herself a series of uncharitable and unthinkable questions flew into her mind.

What if the children turned out like their father?

What if they ... Ciara had difficulty even thinking this ... inherited certain physical limitations from John? Would her son curse her when he grew up and realised? Would a daughter resent the fact that she looked like her father?

She inhaled deeply to calm herself. At least if they took after John they would have the advantage of being intelligent. She decided that even as a consenting adult she couldn't select a partner purely for his physical traits. It was much more important that he be loving and supportive and she had no reason to doubt John on that score.

Ciara squinted at herself in the mirror and nodded, affirming that last thought. She vowed never to drink brandy again. It was obviously a serious depressant!

'Ciara, is there enough hot water for me to take a shower, do you think?' John knocked gently on the door and waited for an answer. Ciara started and swung away from the mirror, turning on the shower as she did so.

'Oh, sure there is. I'll be out in a minute, OK?'

She ducked under the water, scrubbing herself to shake off her hangover. Before wrapping the towel about her body she took one last critical look at herself in the mirror. Her eyes swept briefly down over the swell of her stomach. She couldn't bear to look at where her waist used to be, it was just too distressing.

No wonder her sex life was lousy, she was becoming frumpy and heavyset. She twisted sideways and inhaled, hoping this would make a difference. It didn't. She thought bitterly that she should have had a salad for main course the night before. It was too late to think of that now. No amount of hindsight would lose that stone and get her waist back!

Ciara quickly pulled on her clothes, determined to be fully dressed as she passed John. When she emerged from the bathroom he wasn't in the hall as she'd expected. Instead she found him in the bedroom, propped on the edge of the bed with a very serious expression on his face. He sat, elbows on his knees, chin in his hands, silhouetted against the dull morning light of the curtained window.

Ciara sighed inwardly. It wasn't just their lovemaking that bothered her. She was beginning to realise she wasn't very physically attracted to John. The Lust-fireworks seemed to be missing.

This disturbed her because she cared about him, maybe even loved him, or at any rate could grow to love him. All she could think was that perhaps with time she would get used to the physical thing, and in the meanwhile would just have to be mature about it.

'You OK?' she asked quietly, thinking that he was experiencing some of the feelings she was and between them they could work things out.

John looked at her with an expression of intense emotion. His lips moved slightly and he sighed.

'Ciara, you have no idea how much I longed for last night. How long I waited to make love to you.'

She froze.

How wrong could she be?

John was thinking nothing like she was. He wanted to engage in post-coital endearments!

'Yeah, John. It was ... very nice.' She wondered if he noticed the lack of enthusiasm in her voice. He stood up and stepped forward to give her a quick peck on the lips.

'We were always meant to be together, you know, it'll be wonderful.'

Ciara smiled and felt a shroud of inevitability settle about her. There was no doubt that John was right otherwise why else *would* they be together again? All her feelings of doubt were just a destructive streak she would have to learn to ignore. John would be good for her. After all, he hadn't even commented on the fact that she had put on a bit of weight!

Ciara had heard about couples being comfortable together, accepting little habits and bodily shortcomings, not deriding each other for failures and mistakes. If she could learn to compromise maybe she and John could achieve this.

She reached out and squeezed his arm.

'Thanks, of course it will, but my boss will fire me if I don't get a move on, and you wouldn't like to be going out with somebody who's unemployed, would you?'

He laughed and disappeared off to the bathroom.

It wasn't until they left the building and were working their way down the stairs that Ciara remembered her car. The memory caught at her throat like a cold hand and she had to pause mid-flight to catch her breath.

Poor little Karman Ghia!

'Are you all right?' John stopped behind her, concerned.

'Yeah, just had a car flash. I can't believe anybody would steal Karman Ghia.'

John sighed gently as she moved on down the stairs.

'I'll have to get to my mother's house to pick up the registration book so I can give the police the full details. Maybe I could get out there this evening after work. I'm working late though . . .'

She stopped talking, trying to work out if she would have time and energy to get to her mother's house after work. If she felt anything like she did now all she would want to do was go to bed – on her own!

'I could give you a lift after work,' John offered, slightly breathless from the stairs.

Ciara turned to give him an appreciative smile.

'Would you really? That would be great, thanks. Is it OK if I let you know later?'

He nodded, the earlier look of pleased satisfaction returning to his flushed face. Ciara felt a rush of warmth for him and decided that she was overreacting to the whole physical attraction thing. After all, sex wasn't everything. She gave him a little kiss as he opened the car door for her.

Maybe their life together wouldn't be so bad after all!

John let her off at the end of Henry Street, a few yards from the shop. Ciara knew that she was running three minutes late but hoped Gráinne had something better to do this morning than clock watch.

She hadn't.

'You're late.' Her arms were folded as she stared at Ciara with a look schoolteachers spend years training to achieve. Ciara gave up trying to close the door gently and let it slam.

'Yeah, sorry, car got stolen.' She twisted the truth a little to ease the situation. It seemed unlikely she'd get away with, 'Yeah, sorry, I was shagging the boss and he's a devil to get out in the mornings!'

'Oh.' Gráinne paused for a moment. Ciara could sense that she didn't want to believe her but didn't know her well enough to call her a liar. 'OK, but it's not the first time you've been late, remember that. Hurry up and get changed, the nine-thirties have already left.'

Ciara nodded and moved towards the staffroom to change into her costume. As she did so she glanced enviously at the shop staff who were busily sorting through files and tills in preparation for the day.

She was doing up her costume when Gráinne's voice sounded behind her.

'We've had a bit of a shift in work schedules after yesterday's ... ah ... accident so I wonder, would you be able to work on Saturday?'

Ciara frowned, trying to think that far ahead. It slowly dawned on her that it didn't matter what days she worked, she had nothing planned for the foreseeable future. Gráinne, however, didn't know this as she quickly went on, 'Naturally you'd get double the rate. It is, after all, St Patrick's Day. In fact, all we want you to do is shadow the parade giving out flyers. We can't afford to miss such a great promotional opportunity. We've also sponsored a float in the parade so I think we have maximum coverage.'

Gráinne stopped abruptly, realising there was absolutely no reason why she should be explaining her advertising strategy to a promoter who looked as though she'd had one too many the night before.

It was obvious to her that drinking was the reason Ciara had reached whatever age she was without a career. Gráinne sniffed disparagingly and waited for an answer. Ciara nodded. She would have worked even if it had not been double money.

'Right, hurry up then, you're on North Earl Street this morning.' Gráinne bustled out of the room.

It wasn't until she was about to leave the staffroom that Ciara noticed a newspaper on the table.

Newspaper meant lottery numbers.

She hadn't checked her lottery numbers from the night before!

She scrambled back across the room to get the ticket from her bag. The familiar feeling of anticipation started in her stomach and moved towards her chest. She loved that feeling. It was as though for that minute or so between finding her ticket and looking at the numbers drawn, she was the winner. She, Ciara Bowe, was a millionaire.

The ticket wasn't in her bag. She thought back to the evening before, trying to recall in which of her 'safe places' she had left it.

Suddenly she remembered.

It was in the car!

It wasn't just Karman Ghia that had been stolen. All the hopes and dreams she had invested in the purchase of that ticket had been stolen too. She would never know now whether she was a millionaire or not!

Ciara replaced her bag and, picking up her head and paws, trailed her way despondently out of the staffroom. As she passed through the shop Gráinne handed her a pile of flyers.

'Your break is at eleven-forty-five.'

Once on North Earl Street Ciara checked the next street for another Easi-tel worker. When she spotted one in the distance she raised her arm in salute, wondering if it was Ken. Getting no response she decided that it probably wasn't. She was relieved at this because she felt far too exhausted for small talk, even with a handsome man. All her energy was going into trying not to give in to her desire to sit down and have a sleep. She felt sure that if she could just take one little snooze she would be fine. This might have been something to do with the fact that she hadn't had anything to eat. She didn't want anything to eat, in fact, her stomach felt quite queasy. The memory of how they had drunk three-quarters of the bottle of brandy the night before made her feel even sicker.

She was just considering whether or not she should go and find a quiet place to throw up in when the T2, still in her pouch from the day before, started to ring. She pulled it out and tentatively pushed the button.

'Hello?'

'Ciara, it's your mother.'

Her mother always announced herself like this, evidently assuming that after twenty something years of listening to her voice her daughters would have no idea who was phoning them.

'Hi, Mum.' Ciara didn't even try to sound interested.

'Have you the time to talk now because I can always ring later?'

Ciara looked up and down the street to check if any passers-by were clamouring to get at the Easi-tel flyers. Interest was at an all-time low.

'Yeah, Mum, it's OK. I've got a few minutes. How did you get this number?' She didn't care how but felt it was good to know these things.

'Oh, I phoned John on his mobile phone and he gave it to me.' Ciara could sense that her mother was very pleased at her mastery of modern technology. 'He told me your car had been stolen – that's a wicked shame. What is the world coming to? Who took it?'

'Mum, if I knew who did it would be borrowed not stolen, wouldn't it?'

What was it about her mother that always brought Ciara out in a rash of sarcasm? She quickly moved on.

'I'll have to get the registration book from your house sometime today.'

Her mother had just been waiting for her to finish speaking.

'John told me that and I'm coming into town this afternoon. I could bring it with me. Where would you have put it?'

'In the file marked "car" in the brown box that should be under the bed.'

'That's fine. What time will I meet you later?'

Ciara tried to work out a time and a place but had no idea what time her afternoon break would be or where she would be working.

'Will you call me about two-thirty. I'll be able to arrange something then.'

'Absolutely. I'll give you a wee call just before I leave.'

'Fine. Thanks, Mum. Talk to you later.' Ciara prepared to hang up.

'Ciara . . . Ciara!' Even though the phone was not by her ear anymore she could hear her mother shouting.

'Yeah?'

'The reason I was ringing in the first place was to tell you that I was talking to Ruth, your sister, this morning and she'll be in town later and wants to get in touch with you.' Another habit of Mrs Bowe's was to put 'your sister' after any reference she made of one daughter to another.

'OK, have you given her the number?'

'Yes, but I just wanted to let you know she'd be calling.'

'Thanks, Mum ...'

'She'll probably have called you by the time I meet you this afternoon so ...'

Ciara knew that her mother was going to go on forever and just didn't feel up to it.

'Yes, Mum. I'll talk to you about it later, OK? Gotta go. 'Bye.'

She hung up and heaved a sigh of relief. It was much easier to handle her mother when their conversations were limited to the phone. Besides she'd be meeting her later so she could be nice to her then. Ciara slipped the T2 into her pocket and went back to distributing her flyers.

So Ruth was going to be in town? Ciara managed a little half smile at the idea. She liked her younger sister. Even though she was a bit outspoken they got on well together. Ever since Ruth had been banished from her mother's house and had insisted on remaining banished she'd always stayed with Ciara when she was in town. She lived in Wexford where her main occupation was campaigning against genetically modified foods. She always had some cause or other that she was fighting, living her life in as close to hippy style as she could.

She and Ciara didn't tend to gossip that much on the

phone, instead saving their news until they saw each other. Ciara hadn't seen her for over two months and so hadn't told her all the details of her break up with Gary. She wondered what her sister would say when she heard Ciara was going out with John ... again!

The idea of Ruth's coming to visit had cheered her up enormously. If it hadn't been for a violent thirst Ciara might have forgotten her mid-morning break completely. As it was she had to run back to the shop. Gráinne, checking her watch, for once seemed pleased at this lack of punctuality.

As Ciara burst into the staffroom she heard the mumble of voices. For an instant she thought it might be Ken but one glance at the two men sitting at the table confirmed that it wasn't. She recognised them as being from the group of smokers who had stood outside the shop the evening before.

Ciara felt uncomfortable in their company. The men stared at her coldly and then, with only a cursory nod, fixed their eyes on the table. An awkward unfriendly silence permeated the tiny room. Ciara busied herself at the tap, drinking as much as she could without appearing to linger. Then she made a cup of coffee, hoping it would shock her body into action. As she leaned against the sink and drank it she thought wistfully that if she could live on coffee for two or three days she would lose a few pounds and maybe sort out her waist crisis.

Suddenly, without warning, after a quick mumble to one another the men got up to go. They nodded dourly in her direction. Having made eye contact, Ciara felt she should say something.

'Er . . . excuse me.' She faltered as they turned to look at her sullenly. 'I just wanted to say,' she swallowed, 'that I'm sorry about your, er, friend . . . about Dimitri.' She nodded, hoping that they understood what she was saying.

One of them replied, 'Thank you. I am Dimitri's cousin, it has made us also very sad.' His words rattled like gravel and he turned towards her giving a formal little bow. Then, without looking at her again, the two of them left the room.

So much for being friendly! Ciara thought. So much for making an effort! All the same, she concluded, sitting down at the table and taking another sip of her coffee, it couldn't be easy having your cousin killed like that in a foreign country.

Ten minutes later when Gráinne came in to check the staffroom she found Ciara asleep at the table, her arms cradling her head like a child in junior school taking a nap.

'Ciara Bowe, I believe your break is over. I do *not* pay you to sleep on the job.'

Ciara started awake to the sight of a tight-lipped-arms-folded Gráinne standing over her.

'Gosh, I'm sorry, I didn't mean to . . .' Ciara had gone a deep shade of red and couldn't think of any excuse so she leaped up, gathered the rest of her costume and moved quickly towards the door.

'Your lunch is at one-thirty,' Gráinne called after her in an icy tone.

Ciara cursed her way back to her street, bemoaning her bad luck at falling asleep under Gráinne's critical eye.

She didn't mind if word got back to John, though, he'd probably find it amusing that she was so tired after a night with him.

What she did mind was Gráinne and how she would look at Ciara now, her mean little eyes suggesting that Ciara was incapable even of holding down a job as a leaflet distributor. She would probably work out a way of sending her to work on the motorway, to face certain death! Though she knew that she didn't even have to go on to the motorway to be confronted with death. Standing about under the wrong piece of scaffolding would have just the same effect!

Ciara had just started back to work when somebody touched her lightly on the arm. She swung around, focusing her eyepiece in the direction of the touch.

'Hello, how's bunny business with you today?'

It was Ken, his curly hair a little flat from being trapped inside his rabbit head all morning but his grin as infectious as it had been the day before.

'Fine, fine,' Ciara yelled through the process of pulling the suffocating rabbit's head off. Her face appeared, red and hair-strewn. Without stopping to take a breath, she continued speaking.

'How are you?'

'Oh, you know, fulfilled, satisfied, determined to get ahead in my chosen career. My ambition for today is not to throw any flyers away, no matter how tempted I am.' Ken spoke in a serious tone, eyes sparkling with mischief, his curls starting to reassert themselves. He smiled.

'On a more frivolous note, I'm on my way to lunch and wondered if it's your break time yet?'

Ciara shook her head.

'I'm afraid not, I've just come back from a break. No chance of getting out of here for another couple of hours. Where are you working?'

'Other side of the river. And, yes, the clientele are just as abusive over there.'

Ciara hadn't been thinking about the clientele. What she *had* been thinking was that there was no geographical reason why Ken would have to go down the street on which she was working to get back to the shop. There were only two possible reasons why he was here. One was that he didn't know his way around and the other was that he had come to see her. He didn't seem like the type of guy who wouldn't know his way around so that left just one reason.

The idea gave Ciara a thrill of pleasure.

'Have you had any trouble today?' Ken was still talking to her, his face enquiring.

'No, nothing. Except that I drank a little too much last night and, well, you know ...' She hadn't meant to say anything about the night before, it just slipped out. She realised guiltily that she didn't want to say anything because she wanted Ken to think she was single and available. Before she could work her way through the ramifications of this, he picked up the conversation.

'Do you think that a little "hair of the dog" after work would help?'

Ciara knew what he meant, at least she thought she knew what he meant, but she wasn't prepared to take the risk of being wrong. She wasn't going to risk saying yes to a question that, if looked at objectively, could mean anything.

'What do you mean?' She spoke shyly, awed by the idea that Ken was asking her out. Yeah, OK, he had casually mentioned a drink after work the day before but that was quite different from making an arrangement in the morning to do something that evening.

'I mean, would you like to do something this evening after work? Something like eating or drinking? It's known as socialising.' He was laughing now as he spelt it out. Ciara heaved a sigh of relief. He *was* asking her out and it was all so spontaneous and natural, she laughed with delight.

'Yeah, some socialising would be great but I'm working until seven . . .'

Ken didn't let her finish.

'Hey, remember I'm working 'til nine, so how about we meet up somewhere at nine-fifteen or so?'

Ciara nodded gratefully. At least she would have time to unflatten her hair!

'Meet you outside there,' he said, pointing to the front of a brightly lit, open 'til late café at the other end of the street.

'OK.' Ciara was trying not to show just how pleased she was. Her heart was racing and she felt that if she were alone she would do some sort of bunny dance in her cumbersome costume. Instead she darted a quick glance of agreement at Ken. He was staring at her confidently, waiting to make eye contact.

The smile in his eyes spread to his lips.

'Nine-fifteen then.'

Chapter Twelve

'Hello, Mum. Hi.'

Ciara was almost shouting into the phone. It had taken her so long to find the T2 in her pouch that she was afraid she had missed the call. There was no number on the display screen again.

'So your mother did get in touch with you then?' John's amused voice answered.

'Yes. Er, sorry, John. Mum said she would ring at about two-thirty and it must be that now.'

'It's exactly twenty-five past so I'll make this brief in case she does ring.'

He sounded so kind and thoughtful Ciara thought she would drown in the wave of Ken-guilt that swept over her.

'Oh, don't worry about it. If she doesn't get through, she'll just ring me back.'

Being nice did help to appease the guilt a little.

'How are you feeling?' John seemed determined to continue being considerate and thoughtful.

'Fine. Well, to be honest, a bit ropey. Seems like today is just going to go on forever.'

'I'm sorry to hear that, love.'

Love?

He had called her love!

He'd never called her love before.

Ciara froze. There was nothing wrong with him calling her 'love', it was just unexpected. She had thought people didn't call each other 'love' until they had a mortgage on a house in the suburbs, a family car, two point five children and a dog!

It sounded proprietorial.

John didn't seem to notice her silence and after a quick breath continued talking.

'I was wondering if you'd like to do something later?' Ciara didn't even have time not to answer as he went on, 'A quiet drink or something? Or if you don't feel up to going out, I could cook you something at your place?'

Sheer astonishment forced a response from her.

'Cook?' She was staggered at the suggestion. She couldn't imagine anyone wanting to cook when they didn't have to. She had learned to cook when she was with Gary but that was because they couldn't go out. Why would anyone want to stay in and cook if they had the money and the freedom to go out?

'Yeah, nothing elaborate or anything but I'm a pretty nifty cook now, you know. Italian is my favourite.'

Ciara envisioned an evening of recipe-swapping, or rather recipe-receiving as she couldn't say with certainty that she knew any recipes off by heart. She needed an excuse to avoid this cooking intimacy. And after that she would have to think up a reason to keep the evening free for Ken.

She wasn't going to cancel her date with him, even for her boyfriend!

'Oh, John, that sounds like it would be lovely but I honestly don't think the kitchen in that flat has enough utensils, especially for the kind of cooking you'd like to do. And besides it's in an awful state!'

Ciara crossed her fingers and hoped John wouldn't detect the insincerity. Seemingly he didn't.

'Ah, well, I'm not really in the mood for cooking anyway. Would you like to go out?'

Time for a real excuse, something unanswerable.

'I'd love to, John, but Ruth's in town, my mother just told me, so I'll probably have to meet her straight after work and I haven't seen her for ages. By the time we're finished catching up, I won't be fit for anything.' And then, in case John thought that she might have any excess energy, she added, 'I'm not fit for anything as it is!'

She held her breath, waiting for him to accept or reject her excuse. He accepted it. In fact, he didn't even sound all that put out.

'That's OK, I just thought I'd see if you felt up to doing something. I'd welcome an early night myself actually. Bit worn out.' He worked great emphasis into the last three words as though his being worn out was their special secret, full of deep soft-centred intimacies that reached across the phone network to caress her.

Ciara spoke quickly to shake off the spell of his words and the encroaching guilt.

'Well, that's fine then. Sorry. I'll see you tomorrow.'

She hadn't even finished the sentence when she wanted to kick herself. Why did she have to try to please people all the time? Why did she always say what she thought they wanted to hear? In John's case she knew it was because she felt guilty. He had given her a job, she was living in a flat provided by him, she'd gone out to dinner with him and slept with him. Right up until she'd done that she had been determined to go out with him and as she hadn't officially decided not to she was still going out with him. She was his girlfriend!

'Yeah, tomorrow.' John sounded pleased. "Bye, love, give my regards to Ruth.'

'OK.'

He was gone. Before Ciara had a chance to sort out her emotions or indeed put the phone away, it rang again. She held the little buzzing object in her hand and looked at it, thinking the display screen must certainly be faulty. It was probably John again, ringing to say he'd just had a great idea. Why didn't he pick up a takeaway and bring it around to the flat with a bottle of wine? Then the three of them, himself, Ruth and Ciara, could have a nice meal and a chat!

It struck her that maybe she just shouldn't answer it.

However, with her luck John would just turn up at the flat with a meal for three and discover she'd been lying to him.

She pressed the fluorescent answer button.

'Hello?' She spoke cautiously into the phone.

'Ah, there you are. I thought you must have left your phone somewhere and I'd have to talk to one of those horrible wee message machines.'

Mrs Bowe's voice broke into her trepidation.

'Hi, Mum. No, I just couldn't get it out of my pocket.' Ciara didn't think that another lie was going to make much difference to her day.

'Don't those phones hook on to things? You didn't keep that other one in your pocket, did you?'

'No, Mum, but this one doesn't have ... look, it's not something I want to get into now, OK, Mum? I'm at work.'

Ciara knew that if she didn't change the subject immediately she would end up explaining to her mother how it was difficult to 'hook' a phone on to anything when you were covered from head to toe in a furry costume. In any case, her mother didn't know she was dressed as a rabbit.

Yet!

'Right, well, I found your car details.' Her mother, realising she was being fobbed off, became huffy.

Time for a change of tone.

'Oh, Mum, you're wonderful. Thanks a million. So what time will you be in town?'

Instead of answering immediately her mother allowed a silence to form so that her daughter would know she was fully aware of how she'd been cut short and that it was a great personal sacrifice to let it go. Eventually she spoke.

'What's it now? Half-past two. Sometime between half-three and five. Yes, anytime after half-three.'

'Lovely. My next break is at four-thirty so I could meet you then.'

'Will you have time for a cup of coffee?'

Ciara knew that Mrs Bowe liked nothing better than

to find an untrendy coffee shop that served bad coffee. The sort packaged as 'filter coffee' but which, when passed through whatever machine hummed and slurped behind the counter, tasted like a very weak version of Bovril.

Ciara didn't like Bovril, never mind Bovril-flavoured coffee. She also didn't like untrendy coffee shops. However, as her mother had gone to the bother of finding the car papers it seemed unfair just to meet and grab. It might also be better if her mother was sitting down when she saw Ciara's work outfit!

'OK, someplace near O'Connell Street.'

'Well, that little place up from Clery's does a nice wee cup of coffee. I'll be in there at half-past four. Has Ruth rung you yet?'

Ciara knew that one of the main reasons her mother was phoning and coming into town was in the hope of 'accidentally' meeting Ruth. Mrs Bowe hadn't seen her youngest daughter for five years. When she'd banished her she had assumed Ruth would return within a couple of months and conform to the long-standing family tradition of avoiding the offending subject for the rest of time.

What she hadn't bargained on was Ruth's having inherited her mother's irrational stubborn streak and taking her banishment to heart. Neither of them was prepared to make the first move so the stalemate continued.

They survived on a subsistence diet of monthly friendly

but evasive phone-calls. As much as possible Ciara tried to stay out of the no man's land that lay between them.

'No, no word yet, but you know Ruth, she probably won't ring for days.' Ciara tried to drop the subject.

'Oh, no, I'm quite sure she said that she would be in town today.'

'Yeah, well, I haven't heard from her.'

Mrs Bowe knew she wouldn't get any further and sighed in resignation.

'See you at half-four then. 'Bye, Ciara.'

''Bye, Mum.'

Mrs Bowe put just enough poor-hurt-mother into her voice for Ciara to feel another stab of guilt as she turned off the phone. Was there some spell on the T2 that guaranteed she would feel guilty every time she hung up? Ciara dismissed this idea and instead had a quick bout of well-what-does-she-expect! anger at her mother. On the strength of that she dropped the little phone into her pocket and proceeded to badger passers-by with unwanted mobile phone cardboard cut-outs.

Why did it always have to be like this with her mother? Every conversation was a minefield of what and what-not to say. And no matter how cautious she was, Ciara invariably hit a what-not in every sentence.

When she didn't see her mother for a while she would think of her fondly and imagine all the nice things they should do together, all the things a mother and daughter could share. However, once they'd been together for a few minutes, often even a few seconds, all the good intentions would disappear to be replaced by an impulse to murder or at the very least gag and re-programme.

Ciara remembered one occasion when she had done the mother-daughter thing.

She had taken her mother on holiday abroad.

Mrs Bowe had never been on a foreign holiday. She had visited relatives in Scotland and England but had never gone on a proper holiday. She had never been anywhere that had a different climate or required a passport.

It had always been Ciara's wish to take her mother on a proper holiday. One that included a flight, a stay in a hotel, meals served by somebody other than a relative, and where it wasn't necessary to do the washing up. Growing up, the Bowe family had never been able to afford holidays even though all the neighbours had caravans in various tidy caravan sites around the coast. Ciara knew they were tidy because she had seen the photos year after year when the neighbours' children would come back tangibly more exotic from their sea-side stay.

The next-door neighbours, the O'Rourkes, had offered them the use of their caravan every summer but Mrs Bowe had staunchly refused, humbly grateful but uninterested when offered, defiant and fiercely proud when she spoke about it to her children.

Her family, no matter how poor, was not going to accept charity from the likes of the O'Rourkes with their four-doored car and colour television. The Bowes had a black and white television long after they had gone out of fashion because Mrs Bowe claimed that watching black and white was better for the imagination. Later Ciara realised that it was because of the added expense of a colour licence.

The January after she met Gary, confident of continued contract work, Ciara decided that the thing she most wanted to do with her earnings was to take her mother on a proper holiday. She realised there was no chance of getting away on a proper holiday with Gary, so a holiday with her mother seemed like a reasonable option.

For Christmas that year she presented her mother with the tickets for a two-week holiday in Tunisia. The travel agent had convinced her that she wouldn't have guaranteed sunshine in the Canaries or anywhere on mainland Europe that early in the year. He also argued that Tunisia wasn't that foreign, not really Africa as everybody there spoke French or English. The flight was relatively short and the hotel was on the beach. And he had offered an incredible price for a three-star place!

Her mother, on the other hand, while obviously thrilled

was not so easily convinced. She descended into one of her 'the-likes-of-me' states.

'What would the likes of me do on a holiday?'

'What would the likes of me be doing staying in a hotel?'

The arguments put forward so convincingly by the travel agent now sounded thin and brittle on Ciara's tongue. But she patiently worked her way through all the obstacles.

'But I don't even have a passport!'

'Who'll mind the house if I go away?'

'What'll people think, a woman of my age gadding off?'

'Well, I'm hardly going to start wanting a tan at my age!'

'Won't we need injections to go to a country like that?'

'You know I'm no good with that foreign food.'

'What are you doing wasting your money on holidays?'

It went on all through Christmas until Ciara had wanted to send her mother to be put down. Fortunately Karen thought the holiday was a great idea and told her mother so. As she was the eldest and only sensible daughter (married and to a man with a proper career), Mrs Bowe listened to her and grudgingly gave in. For the next three months she hummed and hawed over the matter but Ciara knew she'd won. Her mother would go on holiday with her.

Tunisia was nothing and everything Ciara had hoped for. On the one hand she'd wanted all the exotic strangeness of Africa as she understood it from films such as *Casablanca* and *Out of Africa*. On the other hand she thought this might be too much for her mother.

What she got was a hotel by the sea with a German-style menu full of varieties of sausage and cabbage. It was serviced by staff who spoke mostly French.

The weather wasn't quite as promised. Something to do with the African land mass and cloud dispersal. It seemed to have dispersed all the clouds over Tunisia. The beach in front of the hotel, while it was perfectly reasonable as beaches go, was wide open to a brisk wind that must have come all the way from Arabia and cooled considerably in the process. Ciara decided that there was nothing so unattractive as goose pimples and a bikini.

Mrs Bowe, though she wouldn't say it, hated the place. It was just *too* foreign.

It was foreign for her to stay in a hotel. Foreign for her to have buffet meals all the time. And foreign for her to be surrounded by noisy tourists, most of whom were German. She was out of her depth so complained more forcefully than ever.

'I don't understand why they can't serve brown bread. That white rubbish would block you entirely!'

'I'll ask again, Mum, but they only seem to have that and the black German bread.'

'And they don't know how to make a cup of tea. It's not that difficult, you know.'

'I know, Mum, I'll get you some hot water and a tea bag.'

'I thought this was a family hotel. How can it be so noisy? I didn't close my eyes last night.'

'It's because we're near the stairs, Mum. I took this room for the sea view but I'm sure we can change.'

'Do I have to give that man money every day if I use a deck chair? Seems a bit unnecessary.'

'Yes, Mum, but if you convert it into Irish money it's only twenty pence.'

'What's wrong with the water in the tap? I'm not going to pay good money for a wee bottle when I know they just took it out of the tap.'

To some things there were no answers.

By the end of the third day Ciara was cured of her wish ever to do mother-daughter things again unless it involved a daughter paying someone to keep her mother out of the way. Fortunately on the fourth day salvation arrived in the form of Mrs Ashton-Marsh, a pensioner-widow retired to Weston-super-Mare and on holiday in Tunisia to avoid a grandchild visiting England from South Africa.

For no apparent reason, the determined widow, Scottish, living in Ireland, and the affluent widow, retired, from the Home Counties, hit it off. As Ciara saw it they had two things in common. They were both widows and they both had to spend time in a place that didn't meet with their approval.

The fact that Mrs Ashton-Marsh was ten years older than Mrs Bowe didn't seem to matter. They bonded on Mrs Bowe's Scottish frugality, strengthened by years of struggling to make ends meet, and Mrs Ashton-Marsh's never-lost post-war waste-nothing attitude. They also discovered they both disliked anything Teutonic and for the rest of the holiday whined their way in harmony from dining room to swimming pool, beach to restaurant, insulating each other against the foreignness.

This friendship took her mother out of Ciara's immediate field of annoyance and she spent the rest of the holiday watching the Tunisian staff torment and in turn be tormented by the tourists they had to suffer as part of their economic survival.

Mrs Bowe never took a foreign holiday again.

Ciara never went on holiday with her mother again.

In fact she hadn't taken another holiday since that trip

to Tunisia. She had done the weekends away with Gary but she had never taken a proper holiday.

No chance of one now, with the state of her bank balance!

The memory of this brought Ciara back to reality. The afternoon seemed endless. Even though her hangover had improved since lunchtime she was now fighting another demon. Her lack of will power! But fighting was the wrong word. She'd already lost the battle. Whether it was joy at being asked out by Ken, or starvation through lack of breakfast, she'd had a burger and chips for lunch. She'd eaten the equivalent of three days' calories in the space of five minutes!

How was she ever going to get her waist back to an acceptable size if she couldn't even say 'no' to junk food?

On her way back to the Easi-tel shop at lunchtime she had been determined to eat only an apple or a banana but when she got there one of the counter girls had declared, 'Hey, I'm off to Burger King. Fancy something?'

Ciara shook her head mutely, afraid to open her mouth in case 'Yes' came out.

The girl gave her a cold look suggesting she thought Ciara's behaviour was unfriendly and left the shop. Ciara went into the staffroom and had a glass of water. The cold tasteless fluid did nothing to ease her longing.

The idea of eating fruit made one last attempt to assert

itself and then died, drowned out by the desire for refined carbohydrates. Ciara grabbed her purse from her bag and left the staffroom.

Gráinne, watching her progress through the shop, called after her, 'Your next break is at four-thirty, Ciara. Drop back if you need more flyers.'

She had raised her hand in acknowledgement and continued on her mission. She went to Supermacs. She got a few odd looks because of her rabbit costume but took her tray upstairs and sat in a remote corner where nobody from her past or present life would see her. She didn't want to be seen eating fast food when it was obvious she needed to lose weight.

To her relief she didn't meet anybody she knew but she had lost the will-power battle!

Now, in post-lunch repentance, Ciara was so caught up in furious feelings of hopelessness that when her phone rang she jumped, dropping the last of her brochures on to the damp ground. She fumbled in her pocket and, pulling out the T2, spoke into it bad-temperedly.

'Hello?'

'Ciara, it's Ruth. Hiya.'

'Ruth, where are you?'

'Why is it that whenever I ring you, you don't ask me how I am or anything, it's always "where are you?"' Ruth's voice scolded affectionately.

Ciara laughed. She liked the fact that Ruth never let her get away with things. She was very like her mother in that way except she didn't load it with condemnation and guilt.

'OK, OK, sorry. How are you? There, I've asked. Now, where are you?'

'I'm very well thank you and I'm about to step on to the bus to Dublin. Should get in about seven. The Home Office said you had a new flat, can I stay for a few days?'

The Home Office was Ruth's title for Mrs Bowe. As far as possible, and to the complete confusion of most people, Ruth never called things by their real name but always made up another that she thought represented their personality and attitude. To those who knew her it was an amusing trait. To those who didn't . . .

'Of course you can. That is, I'm not sure about Elena, and then John . . . It's a long story, but I'm sure it'll be all right.'

'Oh, yeah, I heard the Capitalist was back on the scene. What's going on there?' The Capitalist was Ruth's name for John.

'We were always friends,' Ciara said defensively, and then remembering that she didn't have to be defensive with her sister, added, 'and sometimes, as you know, we're more than friends.'

Ruth chortled at the other end of the phone.

'Umm, I think I'm getting the picture. I take it then that Lassi's gone home?' Lassi was Ruth's name for Gary. Nothing to do with the dog; she'd based the name on the Indian yoghurt drinks which were always described on menus as 'smooth and cool'. Gary was renowned for his cool smoothness.

'Another long story. Look, why don't I meet you in Hennessey's just after seven? I'll take you to the flat. I don't have my car but ...'

'Oh, yeah, sorry to hear about Karmie. Really bad luck!'

'Don't remind me. I ...'

The sound of pips interrupted as Ruth's time ran out.

'Oh-oh, there goes my card. See you lat—'

Chapter Thirteen

'Does John know this is what you're doing?'

Mrs Bowe hadn't yet recovered from the shock of being seen in public with somebody dressed as a giant rabbit. The fact that the 'somebody' was her daughter made matters worse. It seemed to her that at a time in her life when she should be enjoying the successes of her grown-up family it was unfair of her daughters to go out of their way to disgrace her, like this.

'John *gave* me the job, Mum, remember?'

The expression on her mother's face when Ciara had come into the café had been more hurtful than she could have imagined. It was as though she was eleven and had arrived home with a bad maths result. Then, as now, her mother behaved as if her children's choices were her own.

As if her daughters were part of herself, bound to her by some invisible tissue, a virtual umbilical cord, as yet unsevered.

'And how long is this ... this performance going to go on?'

Indignation and hurt were making her mother angry.

'Not long, Mum.' Ciara realised immediately that this would not satisfy her mother so graduated to lying. 'It's just a place to start. By next week I'll be in the office doing what I do best!'

'I won't ask what that is.' Her mother's voice was bitter now. Time to move on to less emotive territory.

'So did you have much difficulty finding the car things?' Ciara stirred some more sugar into her diluted Bovril on the off chance that it might make it taste like the coffee it was supposed to be. Then she decided not to drink it anyway because of the huge calorie increase caused by the added sugar. She pushed the cup away and some of the coffee splashed on to her rabbit's head, sitting on the table, glass eyes staring at her accusingly.

'No. And what's your flat like? I must say I'm a wee bit disappointed in John for giving you a job like this. But I suppose it's not his fault if you dinnae have the qualifications for anything else.'

Her mother threw in a little sigh at the end of this

sentence just to demonstrate how much of a burden Ciara's lack of qualifications were to her.

'The flat's great, I'm sharing it with this girl Elena . . .'

'Oh, and what does she do? Is she an accountant like John?'

'No, she's pregnant.'

This wasn't what Ciara had meant to say.

'Pregnancy is hardly a profession.' Mrs Bowe knew she was being deadpan and was enjoying the moment, confidently controlling the conversation.

'Ha, ha, very droll, Mum.' Ciara was used to her mother's one-liners but rarely managed a smart response to them. 'She's just arrived in the country, she's from the Ukraine, so I don't think she's quite established yet.'

Her mother's face darkened. 'She's not one of those refugees we keep hearing about, is she? One of those illegals?'

She used the words 'refugee' and 'illegal' as though they gave her a bad taste in the mouth.

'I don't know, Mum, what difference does it make?'

'"Behold, therefore I will bring strangers upon thee, the terrible of the nations: and they shall draw their swords against the beauty of thy wisdom, and they shall defile thy brightness!"'

It never ceased to amaze Ciara the way her mother had a quote for almost every eventuality. She knew, though, that attempting to contradict her would bring on another quote or an argument.

'She's probably not one of them,' Ciara said quietly, then took a quick glance around the café to see if anybody was listening. Everybody seemed occupied trying to work out why their coffee tasted like Bovril or agreeing with their companion that their cup of whatever it was did indeed taste like Bovril.

Ciara thought it very politically incorrect of her mother to talk like this. She liked to think of herself as politically correct and her way of ensuring she maintained that was by never talking about things that might have a politically incorrect flavour of any description.

Ciara hated it when her mother got like this which she only did when she was upset. She was usually upset on the days that Ruth rang. This added to the fact that Ciara was masquerading as a rabbit had obviously sent her over the top.

It wasn't that her mother was racist, not really. In fact it was the first time she had ever aired these sorts of views. Usually she would rant about things like vegetable suppliers and what they must be doing to their products to get them to be so uniformly sized, shiny and ever-lasting. Public transport was another favourite. She also found the price difference in toilet rolls compared to the number of metres in each (after she had converted it to feet) particularly engrossing. Immorality was an all-time favourite topic but discussion of it had been curtailed for the last couple of years in case the subject of Ciara and her relationship with a married man should surface. No doubt now that it was clear the affair was well and truly over the path of righteous morality would get a regular pounding once again.

Ciara didn't know what to say to this outburst on immigrants so took her usual attitude of staying quiet and half-nodding until the storm blew over.

It would be relevant but somewhat pointless to explain to her mother that being from Scotland she was a foreigner as well!

'Would you like another cup of coffee, Mum?'

Her mother's frown cleared. 'Oh, no, I don't think so. One is quite enough. I'll be spending a penny all afternoon if I have another.'

She took a quick glance at Ciara's cup and inhaled sharply. 'But you havenae touched yours. That's such a waste. There's nothing worse than waste, you know. And I suppose you have so much sugar in it I couldn't possibly touch it.'

Ciara nodded, wondering if there was any chance she could do anything right, ever.

'Have you seen your sister Ruth?'

Ciara shook her head.

'She said she was coming to town today. Has she not even rung, considering all the trouble I went to to get your number?' Her mother was unrelenting.

'Oh, she rang all right. I'm meeting her later.'

'Is she going to stay with you?'

'Guess so. Yeah. Gosh, is that the time? I've got to get back to the shop to pick up more flyers, I'd better go.'

Ciara started to move her paw-feet from under the table. She'd had enormous difficulty in getting them in there when she'd first sat down. Now, in her effort to get them back out, the table shook precariously. She knew the watching customers were doing little mental bets on whether the crockery would survive. Mrs Bowe, ignoring the ridiculousness of her daughter's predicament, continued speaking.

'Are you coming home at the weekend? It's St Patrick's Day. Your sister Karen is coming over with the children. I dinnae know when you last saw her. When was it? Well?'

Ciara was finally in a standing position, gathering up her coffee-stained rabbit head, her paws and the envelope her mother had given her.

'Don't know, Mum, not long. Can't come by. Working. Thanks for the car things. Talk to you over the weekend. 'Bye.' She bent down and kissed her mother's cheek.

'Goodbye, Ciara, make sure you're eating properly.'

She waved her paw-gloves at her mother and lumbered out of the door. She felt exhausted and her hangover had suddenly worsened. As she moved slowly down the street she counted her flyers and decided it was time to go back to the shop for more. She calculated that if she paced herself and stopped in at the police station on the way she needn't be back distributing until half-past five. That would leave just an hour and a half until she was finished.

An eternity.

But at least an eternity with an end!

Business in the police station did nothing to help things along.

'So you're in a bit of a "stew", are you?' The eyes of the middle-aged guard behind the counter had lit up as soon as Ciara appeared. She ignored his comment and silently presented him with the tax and insurance papers. The guard inhaled through his teeth as he read the details.

'Karman Ghia! That's a "bunny wee" car, isn't it?' He laughed uproariously and turned to wink at the guard on the desk behind him. Ciara made a smile-face and remained silent. He produced a form and proceeded to fill it out. The guard at the desk moved forward and two more who had come into the room stood looking curiously at Ciara. Having an audience did nothing to improve the jokes.

'I'll get the lads here to make out a warren-t for

the arrest of whoever's responsible.' He winked at the men behind him, then turning to Ciara pointed at the form and asked, 'Will I fill this in as Miss, Mrs, Ms or Brer Rabbit?' This drew snorts of laughter from his colleagues.

'Ms,' Ciara snapped, hoping her obvious lack of humour would discourage them. They took no notice.

'Sorry, sorry,' the guard at the counter said contritely, raising his hand appeasingly, 'I'm rabbiting on a bit, amn't I?'

He had to take a break from writing until his mirth subsided.

Ciara sighed impatiently. Ordinarily she enjoyed jokes but she didn't think this was either the time or the place for bad puns. The guard must have sensed her annoyance because he made no more jokes until she was leaving. Then, after assuring her that they would be in touch as soon as they had any news, he added, 'But that's the trouble with cars in the city these days – "hare" today, gone tomorrow!'

Ciara slammed her way out of the station to gales of laughter.

To her relief when she got back to the shop Gráinne wasn't there. In her absence the rest of the staff were much friendlier and assured her that if she wanted a cup of tea or something there would be 'nobody' around until a quarter to six. Ciara was very tempted to spend some extra time in the staffroom but remembered that the unfriendly rabbit on the next street might have something to say about her long absence.

Besides, despite her torment in the police station, she was in better humour now. The day was nearly over, she was looking forward to meeting Ruth and she had a date with Ken! She might be in a dead end job, but at least she had a life.

She might even say hello to little Mr Unfriendly Rabbit later. It could be her Ciara's-such-a-nice-person gesture for the day.

At ten to seven she worked her way on to the next street towards the other rabbit. By the time she reached him she had taken her head off so he could clearly see who she was. Not that he didn't already know as she had taken it off so many times that day she had lost count. He must already have seen her face. She stepped into his line of vision and held out her hand.

'Hi, I'm Ciara. I don't know if we've met but I'm going to head back to the shop now, are you?'

The rabbit, a blue ribbon about his neck, paused for a moment, then raising one paw to his chin pulled off his head. It was Dimitri's cousin, the man who had spoken to her in the staffroom that morning.

'Oh, hi, I didn't realise it was you but we haven't been properly introduced, have we? I'm Ciara.'

The man made a non-committal gesture with his recently revealed head.

'Sasha.' He shook her hand.

Ciara had a distinct feeling that conversation wasn't going to proceed at a dizzy pace.

'So are you heading back to the shop?'

Sasha nodded and silently fell into step beside her.

'How did today go then?' She had no idea what to say to a thirty-something male Russian.

'Very good, thank you, and you?'

It was beginning to sound like an English conversation lesson. Ciara racked her brain for a new direction, heartily wishing she hadn't bothered with her Ciara's-such-a-nice-person gesture.

'Do you think you'll be working the same area as me in the morning? You know, like today?'

'I was not with you this morning. I think I will not be with you tomorrow.'

Even though this sentence sounded somewhat abrupt Ciara was pleased. It was quite a long one and it left itself open to further conversation.

'Oh, really? How do you know about tomorrow, is there some sort of rota? Of course there must be but nobody's shown me. Where is it?'

Sasha looked at her pensively. In fact he looked at everything pensively but now he turned his gaze on Ciara for a moment.

'I know nothing of this "rota". I will not be working tomorrow morning because I must go to the funeral of my cousin.'

Ciara felt as though she had just been simultaneously slapped in the face and exposed as a heartless chatterbox. She didn't know what to say. She hadn't forgotten that Dimitri had died the day before. She had, momentarily, missed the cousin connection.

'God, of course. I'm sorry. Yeah!'

Sasha nodded, his expression even more pensive. In her embarrassment Ciara kept talking. 'Is there any news on who did that ... you know, the hit and run?'

Sasha shook his head.

'No.'

He'd reverted to the monosyllabic. This made her feel even more uncomfortable.

'I mean, it's terrible, isn't it? Somebody just getting run over like that and nobody being caught. It's ... it's ...' She searched for a word in her confused brain. 'Murder. That's what it is.'

She looked at Sasha for verification. She wasn't going to mention that she thought she might be in some way responsible for Dimitri's death. The fewer people who knew about that the better. Besides it smacked of some sort of conspiracy and Ciara wasn't prepared to contemplate this.

Sasha nodded again, no longer bothering to meet her eye.

Ciara wanted to run away. She wished she'd never got herself into this situation. She wanted to disappear into a crack in the pavement! But there was no chance of that.

She now realised what was wrong with this chat. He wasn't asking any questions back. Every time she passed the conversation to him he let it drop and as though it had no natural bounce it rolled off into a corner, far out of Ciara's reach. She knew she couldn't make him play if he didn't want to.

Before she had time to get resentful about this they reached the shop and, with a quick glance at her watch, Ciara quickened her pace and strode in as though she had hurried to arrive at seven.

'How did you two get on?'

Gráinne looked up from her watch. The question was rhetorical but Ciara answered it anyway, enthusiastic now because in a few minutes she would be out the door and off to meet Ruth and, later, Ken.

'Fine.'

She moved towards the staffroom.

'Ah, just a minute.' Gráinne wasn't finished. 'I'm short

a distributor until nine o' clock. Jen's gone home sick, can one of you work?'

Gráinne looked straight at Ciara. She obviously expected her to jump at the chance of spending another two hours on the cold night street.

Ciara froze. She couldn't possibly work on. Her hangover threatened to resurface. Maybe this was a sort of test by Gráinne, some kind of subtle threat. If she didn't comply with the request Gráinne would tell John that Ciara had been sleeping in the staffroom that morning. She would probably make up other offences as well just to make her seem like a real loser. Ciara didn't think that Gráinne liked her very much.

'I . . . um . . .' Ciara opened her mouth to speak but her brain wasn't working fast enough. She was quite at a loss for words. Before she could find any Sasha spoke.

'I will work until nine.'

Ciara swung around fully prepared to hug him. One look at his sullen face, however, quelled that impulse. Instead she smiled gratefully at him but he didn't react. Gráinne's voice, saturated with disapproval, came from behind her.

'Very well, Sasha, if that suits you? You're in at eight-thirty, Ciara.'

With a nod she fled to the staffroom. When she walked into the room a low mumble of voices ceased abruptly.

Three closed faces turned to look at her. Standing together on one side of the room, in the process of changing out of their costumes, stood Anna and the two men who had been with Sasha outside the shop the evening before. They stared at her suspiciously.

'Hi.' Ciara spoke as she moved towards her bag and coat.

The Russians said nothing. They nodded and without a word to one another continued changing, not fully turning away from Ciara at any time, giving the impression they were watching her out of the corner of their eyes. She turned her back, ignoring them, and pulled her purse out of her pouch to put it back in her bag. As she took the bag from its hook she realised something was wrong.

Something was different.

The top flap was open. She never left the top flap open. She racked her brain to remember if after her sudden decision at lunchtime she had broken the habit of a lifetime and left it open. She decided she had definitely closed it.

Somebody had been at her bag.

She swung around and stared at the three silent foreigners. Although she knew they were watching her they didn't look at her directly. She wasn't going to get any information from them. She turned back to search her bag and see if anything was missing. She was glad she'd had her purse with her. She couldn't tell if things had been disturbed because it was always such a mess in there – lipsticks, tissues, compact, hair clips, all piled in together haphazard. She concluded that nothing was missing.

But she knew somebody had gone through her bag and she wasn't going to go on as if nothing had happened. She would complain to Gráinne. It wasn't good enough that she couldn't leave her bag in the staffroom without it being rifled!

Ciara quickly finished changing but even so by the time she was doing up her coat the three Russians had left the room, still maintaining their silence. When Ciara came into the shop they were no longer there.

'Gráinne, I need to have a word with you.'

The manageress ignored her, continuing to issue pragmatic instructions to one of the office staff. Ciara could feel her drive and confidence dissolve.

'Yes? What can I do for you?' Gráinne finally turned to her, her voice cold and formal, peppered with a touch of hostility. Ciara hesitated. It wasn't as though she had any proof that anybody had been through her bag, she just knew.

'I ... I think somebody tried to ... tried to steal my bag.'

Gráinne raised one supercilious, questioning eyebrow.

'When you say "tried", what exactly do you mean?'

Ciara realised that she had said the wrong thing. Nobody had tried to steal her bag, exactly.

'Well, I . . . somebody went through it while I was out at work.'

'Anything missing?' Gráinne asked casually as she busily ticked off signatures on the sheet in front of her.

'No, but . . .' Ciara didn't get a chance to finish as Gráinne cut across her.

'Well, if there's nothing missing, I don't see what the problem is.'

'But somebody opened it!' Ciara was very indignant now but at the same time knew that her comeback sounded infantile.

Gráinne looked at her condescendingly and spoke as if addressing a child.

'I'm sure it's nothing. All the staff use the room, that's a lot of traffic. Somebody probably brushed against it and it fell or got disturbed or something. I mean, if there's nothing missing . . .' She sighed as though this was all too much for her then continued, 'However, if you want to make an official complaint I'll call the police now . . .' She left that hanging between them, almost daring Ciara to do something that would cause so much inconvenience and disruption.

Ciara stared at her in silence for a few seconds, all her anger now focused on Gráinne. She had no intention of having anything to do with the police after their treatment of her that afternoon. Besides, as Gráinne well knew, waiting for them would take forever. Ciara was already late meeting Ruth.

She shook her head slowly. 'No, it's OK. Like you said, it was probably an accident.'

A small triumphant smile hovered about Gráinne's lips as Ciara turned on her heel and left the shop.

Out on the street, to prevent herself from thinking dark resentful ways-to-murder-Gráinne-without-being-detected thoughts, Ciara glanced at her watch. Seven-twenty already! She was late. Ruth would be wondering where she was. Though knowing her sister she would be deep in conversation with some stranger she had just met at the bar.

Ciara recalled one memorable train journey from Cork. She and Ruth had shared a seating area with a visiting German. By the end of the journey he was so taken with the chattering Irishwoman and her sister that he'd started to negotiate how much money they would accept to accompany him back to his hotel room so that he could become, as he described it, 'more intimate with Ireland'!

Ciara broke into a jog, consumed by the fear of sharing life's little secrets with an inebriated stranger. She reached Hennessey's in two minutes and burst in at the door, startling the early-evening drinkers.

'Ciaróg! Over here, Ciaróg.' Ruth beckoned to her from the corner where she sat with what looked like one of those free 'live healthily' magazines in front of her. Ciara hated it when Ruth called her 'Ciaróg'. She had done since she'd first learned the word, aged ten.

Like everybody else in the Irish school system, by the age of ten Ruth was learning proverbs in Irish. Things like the Irish version of 'far away hills are green', 'a good start is half the work', and so on. The one that Ruth liked best was 'one beetle pleases another', which is another way of saying 'it takes one to know one'. She discovered that the Irish word for beetle was Ciaróg. Its likeness to Ciara's name, along with Ruth's penchant for not calling anything by its real name, meant that Ciara swiftly became Ciaróg.

No amount of pleading for change, threats of punishment or even death would induce her to stop. Through habit Ciara ignored the fact that she had just been called 'Beetle'.

'Hi, Ruth, sorry I'm late. How was the journey?'

'Fine, but never mind my journey, I want to hear all about the new job and everything.'

Ciara grimaced, ordered a drink and sat down beside Ruth. Her sister, noticing her reluctance to get started on either the job or 'everything', helped her along.

'OK, how about you start by telling me exactly what happened with Lassi?'

It was an enormous relief to talk. With all that had happened in the last couple of days Gary and the lost job had become very distant, almost forgotten. Ciara had not had a chance to talk to anybody about it because of having to keep a low profile. There was a lot of giggling and I-said-he-said to get through as she exposed the end of the affair to her sister. Ruth was the perfect listener. She had always heartily disapproved of Gary but had limited her disparagement of him to the odd barbed comment, like: 'There's a lot to be said for legalised polygamy, really. At least it would mean you and Lassi could be seen in public together.'

She also liked to build on the Gary-yogurt reference and would comment, 'I'm sure there's some painless way for you to become allergic to dairy products.'

Now she sat and listened attentively, throwing in the appropriate supportive one-liners like, 'You're not serious?!'

'Slimy bollix!'

'The bastard!'

She hooted with congratulatory laughter when Ciara got to the underwear part of the story. 'That's just wonderful – I hope they weren't clean? You should have done that years ago!'

'How dare he speak to you like that, you should have dropped the computer on his foot!'

'They had no right to fire you, it was *his* fault!'

Her reactions were the perfect accompaniment to Ciara's tale. By the time the story was over they had finished their drinks. Ciara checked her watch.

'Christ, it's eight o' clock.'

'What's the matter? It's not closing time for ages yet.' Ruth reached for her wallet to go to the bar.

'No, no.' Ciara gestured wildly for her to stay where she was. 'I haven't time for another drink, I have to, ah, meet someone at nine-fifteen and first I need to change.'

'Oh, yeah?' Ruth looked at her with a well-now-what-have-we-here? expression on her face. Ciara didn't react so she went on, 'Hot date with the Capitalist, is it?'

Ciara shook her head, dying to tell her sister about Ken but afraid that if she admitted to the date aloud she would belittle whatever was going on between herself and John. Especially as they'd just spent nearly an hour talking about Gary!

She decided that not saying it aloud might mean she wasn't really going on a date with yet *another* man! If she didn't say how gorgeous she thought Ken was then he wouldn't be gorgeous and she would just be going for a drink with a guy from work instead of heading off into the colourful land of lust and desire. Guilt crept out of the undergrowth and put its hand across her mouth, gagging her, so that even if she had wanted to, she couldn't have said anything anyway.

'Come on, out with it, who are you meeting?'

Ciara shook her head to release Guilt's grip.

'Just a guy from work, you know.'

'Yeah?' Ruth knew there was more to it than that.

Ciara, however, was not forthcoming.

'Come on, we gotta go. Have you got any money?'

'Some. Why?'

'Enough for a taxi?'

'Yeah, I got my dole this morning.' Ruth lived mostly on Social Security while she campaigned to save the planet. Ciara grabbed Ruth's bag from the floor and, buttoning her coat, headed for the door.

'Right, come on then, let's go home, I'll tell you on the way.'

Chapter Fourteen

'So you're telling me that somebody dropped a generator on you, your car's been stolen, your flat's been broken into, your flatmate's disappeared and today somebody had a good old poke about in your bag? And you don't think this is a bit over the top ... even for you!'

Ruth was sitting cross-legged on the bed, her face set in the defiant expression that reminded Ciara so much of their mother. She wished now that she hadn't poured her heart out to her sister. It had been great to get it all off her chest but now Ruth was turning a few coincidences into a major conspiracy.

'I really don't think they're connected,' Ciara half lied as she balanced, one leg in, one leg out of her jeans. She was in a hurry, she had a date, and she didn't have time to get involved in one of Ruth's endless conspiracy theories. But Ruth, with nowhere to go and nothing else to do, wasn't to be put off that easily.

'But they must be! Things don't just happen, you know. I mean, people think that shit happens all by itself, but it doesn't. People think when they have to pay more for fossil fuels it's because we used them all up to stay warm, or mobile, or whatever we're using them for. But that isn't true! Yes, we've used them up but only because the companies in control of the minerals guarantee that no alternative gets on to the market. I mean, we could be running our cars on alcohol or sugar, something renewable, but that doesn't suit the money makers!'

She paused for breath. Ciara turned away, raising her eyes to heaven, and at the same time inhaled deeply to get her stomach to shrink so she could close the zip on her jeans. They were her favourite pair and they were uncomfortably tight. A line of flesh bulged out over the waistband.

Ruth's voice recommenced behind her.

'And take water supplies ... there is categorical proof that an attempt is being made to monopolise the water of the undeveloped world by buying up the land around the source of ...'

'I don't mean to interrupt, Ruth, but I really don't think that someone going through my bag at work is in any way related to the control of the world's mineral supplies.'

Ciara paused, eye pencil poised, and turned towards her sister for added emphasis. She'd heard all this before. She loved Ruth and respected her complete distrust in the system but she really hated it when she got into one of her lecturing modes.

Ruth had always been like this. When they were young and demanding the important things in life like sweets, permission to go to the circus, a new bike or a Barbie doll, their mother would calmly tell them that they couldn't have whatever it was because they didn't have the money.

This of course was followed by an outcry from the girls about how unjust it was that they never got to do anything that everybody else did. Then their mother would shake her head again and with absolute conviction say, 'Now, girls, no good will come of shouting. Being without's nae bad thing. It will all come to you one day. The good book promises that the meek shall inherit the earth.'

By the time she was eleven Ruth's retort to this was, 'That may be true, Mum, but I bet you that *if* the meek do inherit the earth then the rich will have the mineral rights!'

This declaration and her use of the word 'bet' always ensured she went to bed straight after her supper on the offending days. This happened quite often with Ruth. Ciara was only ever sent to bed when she refused to wear some particularly sensible outfit her mother had bought for her. Karen was never sent to bed early.

'You're not hearing what I'm saying, Ciaróg. Why would all this happen right now if there wasn't something behind it?'

'Well, I don't know. I mean, two weeks ago I lost my job and my boyfriend, is that some huge conspiracy as well? Maybe shit just happens after all!' Ciara pursed her lips to put on her lipstick.

Ruth started to laugh. 'Losing your job and your Lassi wasn't a conspiracy! It was your own fault, you brought it on yourself, even you said so. That underwear routine . . .' Ruth threw herself back on the bed, laughing heartily. Ciara pressed her lipsticked lips together and watched herself in the mirror as her face broke into a reluctant smile.

'It's all right to laugh about it now, but what if she *had* decided to divorce him? I'd have been stuck with him. You'd have had Lassi for a brother-in-law!'

Ruth shrieked hysterically and between chortles gasped, 'Maybe we could have impregnated him with live cultures and turned him into a useful sort of yoghurt. Changed his name to "Actimel" or "Bifidis".'

Ciara was losing track of Ruth's conversation but this

268

wasn't unusual. She was used to laughing at things her sister thought were hilarious but which meant nothing to her. Besides she needed to stop laughing now as it was ruining her makeup.

'Look, Ruth, I've got to go now. You'd better sleep on the floor in here in case Elena comes back and gets a fright. And you needn't answer the door to anyone. I mean, you're not expecting anyone so there's no point, is there?'

Ruth sat up, wiping the tears from her face.

'Are you sure you want me to be in the bedroom? You might want to use it for other things . . .'

'Ruth!' Ciara was annoyed that her sister had guessed she was attracted to 'the guy from work' she was meeting. After all, she had told her that she'd slept with John and she didn't want to appear promiscuous.

Even to her sister.

'OK, I'll sleep in here,' Ruth said in a don't-mind-me-I'm-just-an-imbecile voice.

Ciara laughed and let herself out of the flat, yelling goodbye as she slammed the door. Running down the staircase, she wished heartily that she had asked the cab to come back to pick her up again so that she wouldn't have to walk into town in the dark.

She hadn't asked because she couldn't afford it. If she wanted a couple of drinks she couldn't waste her money on luxuries. Besides it was only a twenty-minute walk and if she didn't get mugged it would probably do wonders for her waistline.

Her head was racing at the prospect of meeting Ken. What would she say to him? What would they talk about? It was one thing to think somebody was attractive but actually to spend time with them ... Ciara felt very out of practice.

She remembered when she'd first started dating Gary. It had been exhilarating and exciting. She had felt as though she was constantly out of breath, caught up in the whirlwind of their romance.

Saturdays were the best. Gary would call by at about midday and they would make love immediately. After this had happened a couple of times Ciara wouldn't even bother getting up on Saturday morning but would lie in the delicious comfort of her bed until Gary came to join her.

After that they would go out of town for lunch or on fine days on a picnic to Wicklow. They would sit by a stream or on a mountainside and talk that delicious mixture of fantasy and intimacy that only ever gets spoken in the first couple of months of an affair.

Ciara had been completely in awe of Gary. He would see her about three times a week but only stay over twice. And he never stayed at weekends. Ciara loved him for this. She thought it was nice to go out with somebody slightly older who understood the concept of space and didn't crowd you at the beginning of a relationship.

The less she saw of him the more she wanted him.

Of course, with hindsight (most of her experience with Gary looked a lot different with hindsight), the reason his time with her was rationed was because he also had to spend time with his family. Sex first thing on a Saturday meant he wouldn't be late home to them at the end of the day.

All the same if there was only one good thing about that relationship it had certainly been the sex. Ciara half smiled at the memory as she glanced at her watch by the light of a street lamp and quickened her pace.

She thought it was funny how impossible it seemed to find all the qualities she wanted in one man. If she could have someone who had a combination of Gary's lovemaking technique, John's dependability and earning capacity, and Ken's eyes and wit she'd have the perfect man. Roll on a future in which a woman could just place an order for such a paragon on the Internet or its equivalent and receive him in the mail within twenty-four hours. It could be called Male-Order!

'What's so funny?'

Ciara had been so engrossed in her idea of an ideal

future that she hadn't noticed Ken waiting for her in the shadows. He was smiling, his curly hair casting a shadow across his face so that he looked like a character out of an old black and white movie.

'Oh ... just ... nothing!' She inwardly kicked herself for being slow and dim-witted.

'I hope it wasn't nothing, I'd like to think there was something behind such a mischievous smile.'

Ciara was blushing now. She hoped it wouldn't show in the dark. Ken sensed her awkwardness, and, realising she wasn't going to share her thoughts with him, changed the subject.

'OK, Miss Nothing, I'm starving. Do you mind if we get something to eat?'

Ciara shook her head, grateful that he had changed the subject and realising that she was hungry too, even though she had thought, or rather hoped, that she would never eat again after her burger and chips at lunchtime.

'Great! Do you have any preference?'

'As long as it's food!'

Ken laughed.

'This is wonderful. A woman who's easy to please. We'll have to keep you on ...'

Ciara could feel herself getting warm at the idea of being 'kept on' by Ken. She hoped the glow wouldn't be apparent in the darkness, revealing itself in a Ready-Brek halo around her body. It couldn't have been because he continued talking.

'... there's that little Italian place around the corner, cheap and cheery, will that do?'

'Perfect.' Ciara smiled up at him and they walked to the restaurant. When they got there the place was crowded but they were shown to a table by the wall immediately and with the aid of their menus created the illusion of a screen between themselves and the bustling room.

'So how was your day at the office, dear?' Ken asked in a mock-serious tone.

Ciara, appreciating the tone but unable to find a humorous answer, decided to play it straight. She raised her eyes to the ceiling and exhaled.

'Endless. I really thought today would go on for-ever!'

'What, you mean nobody pulled your tail?' Ken's eyes were bright with teasing.

'No. They could probably see I was in no mood for tail-pulling today. Did you get hassled?'

'Oh, I'd be very put out if I didn't get hassled at least once a day. I'd take it as a personal insult that I wasn't being seen as enough of a bunny to be tormented. The best one today was from a very well-dressed older gent. He sidled up to me clutching his briefcase and demanded, "What do you call a line of rabbits walking backwards?" I, of course, shrugged so he said, still with a completely straight face, "A receding hareline!" Then he walked away as though he'd never spoken to me. It's probably something he'd wanted to do all his life, tell a rabbit joke to a rabbit.'

'Yes, but I remember one we used to have in school. "What do you call a rabbit who tells jokes?"' Ciara was laughing so much she had difficulty speaking.

'No, I don't know. "What do you call a rabbit who tells jokes?"' Ken tried to keep a straight face.

Ciara took a breath to steady her voice. '"A funny bunny!"'

'Ha, ha, very funny, very school.' He was smiling broadly. 'For your information, out of costume I'm not a rabbit anymore so I don't qualify as a funny bunny. And besides, if you're going to lower the tone that much, I've got another one for you. "What do you twow at a wabbit that's wunning away?"'

Ciara shook her head.

'"A wock!"'

She groaned. 'You're right, that's the pits, I don't have any worse than that!'

Ken raised his hands in surrender. 'Enough then. We'd better order or the waiter will think we're homeless and just came in here for the heat with no intention of eating!'

Ciara bent her head to look at the menu, thinking as she did so how easy it was to laugh with Ken. Even his gibe about the homeless, which would ordinarily have sent her into a spin of politically incorrect paranoia, had fallen lightly into the conversation. An easy joke that wasn't disparaging and meant no harm to anybody.

And the best bit about it was that Ciara got to watch Ken's face as he spoke. His sparkling eyes and animated features made her want to reach out and touch him.

And his hands!

Ruth had presented a theory on men's hands in the taxi on the way home from the pub earlier that evening. For once with her the 'theory' hadn't turned into a lecture on the squandering of natural resources and international eco-conspiracies. Instead she had spoken clearly, succinctly, and seemingly with the research to back up her argument. The subject had come up when they were discussing the recent developments between John and Ciara.

'So you finally got it together with the Capitalist? If you ask me you should have done it years ago and gotten him out of your system.'

'But I couldn't do that, I'd never decided to try and

'make a go of it before,' Ciara said indignantly, not sure that sleeping with somebody just to get them 'out of your system' was the best idea in the world.

'Well, now that you have done "it", are you still determined to "make a go of it"?'

Ciara frowned. Sometimes Ruth could be just too direct. With one wallop she would hit the nail on the head, leaving Ciara to stutter and mumble her way out of probing questions. She decided to come clean.

'You know, I'm not sure, Ruth. I mean, he's really sweet and kind, lovely car, great job and he's intelligent, you know that ...'

She paused and Ruth cut in.

'So if that's what you want, it's all there for you, it's always been there for you – what's the problem?'

'The problem is ... well, I don't know if it *is* a problem. It shouldn't be, sex isn't supposed to be everything ...'

'He was lousy in bed!' Ruth squealed. 'The Capitalist doesn't make the grade between the sheets!'

'Ruth!' Ciara threw a horrified glance at the taxi driver who was obviously thoroughly enjoying this intimate conversation.

'It's no good "Ruthing" me, these things happen. Who'd ever have thought it of the I-can-turn-straw-to-gold Capitalist!'

'Ruth, it takes two, you know. It's probably as much

me as it is him. We probably just need to do a bit of work on it.'

'Well, did *he* seem satisfied?' Another no-holds-barred Ruth question!

Ciara nodded.

'Well, there, you see, that's obviously his usual performance and he's not even entertaining the idea it might need improving. Typical man!'

Ciara didn't want to go on to Ruth's 'typical man' lecture. Suffice it to say that she would start at Adam and Eve and work her way to *Star Trek*, occasionally hitting on a few facts but mostly relying on fictitious representations of men.

Ciara cut in before her sister could draw breath to go on.

'I don't know about the typical man bit, I don't think it's that.'

'Well, what is it then? Did you work that out?' Ruth was back on track.

Ciara paused for a moment and then lowered her voice so that the taxi driver couldn't hear her.

'It's his, you know ...' She waved in the general direction of her hips. 'It's very small. I mean, I don't know, but I think it might be smaller than average and ...' Her voice trailed off in embarrassment. She felt that she was betraying John but had to tell somebody in the hope that they would agree with her that this did constitute a problem and that she was entitled to have doubts about her feelings for him.

Ruth raised her eyebrows, inhaled and nodded her head like a doctor who has finally found the source of a patient's problem.

'OK,' she said on her exhalation, letting the word linger in the car so long that Ciara was afraid the taxi driver might try to include it as an additional passenger. Ruth's voice became matter-of-fact.

'Tell me, what size are his hands?'

'What?' The question had taken Ciara by surprise. She'd expected either ridicule or sympathy, not a change of subject.

'His hands, are they big or small?' Ruth reiterated as though she had just asked Ciara to do a simple addition problem for a school test.

Ciara thought John's hands were small but she wasn't about to leap right in there and say so when she didn't know where Ruth was taking this conversation.

'I guess I'd say they were a bit on the small side,' she said cautiously.

'There, I knew it!' Ruth declared. Then went on enthusiastically, 'There's a definite correlation between the size of a man's hands and his dick.'

Ciara cringed, wishing that her sister could be a little less colourful with her language. She watched in mortification as the corners of the taxi driver's mouth twitched with amusement. And Ruth still wasn't finished.

'I've been researching this for the last couple of years now and there's definitely a connection!'

This time it was Ciara's turn to raise an eyebrow, as, stifling a laugh, she asked, 'Researching? How do you mean, researching exactly?'

Ruth turned to her with a grin.

'Oh, get your mind out of the gutter, Ciaróg. I've done a little research in the field, so to speak, myself. And the rest I got from talking to other women about their experiences. You should have asked me, I could have told you.'

'Right,' Ciara said sarcastically, 'I'll remember that the next time!'

The tone was wasted on Ruth, who went on, 'He'd probably be very popular in Japan, you know, I hear everybody's quite small there so they all match and ...'

Before she could finish her sentence the taxi came to an abrupt halt. For a second Ciara thought it was because the taxi driver was going to get out and thump Ruth for insulting the male species but in fact it was just that they had arrived.

As Ruth paid the driver Ciara took a quick look at his hands.

If her sister's theory was correct this man should have nothing to fear from her research.

The same was true of Ken. Even if she didn't have a special interest in hands at the moment her eyes would have been drawn to his. They were square hands, the palm and the fingers appearing to be equal in length, but a nice length. And they were a good size, didn't look abnormally big or abnormally small. They looked strong, as though if they had to they could chop logs or build a timber hut in the wilds. They were capable hands.

Ciara wondered about what Ruth had said. Were the size of a man's hands really related to other things? She lowered her head behind the menu, afraid that by some untimely change in his telepathic senses Ken would discover she was sitting opposite him, on what might or might not be their first date, thinking about his penis.

'What would you like?' Ken didn't sound as though he suspected anything. Ciara concentrated on the menu for a moment. What she would like was a mountain of pasta smothered in a rich cream and meat sauce and topped with spoonfuls of grated Parmesan. What she would order was a light tomato sauce on a specially ordered small portion of pasta and hope they would have the wit not to bring any cheese to the table. She could feel her stomach bursting against her jeans in an effort to make itself noticed by the rest of the world. Ciara pulled it in and vowed she wasn't going to spend the rest of her life without a waist.

She had a flash then of what it would be like, always wearing baggy clothes in an effort to disguise her shapeless middle; never being able to wear a bikini if she could ever afford to go on holiday again. She probably shouldn't be touching pasta at all but couldn't just sit there eating nothing. She listened as Ken ordered a pizza with double everything and remembered John ordering the food she would have liked to eat the night before.

She felt a stab of guilt at the memory and looked furtively around the restaurant as though he might be sitting at one of the tables watching her, feeling hurt and betrayed because she was having lustful thoughts about another man.

'See anyone you know?' Ken's voice was curious. Ciara's eyes flew back to his face. He was smiling slightly as though amused by her lapse of attention. The idea crossed Ciara's mind that being so handsome he probably wasn't used to women losing attention when they were out with him. And despite her momentary lapse just then she had no intention of being the first.

'Oh,' she responded inanely, 'I was just checking out what sort of people eat Italian on a Thursday night ... lateish.'

What was the matter with her? Why couldn't she

think of any sparkling witticism to impress this man? Maybe fate was taking a hand in ensuring a monogamous lifestyle for her.

But Ken was laughing, eyes dancing by the light of the candle between them on the table.

'And do they live up to your expectations?'

Ciara joined in his laughter, relieved he didn't think her stupid or humourless. A little while later, after a few glasses of wine, she had forgotten her awkwardness and the meal progressed in a steady stream of light banter. She told him about the car theft and her suspicions about her handbag being searched, but in a jovial tone as though they were just a couple more funny events. It wasn't until they were having coffee at the end of the meal that the conversation returned to work.

'Do you think you'll stick this job for long?' Ken's voice was a mixture of concern and interest.

Ciara shrugged. 'I don't know. The plan is to get some cash together to, you know, sort a few things out.' She still hadn't told him that her unemployment had come on her rather suddenly or that she was totally broke and that it was pointless her looking for a 'real' place to live because she simply couldn't afford it. She had told him that she'd found her current flat through some friends. She'd been on the point of telling him about Elena but had decided this would lead to questions that might eventually pinpoint John.

The one thing she didn't want to do was tell Ken about John.

She felt guilty about this both for John's and for Ken's sake but until she'd sorted out what exactly was going on she wanted to keep the two men completely separate.

'I never did ask, how did you find this job? It sounds like with your experience you could have gone into a more comfortable line of work.' Ken waited for an answer.

This was a difficult question. If she claimed to be in the job for any reason other than that a friend had given it to her, it would make her look like a loser with no prospects. Mentioning the 'friend' would lead directly to John, either as boyfriend or boss, both of which smacked of a form of social nepotism Ciara didn't want to admit to. She racked her brains.

'Actually it was my mother,' she said shortly.

'Your mother?' Ken looked surprised.

'Yeah, you know, I stayed with her for the last couple of weeks since my ... ah ... lease expired ...'

Ken nodded.

Ciara was sure that the lie-police were going to burst into the restaurant at any moment now and arrest her for flagrant and repeated breaches of the truth. She glanced furtively towards the door but it remained unopened.

She looked back to Ken, then lowered her eyes and toyed with her spoon.

'Well, she was talking to a friend of my sister's who has a teenage daughter who'd heard about it through some friends and she suggested I give it a go ... My mother has never really understood what I do. She figures that PR *is* advertising, and this job's advertising so ...'

She glanced quickly at Ken to see if he was swallowing this. He was nodding slowly, his face revealing nothing of what he was thinking.

'So you didn't know anybody on the job?' Ciara thought this question rather pointed but then decided she was just being paranoid.

'God, no. Nobody.'

She took a quick furtive look about her. She expected to be struck down by a bolt of lightning. Surely such barefaced lying couldn't go unpunished? She listened for the sound of the great thunder roll of God's wrath or the rising all-consuming flames of the Devil approaching. Above the bustle of the restaurant, however, the world was strangely quiet.

'So did *you* know anybody on the job before you started?' Ciara was frantic to divert the questioning away from her as soon as possible.

Ken hurriedly shook his head. 'No, not a soul. Should we go?' The suddenness of his suggestion startled Ciara.

It seemed he wanted to change the subject as much as she did. She nodded gratefully and they got up to go, light-heartedly arguing over how to halve the bill, Ken insisting that the wine was his treat. Ciara gave in easily on that one. Outside, closing their coats against the March night air, they both turned to walk in the same direction.

'By the sound of things you live pretty near me, can I give you a lift?'

'You have a car?'

When they had talked about her car being stolen she had presumed Ken didn't have one. He hadn't mentioned it.

'Oh, yeah, it's from a former life when wages were more steady. It's nothing swish but it gets me there!'

'Yes, please.' Ciara had not been relishing the prospect of a walk back through the dark.

'Well, I'm parked about three streets away, near one of those building sites where they haven't started charging for parking yet. Long may it last!'

Ciara followed his lead, looking in the windows of pubs and restaurants as they passed. Then she glanced at Ken's profile, as he looked straight ahead, concentrating on where he was going. She smiled. This was the first time in weeks that she'd felt normal, part of the world around her. Not some misfit who was forever more going to be on the outside, nose pressed against the window like a Dickensian urchin, watching but separated from the world.

She turned once again to look into the pub they were passing. A movement caught her eye and she focused her attention on it. Somehow it seemed familiar.

She must have gasped. Certainly she felt as though all her limbs had seized up even though later she discovered that she had kept moving.

Inside the window sat John.

This wasn't unusual, John liked pubs.

What was unusual, indeed a shock, was that he was with a woman. And he wasn't just with her, he was gazing into her face as she stroked his with the palm of her hand. There might have been nobody else in the world but them.

The woman leaned over and brushed her lips against his. Then she lowered her hand and reached out to pick up her drink, and as she did so she turned her face towards Ciara.

There was no doubt.

There could be no mistake.

The woman was Gráinne.

Chapter Fifteen

'Ciara, are you sure you're all right?'

They had reached Ken's car. Ciara was leaning against the bonnet as Ken unlocked the doors and cleared the front seat of newspapers. The inside of his car reminded her of Karman Ghia. A little stab of loss fought unsuccessfully to take over from the memory of John's intimate moment with Gráinne.

'Yes, I'm fine really. Probably just tireder than I thought – all that standing about at work.'

Ken continued to be concerned.

'You were so pale, I thought you were going to faint.'

Fainting had not been an option for Ciara as she had stood outside the pub in a state of shock. If she caused a commotion people might come out on to the street to see what was going on and she would have to come face to face with John and Gráinne.

Ken's attention had been drawn by the small noise she had made in her throat. When he'd seen the stricken expression on her face he had reached out a supportive arm to steady her. Once she had recovered herself Ciara couldn't tell whether the quickening of her heart was because of what she had just witnessed or Ken's proximity.

Whichever it was, she didn't want him to let go.

Ken held her arm all the way back to the car, causing a disturbing conflict of emotions because despite her exhilaration at his touch, Ciara's mind could not relinquish an image of John and Gráinne in the pub, oblivious to those around them.

Did this mean that while professing undying love to her, John was also having an affair with Gráinne, Manageress from Hell?

If this was the case, why had he given Ciara a job?

Why had he found her a place to live?

Why had he taken her out for dinner?

Why had he slept with her?

It made no sense.

Was he going out with Gráinne? If so, how long had it been going on? Did Gráinne know that he had gone out with Ciara too and was that why she was so persistently horrible?

'A penny for them?' They were stopped at traffic lights. Ken turned towards her, his eyes warm, his voice caressing.

Ciara shook her head slowly and answered, 'I doubt you'd get your money's worth.'

'I'm not looking for value, I'd just like to know what's wrong and if there's anything I can do to help?'

His voice was so sympathetic, his words so well-meaning, it took all Ciara's willpower not to blurt out her troubles. But she realised this would be a mistake. It would uncover all the lies and little omissions she'd made during their evening together. She had created an image of herself and now wasn't the time to deconstruct it, no matter how distressed she was. She changed the subject.

'The next left and left again will take you to my place,' she mumbled, not wanting the journey to end. She wished that Ken would just keep driving until they'd driven out of her life and into some better place where everything she touched didn't get destroyed or become in some way sordid.

This John and Gráinne thing was the last straw.

How dare John think he could waltz into her life after all these years and two-time her! What did he think she was? Some easy pick-up? He would help her get a lousy job and an even lousier flat and she would be so grateful she would sleep with him? And she'd believed she was the only woman for him! Why else would he have kept coming back all these years?

By the time they got to the other side of town Ciara was getting over the shock. Like a fading anaesthetic the numbness she had felt since she had seen John and Gráinne in the pub was disappearing and her emotions were surfacing. Feelings were clawing their way back through the raw nerves.

And what Ciara was feeling was betrayal.

Betrayal and hurt.

But it wasn't coming out as betrayal and hurt, it was coming out as anger.

Ciara Bowe was furious.

She was so furious she had the distinct impression there might well be steam coming out her ears. She turned to Ken to check if he would react like a man who could see steam coming out her ears.

He didn't. In fact he had just stopped the car. Having turned the engine off he was now shifting himself sideways in his seat so that he could give his full attention to her. Ciara could feel her anger getting sidetracked.

'So, Ciara, I don't suppose you feel up to making a man a cup of something?'

He said this with a half smile on his face and in a tone that suggested he didn't expect an invitation but just thought he would check.

Ciara would have loved to give him a 'cup of something' but she hadn't been thinking this far ahead so the suggestion took her by surprise. She'd been so engrossed in duelling with her anger that she hadn't considered how her evening with Ken would end.

'No, sorry, I . . . my sister is staying and she's probably asleep . . . in the living room.'

Another lie to add to the myriad!

'That's OK, don't worry about it. I didn't really think . . .' He grinned ruefully and met her eye. 'Can't blame a man for trying.'

Blame!

There was no question of blame. Ciara was thrilled. Here was a handsome entertaining man making no bones about the fact that he wanted to be asked in after . . . well, after their first date.

And, yes, she decided in a flash of hot anger, it *was* a date! Any hint of guilt had been buried in the avalanche of bitterness caused by the spectacle of John and Gráinne together. There was now no reason why she shouldn't consider an evening spent with Ken as a date. After all, John was out on a date. And if he could do that, she could too.

She looked at Ken in the half-light, his handsome features accentuated by the shadow of stubble on his chin which gave his features a more rugged appearance.

'Ciara, I had a great eve—'

Suddenly, driven by impulse, she reached out and put her hand under his chin. Then, drawing his face towards her, she leaned forward and kissed him on his still-parted lips. Ken didn't object. In fact after a few seconds he warmed to the idea and reached out to put his hands to either side of her face so that when their lips parted it was only for breath and the next kiss was even more intense.

Ciara was transported. She had no idea where to, she just knew that kissing Ken had moved her into unfamiliar territory. Or maybe not so much unfamiliar as forgotten. She had kissed Ken because she wanted to and because she was angry with John but now it had become something else. The sensation took her over completely. She was bobbing on a tidal wave of lust, swept along by sheer surprise. This was something she had not expected.

The second kiss lasted forever.

Finally they came up for air.

'Wow!' Ken said, somewhat breathlessly. His wide-eyed gaze was almost startled. Ciara had difficulty focusing. He took a deep breath.

'Are you absolutely sure you don't want me to come in?'

Ciara wasn't at all sure. Her hormones were in such disarray she wasn't even sure where she was, never mind what she wanted. She swallowed hard and, just to prove to herself that she could, shook her head to say no. Ken's disappointment was almost tangible.

'Yeah, well. Are you OK the rest of the way on your own?'

She nodded and reached for the door handle.

'Thanks, I had a great time too.'

'Don't mention it. Maybe we'll do it again sometime.' His voice had an edge to it and when Ciara looked over her shoulder at him she could see that his face had set into disappointed lines.

She decided to ignore his tone.

'I'd really like that.'

Ken didn't answer, just nodded, the dim light through the windscreen accentuating his frown. Ciara couldn't think of anything else to say so she pushed the car door open and climbed out.

'See you tomorrow then.' She raised her voice as she closed the door. He waved his hand and put the car into reverse.

As he drove away Ciara crossed the yard towards the block of flats. She kicked a pebble disconsolately as she walked, convinced that she had blown the only opportunity she would ever have with Ken. It was just her luck to meet a man she really liked when she had started going out with somebody else.

Somebody else . . . John! The two-timer! His infidelity

was what had driven Ciara to kiss Ken in the first place. She owed him nothing.

She wondered if she would have said no to Ken had Ruth not been sleeping on the floor of her bedroom. If there had been no chance of a witness would she have allowed him to come in?

Maybe.

Ciara slowly climbed the stairs and let herself into the flat. Everything was quiet; the door of Elena's room still stood open. Ciara peered in to see if there were any signs that the girl might have returned, but nothing had changed. The room was still in turmoil with no sign of anything having been touched since she and John had found it the evening before.

John! There he was again, constantly popping into her head to infuriate her! How could she have been so taken in by him? How could she have believed all those things he'd said to her? How could he have made her believe that he was still mad about her after all these years? How could he have slept with her and then be all lovey-dovey in that pub with Gráinne the Marketing Guru!

It was just too much!

Maybe it was an elaborate revenge plotted by him to punish Ciara for all those years when she would never commit to him. He had lured her into a humiliating job and then seduced her, and now he and his plain girlfriend were having a good chuckle about it.

Ciara rediscovered the anger she had diverted during the excitement of kissing Ken. She slammed furiously about the flat looking for what remained of the bottle of brandy from the night before. Then she remembered that it was in the bedroom. No doubt John had wanted it on standby in case Ciara had any second thoughts! She went in search of it.

'Hey, watch it!' A muffled voice came from somewhere under Ciara's feet. Ruth erupted from beneath a mound of covers, eyes squinting against the light that streamed in from the hall.

'Sorry, Ruth, sorry, I couldn't see. Did you notice a bottle of brandy about when you were doing your bed?'

'Yeah, it's on the floor over there.' Ruth paused and peered up at Ciara's face. 'Is there somebody with you?'

'No. I just want a drink, OK?'

'Fine by me. Is there enough for two?'

Ciara nodded and went to the kitchen to fetch some cups. When she came back Ruth was propped against the wall, swaddled in blankets. She looked like an old Indian chief about to have a pow-wow. As Ciara poured, Ruth spoke.

'So, Ciaróg, how was the hot date?'

Ciara scowled and before answering handed Ruth a cup, threw herself on the bed and took a drink.

'I don't know, Ruth, I just don't know.' She shook her head and looked miserably into her brandy.

Ruth was taken aback by this response. She'd been expecting some light-hearted banter, a bit of teasing, not this near-tearful apathy.

'What happened? Ciaróg, what's the matter? Was he just horrible? He didn't do anything to you, did he?'

She shook her head, managing to force a laugh at Ruth's concern.

'No, it's not him, he was great. It's John.'

'But you weren't seeing John this evening. Oh, no, did he see you with the guy from work and get all territorial?'

Ciara shook her head again, laughing outright at that idea. She went on to tell Ruth what she had seen through the pub window.

'Are you sure? Could you not have been mistaken?'

Her tone was incredulous.

Ciara shook her head.

'Maybe he was just taking something out of her eye?'

Ciara snorted.

'And she then had to take something out of *his* eye in return? I really don't think so. Besides you don't need to kiss someone when you're taking something out of their eye!'

Ruth grinned ruefully. 'I guess not, but I can't imagine the Capitalist having the balls for this. He just never struck me as the sort who would two-time — who *could* two-time!'

'Well, he is and he has!' Ciara snapped and finished her brandy. 'More?'

She held out the bottle like some kind of threat. Ruth glanced into her cup and nodded.

'Well, maybe he'd been going out with her and was meeting her to tell her he'd got it together with you and so couldn't go out with her anymore. Maybe it was some sort of final meeting.' Ruth sounded as though she had just made that up.

'Do you think so?' This idea had never crossed Ciara's mind.

'Why not?' her sister answered in an anything-is-possible voice. She really didn't think so but she hated seeing Ciara so upset about John. Ruth had always believed that Ciara and the Capitalist were totally unsuited and it was taking all her will-power not to declare that he was a rat and Ciara should have nothing more to do with him.

'Maybe.' Ciara didn't sound in the least bit convinced. She paused for a moment, visualising the scene in her head. 'No, you know, I really don't think so. You don't go stroking somebody's face if you're leaving them, do you?'

'I don't know, people break up in different ways.' Ruth was still placatory.

Ciara thought about this for a moment and then her face set in anger.

'But he could have told me if that was the case. He could have told me last night or at any time in the last couple of days. He made me believe he wasn't seeing anyone. It's his dishonesty I object to the most!'

Ruth looked thoughtful for a moment and then her face broke into a slow smile.

'And you're going to tell me that you were always honest with him whenever you went out before? That you never two-timed him? You just never got caught, that's all!'

Ciara looked at her sister indignantly.

'That was different! We were much younger and things didn't matter as much then. Besides, I've no idea what you're talking about!'

Ruth continued laughing.

'Oh, yes you do. And the only reason it was different is that you were the one doing the two-timing!'

Ciara squealed, 'You're such a liar, Ruth Bowe! That's not true, how could you say such a thing?'

But Ruth wasn't letting her off with a denial. She lowered her voice.

'Well, what about the Conquistador then, eh? That

wasn't two-timing at all, was it? Even though John nearly found out, didn't he?'

Ciara contorted her face into an expression of horror and fell back on to the pillows, giggling uncontrollably. Ruth was right. Her brief fling with José the handsome enigmatic Spaniard, nicknamed the Conquistador by her sister, could qualify as two-timing.

It had happened the first Christmas after John went to America. He was home during the summer and they had gone out together then. It had been fun because he was full of stories of his different life and they both knew they only had two weeks. The time together had an urgency and vibrancy about it. When he was leaving he had said he would let her know if he would be home for Christmas and if he was then maybe they could take up where they'd left off . . . Ciara had nodded and waved, animated by the drama of his departure, confident that she would be waiting for him at Christmas.

By mid-November John confirmed he would be home for Christmas, and asked if they could see each other then? Ciara was delighted. She had only gone out with one person since the summer and that had been a disaster. She looked forward to presents from New York and the dogged devotion that was so much a part of John.

Then a week before the end of November lightning struck.

Or rather José Gomés struck.

He was a Spanish law student working with a Dublin firm to improve his English. As far as Ciara could tell his English was fine: a little accented perhaps but this only added to the attraction. Nevertheless his father had insisted that he spend time in Ireland working with a legal firm. It was probably more to do with business expansion than improving José's English. He in turn, with few responsibilities at work, had partied his way through his time in Ireland.

Ciara and José met at a party three weeks before he was due to go back to Spain. For her it was lust at first sight. Never before had she seen such liquid dark eyes, such clear olive skin, such shiny, happy hair. His soft accent with its occasional idiosyncratic translation was like the caress of a lover. And while he wasn't very tall, he was well-built, his continental clothes complementing his toned body.

They had spent the entire party talking to one another and at the end of the evening José had walked her home. She didn't ask him in because she was living in a flat with four other girls who were not only inquisitive but also oblivious to dirty dishes and over-full rubbish bags.

With a suaveness that Ciara was unused to in Irish men he'd drawn her into the shadows of the neighbouring house, folded his arms about her and gently but firmly kissed her on the lips. She thought she'd died and gone to heaven; even the way José smelled was different from the Irish men she had gone out with. His clothes were a different texture. He wore a subtle aftershave that seemed to come from his pores rather than a bottle. He was a truly exotic creature.

Finally, with thumping hearts and heightened senses, they had stopped kissing and he'd held her close to him, his breath warm on her forehead.

'Ciara, I must see you again. Tell me you don't have a boyfriend? Tell me that tomorrow we can meet without this wondering whether I should kiss you or not?'

If she'd had a hundred boyfriends Ciara would have denied them all in that instant.

'Boyfriend? Of course not, what made you think I had a boyfriend?'

He fixed his black eyes on hers.

'A woman as beautiful as you will always have a boyfriend. Only a fool would not want you.'

She felt a tingle running through her. Nobody had ever spoken to her like this before, she could get used to it. All the same she didn't want him to think that she was a pushover so she toughened her voice and asked, 'And you? Don't you have a girlfriend?'

José hadn't answered immediately. He held her a little closer and breathed some more magic into her hair. Then he nodded gently.

'Yes, I have someone. It is my fiancée in Barcelona. We have been together since we were very young and some day we will marry. Already she is part of my family, my father's favourite. We will spend Christmas together. I love her . . .'

Ciara at this point had struggled to free herself from his embrace but he wouldn't release her.

'. . . but this does not stop me loving another. Why must love be exclusive? We are young, why cannot we just enjoy our youth? Say you'll meet me tomorrow? Don't tell me there is nothing between us, Ciara. Meet me in Dwyer's at eight.'

Then he released her and walked her silently the few yards to her door. As she let herself in she glanced over her shoulder. He was standing motionless in the shadows, his face a landscape of tragedy, handsome head tilted to one side in pleading. Their eyes met.

'I will be waiting for you.' His voice carried softly on the night.

And he was.

When Ciara arrived at Dwyer's the following evening at 8.15 he was sitting alone in the corner, watching the door. His face lit up when he saw her.

'Ciara, I am so happy – you have no idea. I am so happy.'

And he was. She worked out soon enough that José was

the sort of guy who was always happy and who always got what he wanted but that didn't matter because what he wanted during his last few weeks in Ireland was Ciara.

Naturally she had been disturbed when he'd said that he was engaged but she had rationalised that it was part of another life far away in Spain. John would be coming back at Christmas but by then José would be gone. She could have the best of both worlds.

Ciara's arrival in Dwyer's heralded three weeks of undiluted romance, wooing and seduction. José's charm and technique were unrelenting. The fact that it was destined to be such a short romance only fired its intensity.

José's fiancée wasn't mentioned again.

During the second week of December John rang to say that he would be arriving in Ireland on the twentieth. José wasn't leaving until the twenty-third. Ciara wasn't prepared to tell John about the handsome Spaniard because she suspected he would be unimpressed and quite probably quarrelsome about the matter. She was aware that there was an overlap of three days but was so caught up in the fling with José that she ignored this.

On the evening of the twentieth she was in a frenzy of dressing to go to yet another party with the romantic Spaniard when the phone rang.

'Hi, Ciara. It's me, John.'

'Oh, John, hi. How's the US of A today!' She was in high spirits and thought this very funny.

'I wouldn't know. I'm in Dublin. I thought you might have come to the airport to meet me.' He sounded bad-tempered.

'Oh, God, John! I completely forgot what day it was.'

This as it happened was the truth. Ciara had difficulty remembering what year it was, she was so enthralled by her foreign affair.

'OK.' John's voice was forgiving. 'Well, I'm here, so why don't we meet up later?'

Ciara knew there was no hope of that but she couldn't tell the truth.

'Oh, John, I'm sorry. One of the girls from work has asked me to a Christmas party, I'm just on my way out to it now!'

He was unfazed.

'That's OK. Tell me where it is and I'll meet you there later.'

Ciara felt cold panic wrap itself about her heart. She had no doubt that its frosty macabre laughter must be audible down the line and slapped her hand across the mouthpiece.

'Ciara? Ciara, are you still there?'

'Yeah, sorry, John, the receiver slipped. Er . . . no, you can't come. It's a girls' night only, you know, the equivalent of a slumber party only it's for twenty-somethings.' She added a laugh at the end of this to give the statement some levity.

'Oh, right.' John didn't sound totally convinced. 'Tomorrow then?'

'Yeah, OK, I'll give you a ring in the morning. I'm running late now, 'bye.'

With that she had dropped the phone. She was in the enviable but awkward position of having two boyfriends.

She would have given anything for another two and a half days clear of John! She had managed the inconvenience by having lunch with him and spending the evenings with José. She told John that she had a sort of 'flu that got worse at night and that if she went to bed early for a couple of days she would be over it by Christmas.

On the twenty-third she had gone to the airport with José. Theirs was a heart-rending parting.

'I will never forget you, Ciara, my Irish love. You will always be in my heart and in my dreams. Nobody can take these away from me. I will try to come back to be with you but, you know, my studies and my father. It will be difficult . . .'

No mention was made of the fiancée!

She watched his plane take off with a tear in her eye and an ache in her heart. She never heard from him again.

After the romance with the handsome Spaniard, Christmas

with John had been very dull. Ciara compared everything he did with how José would have done it and there seemed to be an incredible shortfall. John, hurt and confused, had become argumentative and petulant. They had made no promises to one another when he flew back to America in the New Year.

Chapter Sixteen

'So how are you this morning?'

Ken wasn't his usual smiling self but his voice was warm.

'OK. And you?'

Ciara had a feeling she ought to be embarrassed by the memory of her 'romantic' moment with him the night before. But she didn't feel embarrassed or awkward, just shy, and her heart had leaped when she'd met him in the street outside the shop.

'I'm fine.' Ken's tone was serious. 'To tell you the truth, I thought there might be some official time off for Dimitri's funeral this morning but the family have said they didn't want a crowd.'

Ciara was taken aback. Here they were meeting for the

first time after being fairly intimate and he was talking about a funeral, one he wasn't even going to! Maybe it was his way of avoiding any mention of the night before. His way of saying he was still annoyed but mature enough to let it go.

'Oh, really?' She didn't want to have this conversation. Ken, sensing her discomfiture, changed the subject.

'How did this morning go?'

It was eleven o'clock. Ciara had just finished her morning break and was heading back on to the street. Ken, it seemed, was on his way into the shop for his break. Ciara had been wondering all morning what they would say to each other when they met. Now she was disappointed but could hardly have expected they would throw themselves into each other's arms with gay abandon and rediscover the excitement of the night before.

It would have been nice, though.

Instead they had an inane conversation about work and funerals.

'Great. Well, you know, boring, but no catastrophes or anything.' Ciara worked on sounding nonchalant.

Ken nodded, his mind obviously not on the subject. Ciara decided it was time to be brave and edge the conversation in the direction she thought it should go in.

'And you got home all right last night, after . . .'

Ken looked at her quickly, unsure if she was being facetious or even sarcastic.

'Yeah, got home OK. Didn't have far to go.' He had the appearance of a man who wanted to say more but didn't know how. 'I had a great evening . . . all of it.'

His face broke into a soft smile as he said this and once again the familiar Ken started to appear. Ciara smiled also and they stood outside the door of the Easi-tel shop, two adults dressed in rabbit costumes, smiling at one another.

'I don't believe I'm paying you to stand about and gossip.' Gráinne's strident voice broke into their moment.

Ciara started. She had successfully avoided speaking to Gráinne all morning, and except to bark the name of the street on which she was to be working that day, Gráinne hadn't addressed her.

Ciara didn't want to speak to her. Didn't want to see her. She wished Gráinne would cease to exist, be kidnapped by aliens, vanish like mushrooms exposed to sunlight or simply disappear in a little puff of smoke. Anything that would mean Ciara didn't have to acknowledge her.

No chance of that.

'Did you hear me, Ciara? Shouldn't you have been back five minutes ago? I'll have to start deducting from your wages if you're not doing the work, you know!'

Ciara scowled and looked the other way.

Ken, who had stared embarrassed at the ground as soon as Gráinne had spoken to them, regained his composure.

"Bye then, Ciara, I'll talk to you later.' He unsuccessfully tried to catch her eye but she didn't notice as under his manager's don't-you-dare-disobey-me glare Ken stepped lightly into the shop.

Outside Ciara pulled on her rabbit's head so that she wouldn't have to make eye contact with Gráinne and shuffled off back to work. The very idea of Gráinne disturbed her. Ruth had cheered her up enormously the night before while also reminding her that relationships rarely run along straight lines. Ciara had accepted this and by the time she had woken that morning, with a slight headache from the brandy, John's probable infidelity didn't seem to be that big a deal after all.

That was until she saw Gráinne.

When she saw her Ciara had the severest case of the 'other woman'. She wanted to do horrible things to her, the very least being to call her 'Shorty' and pull her hair. Or better still pluck it all out and call her 'Baldy'.

She wanted Gráinne to have a nasty fatal accident.

She wanted . . .

Just then Ciara's pouch started to vibrate. Her T2 was ringing. She reached in and pulled out the little phone, taking her rabbit's head off as she did so. The T2 lay in the palm of her hand, quivering. It struck Ciara that there must be some way of making the display screen work but she would probably need an instruction book!

What if it was John calling?

This morning she had decided to go on as though she hadn't seen him the night before. After all it was going to be difficult to explain what she was doing in town after she'd said she was staying at home for the evening.

Now, though, having experienced the fury that the sight of Gráinne had induced, Ciara wasn't at all sure how she would react to John.

She pressed the fluorescent button.

'Hello.' Her voice was cautious, neutral in the extreme.

'Hello, Ciara, what took you so long to answer? What's the point in having a mobile phone if you're no' going to answer it?'

Ciara breathed a sigh of relief.

'Hi, Mum, what's up?'

'Well, I don't know, Ciara. Ruth just rang me for your number and I thought I should let you know she'll be ringing you. I gave her the number yesterday but she said she'd lost it. Do you think she's having a breakdown?'

Because she hadn't seen Ruth for a couple of years Mrs Bowe had no way of really gauging her daughter's well-being. Her assessment of health, mental and physical, could only be made by seeing her children.

'No, Mum. She was sound asleep when I saw her this

morning and she was grand when I spoke to her last night. I'd say she's fine.'

'But do you no' think it's odd that she'd lose your number when I only gave it to her yesterday?'

'No, Mum. You know Ruth. She's always losing her bits of paper. Honest, she's fine.'

'I just don't know about that girl ...' Her mother left the sentence hovering darkly, her silence painting unmentionable pictures.

'And you'll still no' be coming by tomorrow for St Patrick's Day?'

'No, Mum. Like I told you yesterday, gotta work.'

'Right, well, I'll call you tomorrow anyway, and you'll let me know if there's anything about Ruth I should know, won't you?'

'Yes, Mum. OK. 'Bye.'

Ciara pressed the button to silence her mother. She was about to return the phone to her pocket when it started to vibrate again. This time she didn't even consider who it might be.

'Hi, Ruth.'

'How did you know it was me? Is that some sort of magic phone?'

'Bush telegraph.' Ciara's voice was deadpan.

'The Home Office! I don't believe it, I only got off the phone to her a second ago!'

'One of the miracles of telecommunications, your mother can always find you!' Ciara teased.

Ruth sighed. 'Some things never change. You were up and off very early this morning. I wanted to ask you if you could have lunch with me? I don't know how late I'll be working tonight.'

'Sure, yeah, that would be nice. My lunch break is at twelve-thirty.'

'OK, I'll meet you at that French place on the quays then, is that all right?'

'Yeah, see you later.'

Ciara put the phone back into her pouch and pulled out a pile of flyers, shuffling and sorting them before she put on her head and paws. She didn't feel like it but she really had no option but to work. She was just about to pull her head on when a voice spoke from behind her.

'Ciara?'

She swung around and there, standing some feet away, was Ken, his head held under his arm. Even in his rabbit costume, his body gave every impression of being apprehensive. His eyes met hers and he smiled hesitantly.

'Sorry about that back there. The woman's an awful tyrant but she's the boss!'

Ciara, relieved that they weren't still talking about funerals, shrugged.

'My break was over anyway.'

Ken nodded, seemingly eager now to talk.

'I'm just on my way back from mine but I thought I'd come this way and say hello.' He paused but evidently hadn't finished speaking. 'I wondered if maybe we could do something after work later? If you like. I feel as if we left things a bit up in the air last night, you know.'

Ciara nodded, agreeing wholeheartedly but not trusting herself to speak, delighted that he wasn't just going to ignore the fact that they had kissed.

'So maybe around eight? Does that suit you?'

'Yes, eight would be fine.' She wanted to skip for joy but decided that it would not be appropriate.

'Same place as last night then?'

'Yeah, sure, fine.' She nodded, trying not to laugh outright with delight. Ken smiled and for a moment looked as though he was going to hug her. But, restraining himself, he raised his hand in a salute instead and said, 'See you later then.'

'Yeah, 'bye, Ken. See you.'

Ciara watched him walk away until he disappeared around the corner, his furry little tail swaying slowly to and fro. The sight was so comical that she did finally laugh outright, wondering as she did so whether she was mad to be attracted to a man with such an undignified job. All the same, she thought as she started passing out flyers, she was in no position to comment on other people's career choices!

Her day had improved one hundred per cent.

She had not wanted to come to work that morning. She didn't want to have to face Gráinne and possibly John, knowing as she did now that they were more than just colleagues. She shuddered involuntarily every time their face-caressing moment in the pub came to mind. She felt hugely angry about the entire matter especially when she remembered how highly John had spoken of Gráinne when he had been out with Ciara.

'Gráinne's great at that side of things. In fact, she runs the whole on-the-ground operation, don't know how she manages it.'

She had been right to be jealous! There was something going on between them. He didn't just admire his manageress for her ability to do sums and conjure up profits!

The prospect of her own date with Ken soothed Ciara's anger. That would show John he couldn't just keep her as the second option on the girlfriend front, to be called upon on evenings when Gráinne had something more interesting to do.

Indignation at his treatment of her and delight at the prospect of an interesting and exciting evening with Ken made the rest of the morning speed by. At exactly twelve-thirty Ciara stepped into the little café on the quays.

'Nice outfit, Ciaróg. Good to see you haven't lost your taste for designer labels with your career change!' Ruth was waiting for her at a table inside the window.

Ciara rolled her eyes and wedged herself in on the other side of the little table.

'I've gone ahead and ordered soup for two, OK?'

'Lovely, thanks, Ruth.'

'So how was the morning?'

'Fine. Well, you know, boring as usual.'

'Any sign of John?'

Ciara shook her head and poured herself a glass of water. 'No. Gráinne was there, of course.'

'Did you say anything to her?'

'Of course not, Ruth. I don't even know if she knows that John's going out with me, or went out with me, or whatever it was we were doing. And besides she's horrible, I'm hardly going to pour my heart out to her!'

'Well, what *are* you going to do?' Ruth piled butter on to a piece of bread and ate it. Ciara watched her enviously, determined she wouldn't touch the bread before the soup arrived. And then it would be without butter!

'Don't know.' Then, because she was dying to tell somebody and there didn't seem to be any harm in it, she blurted out the latest development with Ken. 'That guy I saw last night has asked me out again tonight.'

'Mr Anonymous "just a guy from work", is it?' Ruth asked mock-innocently.

'Yeah, the same one,' Ciara confessed a little shame-facedly.

'Ah, so I was right, there was more to it than "just a guy from work"! Come on, out with it!'

'OK, OK,' Ciara giggled, 'he *is* a guy from work but he's really nice and he kissed me goodnight last night.' She didn't want Ruth to think that it was she who had done the kissing in the first place – though she had.

'Wow! You don't hang about, do you? All the comfort and advice I gave you last night and you'd already gone and got your tongue down somebody else's throat!'

'Ruth, it wasn't like that! And there's no need to be, well, so rude!'

'What, are you telling me there were no tongues? If there were no tongues don't go out with him again, that's my recommendation!' Ruth's eyes shone with mischief and Ciara had no choice but to laugh.

'All right, all right, but it's nothing serious. He's just really good company and, believe me, I need a bit of that right now!'

'And are you going to tell John that you're engaging in a bit of "good company"?'

'Why should I?' Ciara was defensive now. Even though she was angry with John for going out with Gráinne she still felt guilty about seeing Ken, as though somehow she was being unfaithful.

Ruth shrugged. 'I just don't see the point in getting your knickers in a twist this early in the relationship.'

Ciara became sulky. 'It's not *that* early in the relationship, we've known each other for years. And we've slept together. It's not like nothing's happened.'

'So *are* you going to talk to him about it?' Ruth moved the conversation on, unwilling to let things stay as they were. Ciara, still sulky, frowned into her soup and didn't answer.

'Well?' Ruth persisted.

'Why should I? He's the one seeing someone else. Why should I be second best *and* look for an explanation?'

'You just spent the last three years with Lassi being second best and I didn't see you getting into a sulk about that until quite recently. Why should this be any different?' Ruth's voice could have cut through wood it had such an edge. Ciara inhaled sharply, surprised at such directness. Even from Ruth this was a harsh fact to throw into a lunchtime conversation.

'I . . . I . . .' she stammered. 'That was different!'

'Why?' Ruth was matter-of-fact now. 'Lassi had a wife and child. It took him two or three months to tell you about them but when he did it was all hunky-dory. "That's fine, Gary, I don't mind being second best, I'll be fine as the other woman, don't mind me!" And now John may or may not have something going with this Gráinne and you're out for his blood! What's going on here?'

Ciara fixed her eyes on the pepper mill and bit her lip. Put like that, she had to acknowledge that Ruth was right. Maybe she was over-reacting. Maybe she should just talk to John about it, sort it out. Find some way of explaining to him how she had seen him in the pub when she was supposed to be at home catching up with her sister.

But she wouldn't talk to him immediately. She'd leave it a couple of days. She'd go out with Ken and have some fun, show John that she didn't need him, that other men found her attractive. And then when she was ready she'd talk to him and see just what he had to say for himself!

Ciara looked up at Ruth who was waiting, spoon poised, for a reaction to her attack. Shaking her head with a half smile, Ciara said, 'I don't know why I keep you as a sister, you're so horrible to me, you really are!'

'Ah, yes, but it's for your own good!' Ruth replied in a mock-serious voice. Then, switching back to her normal tone, she asked, 'Do you want that piece of bread or can I mop up the last of my soup with it?'

Ciara passed the bread to her, still shaking her head. Then she checked her watch and said, 'I'd better go, I've got to pick up some flyers at the shop on my way.'

Ruth mumbled through a mouthful of bread, 'If you

hang on I'll walk you there, I'm heading that way any-way.'

As they made their way through the crowded lunchtime streets to the shop she slipped her arm through Ciara's furry one and asked, 'So what are you and Mr "just a guy from work" doing later?'

Ciara shook her head. 'Don't know yet. We've only arranged to meet.'

'Just be careful he's not some sort of axe murderer, I don't want to have to stay with Karen-I'm-married-to-a-consultant-and-have-a house-in-Castleknock every time I come to town, you know!'

Ciara patted her hand consolingly. 'At least you'd have less chance of getting mugged on the way home! Don't worry, he's far too good-looking to be evil. And if you play your cards right you might even get to meet him.'

'Sounds to me, Ciara Bowe, as if he's going to get invited in tonight. Am I right?'

'We'll see,' she said evasively.

'Don't worry about me being there anyway, whatever you do.' Ruth was serious now.

'Why, where will you be?' Ciara was disappointed and slightly panicked.

'You know I'm in town for the St Patrick's Day parade tomorrow? Well, we have to put the float together for our anti-GM campaign. We're a bit behind so a few of us will probably work very late to get it done, maybe all night. The workshop's in Wicklow so I don't think I'll be back tonight.'

Ciara was taken aback. She did not want to spend the night in that flat on her own.

'Will you be around tomorrow or are you going to the Home Office?' Ruth was still talking.

'I'm working, covering the parade. Maybe I'll see you during the day?'

'Great. Of course you will. You won't be able to miss us. We've made a giant automated gene-monster being orbited by skull and crossbones helium-filled balloons. I think you'll notice us!'

Ruth was obviously very excited about the group's creation for the parade the next day. Ciara secretly thought that the last thing the anti-GMers would want was a mobile phone bunny hanging about with them, spoiling their image! She didn't mention this to Ruth.

Instead she said, 'Will you stay for the rest of the weekend?'

'Try and stop me! You'll be so glad to get rid of me on Monday.'

By now they had reached the corner across the street from the Easi-tel shop. Ciara stopped and turned to Ruth. She nodded her head towards the shop.

'That's the witch's den over there. If you're lucky

you'll catch a glimpse of her as she whips the workers into shape.'

'I'm sure she's not that bad, you just have it in for her because you think she's "after yer man".'

'I hated her long before I knew she had anything to do with John,' Ciara half-seriously defended herself.

'Whatever his employees are like, I have to hand it to the Capitalist. He's doing all right judging by the crowd in the shop.' Ruth paused, tilting her head to one side, and added, 'if you're into that sort of thing.'

Having had a lunchtime devoid of conspiracy theories and world exploitation, Ciara was eager to get away before Ruth gave in to the temptation to launch into the environmental implications of mobile phones. She turned and gave her sister a peck on the cheek.

'See you tomorrow then, Ruth, OK?'

'OK, Ciaróg.' Ruth leaned forward to meet her kiss. Then, focusing on something in the distance over Ciara's shoulder, added with a frown, 'Goodness! What's he doing dressed like that? It's very strange!'

Ciara looked at her sister in surprise, then following the direction of her gaze turned and looked at the Easi-tel shop just in time to see Ken disappear through the door.

'What do you mean? Who?' Ciara glanced up and down the street in case she had looked in the wrong direction.

'Ken Meagher ... I'm sure I just saw Ken Meagher go

into the shop in one of your outfits. What's he doing working with you? He's a journalist, and a good one. He's written some great stuff for us. Do you know him?'

Chapter Seventeen

'No.' Ciara was speaking very quietly so her voice wouldn't carry into the staffroom where Ken was. Gráinne looked at her impatiently. Ciara, realising she must have spoken too quietly, raised her voice.

'No, I haven't seen tomorrow's timetable.' She glanced furtively towards the staffroom.

Gráinne, deciding to ignore her odd behaviour yet again, swept a sheet of paper from underneath the counter and slapped it in front of Ciara.

'Here's a list of everybody who's on. I want you dotted all along the parade route and on the street by ten when the crowd starts to gather, OK?'

Ciara looked at the list. There were eight names on it but she was only looking for one. And there it was!

There was one 'Ken' on the list. Only the name was not Ken Meagher, it was Ken Brown! Not only had he lied to her, he was also using a false name for the job!

When Ruth had asked her did she know journalist Ken Meagher, Ciara had shaken her head and said nothing. Although she didn't say it to Ruth she knew her sister must be mistaken. It must be a different Ken!

Why would he lie to her? Or rather, as he had not *really* lied, why would he not tell her the truth? Working in 'printing' was hardly the same as being a journalist, now was it?

'But you must know him!' Ruth had said. 'He's just gone into your shop in a rabbit costume and he's not the sort of guy you wouldn't notice – he's got the most amazing blue eyes. Very popular with women!'

Ciara shook her head again. 'He's probably just started, we have new ones every day. I'll meet him later, I'm sure.' She needed time to work this out and didn't want her sister to know that she had gone out with and kissed a man without even knowing his last name. It just sounded too sordid!

'What I want to know is, what's he doing working as a rabbit?'

'Maybe, like me, he felt the need for a career change!' Ruth, ignoring Ciara's answer, went on enthusiastically, 'I know what it is! He's doing an article, although he usually covers more controversial topics than mobile phones. You should ask him what he's doing, Ciara.'

She was too confused even to talk about Ken.

'Look, I'd better go, I'm awfully late.' She had to get away.

'OK, I'll see you tomorrow then.' With a wave Ruth disappeared around the corner, leaving Ciara to return to the shop apprehensively.

She didn't want to meet Ken until she'd worked out just how to react now that she knew who he was. Although she had never asked his last name it was completely unacceptable that he should use a false one. He had deliberately deceived her! But at least she knew now he was lying.

Ciara was furious. It was one thing to lie to Gráinne, or any employer really, but to lie to somebody you'd gone on a date with and even kissed was totally unacceptable.

Especially when that somebody was Ciara Bowe!

And he had asked her out again. Just how long and how far had he intended to go before revealing that he wasn't himself? A horrifying idea crossed Ciara's mind. What if he had never intended to tell her? After all, why would a successful journalist want to go out with a mobile phone street advertiser? It had all just been pretence. He had been using her!

'So is that entirely clear then?' Gráinne's demanding

voice cut into Ciara's traumatised musing. For the first time that day she looked at her manager.

'Yes,' she said. 'It's all quite clear.'

Gráinne, taken aback by the change of tone, nodded then stated brusquely, 'Right then, I think that's all. You'd better get back to work, your break is at three-thirty.'

Ciara went back to work in a daze. She had difficulty accepting that Ken, cheery, intelligent warm-hearted Ken, had been lying to her since the moment they had met. Compared to his cold-blooded deception John going out with another woman seemed relatively harmless. It might just be, as Ruth said, that John was finishing with Gráinne and that's what she had witnessed the night before. Perhaps he had not wanted to upset Ciara by mentioning it. Ken on the other hand had quite obviously set out with the intention of total deception. And she had fallen for it!

Before she could wallow further in self-pity the T2 started to ring in her pouch. She pulled it out and stared maliciously at it. Why, she wondered, did it never show a number so that she could at least have a hint who was ringing her? It was probably her mother, still determined to have Ruth certified for losing bits of paper with phone numbers on. She pressed the button.

'Hello,' she said shortly, deciding on a no-nonsense approach from the outset.

'Ciara, are you all right?' John's voice was full of its usual concern.

Her heart skipped a beat. What was she going to say to him? How was she going to handle this?

'John, hi.' She spoke more slowly now, allowing herself time to work out a strategy.

'How're things?' His tone was casual. He obviously had no inkling that anything had changed between them since he had spoken to her last.

'OK.' Ciara was still playing for time.

'Any news on the car?' He was reminding her that there were other disasters in her life besides lying boyfriends.

'No, they said they'd ring if they had any. Nothing so far.' To Ciara's surprise she realised she was having a normal conversation with him. The inclination to shout at him and scratch his eyes out had been lost somewhere in the more recent Ken-revelations.

'Sorry to hear that. I'm sure there'll be some news in the next day or two. Do you feel like doing something tonight to take your mind off things? We could go to the cinema or something?'

John had just asked her out!

It had been bound to happen but Ciara was not sure what she should say to him. One thing she did know for sure was that she would not be keeping her appointment with Ken Meagher/Brown later!

She decided that in the circumstances the best thing to do was to go out with John. At least she would not be on her own in the flat and would not be there if Ken decided to call by later in a you-stood-me-up fury. There was also the possibility that she and John could clear up all this Gráinne business.

'Yeah, that would be nice. Thanks, John.'

'Is Ruth still about, would she like to come?'

He was so thoughtful. Ciara was already starting to doubt what she had seen in the pub the night before. Surely he couldn't be so attentive *and* be having an affair with another woman? 'No, Ruth's not around this evening . . .'

'OK, I'll pick you up at eight at the flat, how about that?'

Before she could stop herself Ciara blurted out, 'Seven-forty-five. I mean, that is . . . I should be ready by seven-forty-five. Most of the films start at eight, don't they?' She tried to sound reasonable as she said this. She didn't want Ken turning up on her doorstep if John got delayed or simply decided to sit in the flat and chat for a while.

'Good thinking, Ciara.' John's voice hadn't even a whisper of suspicion in it. 'See you later.'

He was gone.

Ciara slipped the little phone into her pouch and went

back to work. Her mind, however, was not on the job and by breaktime she still had a pouch full of flyers. She didn't dare go back to the shop in case Ken was about. With her luck he would be leaving just as she arrived or arriving when she was leaving and the last thing she wanted was to have to face him or indeed ever speak to him again. She walked around the block a couple of times and then returned to her absent-minded distribution.

For the next hour and a half all she could think about was how she would get changed at the end of the day without bumping into him. She decided there was only one thing for it. She would go back to the shop half an hour early, pretending to be sick and needing to go home. She would have to face the wrath of Gráinne but this was nothing compared to her desire not to meet Ken.

At 5.30 she shuffled into the shop clutching her stomach. She couldn't even feel it through the costume padding but hoped she looked convincing nonetheless.

'What are you doing back so early?' Evidently Gráinne was not very good at reading giant bunny body language. Ciara pointed to her stomach and shook her head, holding her breath as though she was in pain.

'Cramp . . . don't know what it is . . . must be something I ate. Think I should go home.'

Gráinne looked at her disapprovingly.

'You can't just go dashing off home because you

have a pain in your stomach. Have you taken anything for it?'

Ciara nodded. 'Yeah, hasn't helped. I think it's getting worse.'

Gráinne gave in grudgingly.

'I suppose you'd better go home then. Just don't be missing tomorrow.'

Relieved, Ciara headed slowly across the shop, remembering to stay slightly hunched. She mumbled, 'Thanks, Florence,' under her breath as she went through the staffroom door. Two assistants standing nearby heard her and broke into giggles. One of them turned to the shelf behind to hide her grin from Gráinne, while the other ducked under the counter.

Once in the staffroom Ciara changed as quickly as possible. Then, hunching her shoulders and keeping one hand on her stomach, she shuffled painfully out through the shop. Gráinne did not look up as she passed.

Outside Ciara turned up her collar against the biting March breeze and walked home. She was relieved that the working day was over and that she would not have to worry about meeting Ken again until the next morning.

As soon as she stepped into the flat Ciara knew she wasn't alone. She stopped and stood very still, listening. She could hear nothing. She took a few quiet steps into the hallway and peered in at the open door of Elena's room, still listening. There was nobody there. Then she heard it: a faint shuffle as though somebody had moved something a short distance across the shiny floor. And the sound was coming from *her* room! Her scalp tingled in fright. She stood quite still, wondering if she should call out or if this would just draw unnecessary and unwelcome attention to herself. Suddenly she noticed the door of her room start to open slowly – so slowly it was difficult to tell if it was moving at all at first. Ciara flung herself back against the wall and held her breath. Now she was debating whether or not she should run.

Before she could decide Elena stepped cautiously through the partially open door. Both she and Ciara started and gasped at the sight of each other.

'Oh my God! You frightened the life out of me, Elena!'

She put her hand on her heart and took a couple of deep breaths. 'I'm sorry, I did not expect you home so early. I did not know who was here!' There was real fear in her voice but Ciara was too relieved to notice.

'Where have you been, Elena? I've been worried about you – you just disappeared. We were burgled, you know. Are you all right?'

Elena raised her hands to stop the flood of questions.

'I'm fine. I forgot to tell you I stay with friends for a couple of days. I'm sorry you worry. I just come back and see everything on the floor so I go into your room to see if it is the same there and then ...' Elena gestured with her hands.

So that was why she had been in Ciara's room!

'Yeah, sorry about that, Elena, I'm a bit nervous since the break-in. I really thought that maybe something had happened to you.' Ciara was still not quite satisfied with Elena's vague explanation for her disappearance.

'I'm sorry, I saw nothing strange. Everything was all right when I left.' Elena was almost pleading now and looking very uncomfortable standing for so long in her heavily pregnant condition.

Ciara decided they ought to stop apologising to one another and she had better start getting ready to go out.

'You ought to sit down. Can I get you a cup of something? You're very pale.'

Elena looked relieved and, nodding, moved towards the living room. 'Maybe a cup of tea.'

'One cup of tea coming up.'

Ciara ushered her on to the sofa, dropped her own bag on the floor and went into the kitchen. She filled the kettle and plugged it in. Then, salvaging two teabags from the little teabag pile on the counter, she went to the fridge for milk. There wasn't any. The only milk in the kitchen was congealed about the sink, its empty torn container on its side on the cooker.

Ciara slammed the fridge door shut, cursing herself for forgetting to buy milk. Then she remembered the coffee episode. Elena did not take milk in coffee so perhaps she did not take it in tea either. She went into the living room to ask.

As she came through the doorway she stopped in surprise.

Elena was sitting on the sofa going through Ciara's bag!

She must have noticed a movement or a sound because she looked up with a startled expression as the bag fell from her hands, its contents spilling out over the floor.

'Oh!' she gasped, a look of sheer terror on her face.

'What are you doing?' Ciara demanded, swooping on to the floor to gather up the messy pile of powder-coated lipsticks, a comb, her compact, mascara and eye-liners.

'I ... I ... wondered if you had a cigarette.' Elena sounded as though she had said the first thing that came into her head. 'I'm so sorry, sorry, I did not want to ask ...'

'So you thought you'd steal!' Ciara's voice was harsh and she immediately regretted her tone as she watched the younger woman's eyes fill with tears. 'Why didn't you just say?' Her voice was more kindly now.

Elena looked down at her hands clenched in her lap. 'I

did not want to be a beggar. And ... I should not smoke for the baby.'

Ciara sat back on her haunches, her bag on the floor in front of her, and spoke softly. 'You know, you're right, you shouldn't smoke. But asking me for a cigarette isn't begging, I wouldn't mind in the least. Unfortunately I don't smoke. Tell you what, let's forget about it and I'll get that tea. Is it all right without milk?'

Elena nodded, still shamefaced, and Ciara moved towards the kitchen, embarrassed now that the other woman had been too shy to ask her for a cigarette. She quickly finished making the tea and was carrying the cups from the kitchen when she heard the front door close quietly. When she went into the living room it was empty.

'Elena?' There was no answer. 'Elena?' She raised her voice. There was still no answer. She looked into Elena's room but there was nobody there. She wasn't in Ciara's room either. Ciara went back into the hall and looked at the closed front door. Elena had obviously left the flat.

'Well, don't say goodbye or anything!' She spoke to the door. 'And I suppose you won't be wanting your tea then.'

She dumped it in the sink. John had been right, she thought, when he'd advised her not to pay any attention to what Elena said. She was most definitely strange and evidently not very honest.

Ciara had a shower and as she stepped out of it realised that she was starving. She'd had nothing to eat since her soup at lunchtime. The upset had kept hunger at bay but now she was ravenous. There was no food in the house and all she had to look forward to was popcorn if she and John went straight to the cinema. But maybe that wasn't such a bad thing as it was notoriously unfattening. Besides clothes felt much better when they were not so tight about the waist!

As she got dressed she became nervous. Even though she was not nearly as angry with John as she had been that morning, she still had to sort out how she was going to handle the whole Gráinne business. Should she just ignore it and follow him for a couple of days to make sure it was a one-off thing? Or should she confront him about it, put him on the spot and demand the truth? Or maybe there was some way of bringing up the subject using subtle hints and allowing him to take the bait and talk about it without Ciara's having to admit to seeing them together.

Although she preferred this last option she couldn't work out a way of achieving it. As she put on her makeup she practised leading statements.

'You know, John, monogamy has always struck me as peculiar, what do you think?'

Very general, perhaps a bit too polite.

'Have you gone out with anybody besides me since you got back, John?'

Too inquisitive, overly sweet.

'Tell me, John, have you ever gone out with anybody you work with?'

Bit specific, too pragmatic.

'Did you have a nice quiet evening in last night, John?'

Obviously leading, probably bitchy!

None of these worked and John arrived as she was still trying to find one that did.

'Sorry I'm late, had to take a call.'

Late? He was late? Ciara looked at her watch. He was late! It was almost eight o'clock. This was cutting things a little too fine. What if Ken was the impatient sort or suspected immediately that she'd stood him up? He could arrive at the flat any time now! In fact, he was probably going from door to door even as she thought about it.

'God, we'd better go or we'll miss the film.'

'But we don't even know what we're going to see or where. I have a newspaper in the car, we can check when we get downstairs.'

'Good idea. Let's go now.' Ciara grabbed her coat and bundled him out of the door. Once in the car she convinced John to drive while she read. She chose a movie that allowed just enough time for them to get there. She didn't want any chance of a passing Ken seeing her outside the cinema.

Before she sat down Ciara bought the largest tub of popcorn available. She held it on her lap throughout the film in case John wanted to hold hands or attempt any other sort of physical intimacy. As it turned out it was not the kind of film to encourage any sort of romantic feeling. It started with a huge explosion that seemed to wipe out the whole cast and continued in a like vein until only the hero was left alive, blood-stained and defiant, in a landscape of dismembered bodies.

Ciara did not enjoy it at all but as she had chosen it did not feel she could walk out or even object. As she stumbled, numb and almost deaf, out of the cinema John turned to her. Taking the half-empty popcorn container out of her hand, he said, 'Great choice, I've been meaning to get to that one for ages.'

Ciara nodded and smiled and quickly suggested they go for a drink. As they walked into the bar she cast a furtive glance around to ensure Ken was nowhere in sight.

'Is something the matter, Ciara? You've seemed a bit on edge all evening.'

'No, no, nothing.' She smiled again, unconvincingly.

'Are you working tomorrow?'

Ciara nodded. 'Are you?' she asked conversationally rather than from interest.

'No, nothing for me to do. Most businesses are closed. I'll be about, though. It's a big day for advertising. You probably have to be up early so I promise not to keep you out late. In fact we should go home straight after this one.'

Ciara wondered what he meant by 'we' and 'home'. It all sounded a bit too cosy when the Gráinne matter had not yet been settled. But what was she going to say? 'Hey, John, what's this "we" and "home" business?' Or, 'Don't you have something to tell me before we can get on to going "home"?' But she said nothing of the sort and the moment was lost through her indecision.

Their conversation moved on with John behaving as though he had not been out with another woman the night before; as though there was no reason why things should be different between himself and Ciara. He was very attentive and even slipped his hand around her waist as they left the pub. She stiffened but John did not seem to notice and did not remove his arm until he opened the car door for her.

On the way home they made small talk. It was not until they were parking in front of the flats that he changed the subject. He smiled at her sideways and said, 'I could really murder a cup of coffee.'

'I don't have any, it got spoiled in that break-in,' Ciara responded quickly.

'It doesn't have to be coffee — tea will do. You know what I mean.' John had chosen to overlook her short answer and continued smiling at her, leaning a little closer.

Ciara felt a surge of anger. How dare he think he could just invite himself in after the way he had behaved the night before? How dare he carry on as though he and Gráinne hadn't been fawning over each other in that pub?

'And what would Gráinne have to say about you coming in for tea?' she snapped before she knew she was going to speak.

So much for taking a subtle approach!

John sat back as though Ciara had just slapped him, his face frozen in a look of astonishment.

'Gráinne? What do you mean?'

Ciara may have brought the subject up but she still was not prepared to admit that she had been in town the night before.

'You know what I mean.' She decided to try ambiguity. It worked.

John's look of astonishment faded. He pushed his glasses higher on to his nose and sighed. Then he sighed again.

Ciara felt faint stirrings of irritation but resisted any impulse to speak further. He could sigh all he wanted, she was not going to help him out on this one. John sighed some more.

Eventually he spoke.

'I'm sorry, Ciara, I didn't mean to hurt you.' She did not like the sound of that at all but remained quiet, waiting for him to continue. 'I've known Gráinne for a couple of years, she used to come to Russia on contract work. We started going out then. Nothing regular. She was the obvious choice for Easi-tel when I started up. But we still weren't seeing each other steadily or anything. I met her last night to tell her there was somebody else. It's all over now. I'm sorry I didn't tell you before. I thought you might be upset. That you'd think badly of me.'

He paused.

He sighed.

Ciara didn't know what to say. So Ruth had been right! It was just an overlap thing. But did that mean she was supposed just to forget about it? After all he had lied to her ... sort of.

John sighed again and looked at her, his eyes full of please-understand-me-I'm-such-a-nice-guy.

'Ciara, you know you're the only one I've ever wanted. The only one I've ever really loved, all these years. And now suddenly it's all happened so fast. You have no idea how happy I was about making love with you. It meant so much to me. Don't let my ... my mistake take that away from us.'

She was speechless. What could she say to such a declaration? A little bit of her had been hoping he would deny Gráinne so that she could accuse him of lying and therefore get off the hook over their physical incompatibility. But instead, here he was saying he loved her and always had. It was quite possible that he always would love her. How could she let that go?

She had been attracted to Ken who had turned out to be so deceitful he hadn't even given her his real name! And here was the man she had chosen to sleep with two days before, because she hoped he was The One, practically declaring undying love.

Time for that decision.

Time for that compromise.

Time to admit that she could make things work with John.

He reached out and took her hand.

'Say you forgive me? But the car isn't the place to discuss this. Let's go inside. I don't need tea or coffee or anything, just you. Say it's all right, that it'll all be fine?' His voice was soft and pleading.

Ciara looked at him for a moment, then nodded.

Chapter Eighteen

It had happened again!

Sex had been a disaster. Even though Ciara thought she was prepared this time she had still not expected it to be such a disaster! As she lay in bed watching the morning light filter through the curtains she had to accept that it had not just been a first-time thing. This was a repeat performance and she knew now that there was no way of ignoring the issue.

She and John Murphy were physically incompatible.

He was caring, thoughtful, intelligent, industrious and he loved her. What more could she ask for in a man? Surely a relationship based on liking and trusting one another could see its way through a little problem like the 'little' problem John presented her with during lovemaking? Ciara had always been told: 'It's not what you've got, it's what you do with it!' A niggling, soft-spoken but articulate doubt suggested that this statement probably came from the same people who claimed size didn't matter.

She threw the doubt out as a dissenter. This was not what she needed to hear as she worked towards a compromise! As she expelled Doubt he raised his soft voice to reiterate his opinion. 'Maybe it's just another lie to make you settle for less. Maybe it's . . .' She slammed the heavy door of denial in Doubt's face, blocking him out.

She had to find a solution to this problem. Perhaps it wasn't even a problem at all but something a bit of discussion could sort out. She took the day before as an example. She had been upset and angry at what she saw as John's infidelity but she had been wrong. He had been clearing up his past so that he could be free for her. And he had not mentioned Gráinne because he knew it would upset Ciara. He had proved himself to be considerate as well as thoughtful.

Maybe she should just talk to him about the matter.

She stirred, rolling over so that she faced the sleeping John. His regular deep breathing stopped as soon as she moved and his eyes opened sleepily.

'Hi, love,' he mumbled. He reached out and let his hand fall on her waist. 'What time's it?'

Ciara glanced at her watch. 'Nearly nine.'

Her I'm-so-awake voice roused him a little more. He propped himself up on one arm and turned to her, eyes oddly vacant-looking without his glasses.

'Awake long?' His voice was sleep-coated.

Ciara nodded. John sensed there was something on her mind.

'Anything the matter?'

Ciara exhaled, rolled on to her back and stared at the ceiling. She didn't know how to talk about this. She didn't want to talk about this. But talking had sorted out the Gráinne thing so there was no reason why it couldn't sort out this sex thing.

'You know when you sleep with someone, John? Is it different with each person?'

He laughed, thinking this an odd question. 'Of course it is! Isn't it for you?'

'Well, yeah,' Ciara said, not expecting to be asked the same question back. 'Of course, but I was just wondering if it's better with one than it is with another? You know . . .'

John, realising she was serious, didn't laugh this time.

'Yes, naturally.' Then his face cleared. He knew what was going on here. 'With you it's fantastic, don't worry about that! I think you're great in bed.' He leaned across and gave her a peck on the cheek.

Ciara nearly choked. This was not what she'd meant. He

thought she was compliment-hunting! How embarrassing. She was ready to drop the subject completely. This conversation was just too difficult. However she knew if she abandoned it now she wouldn't have the courage to start it again.

Ever.

'Um ... well, that's not exactly what I meant. It was more, well, more ... I don't seem to be ... I'm not that happy about the bed ... stuff.'

Ciara didn't feel she was expressing herself very well but John seemed to get the message. He withdrew his arm from where it lay across her stomach and the contented lines of his face turned to a frown.

'Oh,' was all he said.

He didn't even sigh.

He wasn't taking this at all as Ciara had hoped he would. She'd just wanted to start a general discussion that covered topics like expectation, desire, and if necessary technique. All in the nicest, friendliest, most mature sort of way. This had not happened.

Silence had gathered about the bed. Like relatives at the side of a dying loved one, it waited quietly for any sign of change.

Ciara wanted to say something, do something, to change the atmosphere. In fact she wanted to take back what she had just said but she couldn't do that. She did not know what to say that would not make the situation worse.

Suddenly John threw back the bedcovers and got out of bed. He gathered up his clothes and stomped out. He went into the bathroom, slamming the door behind him.

So much for talking about it!

Ciara got out of bed and picked up her own clothes from the floor. She wondered if there was anything she could say that would sort out the situation. Maybe a little time in the bathroom would help him calm down and then she could explain things better to him.

John came out of the bathroom. Before Ciara had time to leave the bedroom he had stormed out of the flat, slamming the front door loudly.

Ciara had had no idea he would take the matter so seriously, react so strongly. How dare he just walk off in the middle of a discussion? It wasn't as if it was something she wanted to talk about either but this was hardly the way to behave!

And he had gone without even offering her a lift to work!

It was 9.20, she would have to get a move on. Even as she dressed she could not get John's extreme reaction out of her mind.

Did this mean he was gone forever?

Did that one little query, one little statement of

dissatisfaction from her, mean he had left for good? She couldn't believe that but it seemed pointless for her to stay angry about it. John was just hurt and embarrassed, too upset to discuss it now. But she would ring him and see if he wanted to talk.

Yes, she would ring him later.

Ciara was so caught up in working out a strategy for dealing with John that it wasn't until she'd left the flat and set off into town that she remembered she had to avoid meeting Ken if at all possible. As the memory of his deceit flooded back she realised there was no 'if at all possible' about it! She had to avoid Ken. The only way she could think of doing this was to get into work before her actual starting time and get out on the street before anyone else arrived. She also needed to check that she would be working as far away from him as possible. He probably knew by now that her standing him up meant she knew more than she ought!

Ciara broke into a jog. She wasn't able to maintain it for any distance but in between bursts of running she walked as fast as she could. She got to the shop just before five to ten, panting. Gráinne, evidently opening late because of St Patrick's Day, had just arrived and was standing inside the door, the keys still in her hand.

She took a quick glance at her watch to verify she wasn't late.

'Ciara, you're very punctual today!'

She nodded, too out of breath to speak. She pointed at the staffroom as she headed towards it, miming she would go and put on her costume. Gráinne half shrugged, half nodded and proceeded to turn on her laptop.

Within a minute Ciara was back in the shop in costume, breathing a little more easily now.

'Could I just have a quick look at that list? I can't remember where I'm working ... Gráinne.' It killed her to have to say the name. She couldn't bear the idea that this woman had slept with someone that she had slept with, no matter how unsatisfactory the experience had been for her.

Instead of producing the list from the day before Gráinne pressed a few keys on her computer and looked closely at the screen. She nodded and said, 'Dame Street. You're on Dame Street.'

Ciara nearly exploded with frustration! She couldn't see what was on the screen and there was no point in asking Gráinne where Ken would be working, she would be bound to say it was none of her business. Besides Ciara did not have time to stand and chat about it, she had to be clear of the shop before the others arrived.

'Thanks,' she said through gritted teeth, grabbed a pile of flyers and moved quickly towards the door.

'Oh, Ciara . . .' Gráinne raised her voice. Ciara stopped and looked around. 'Don't bother coming back during the day, just take these extra flyers. You needn't stop for lunch and you can finish at three.'

Ciara nodded and took the extra flyers, silently cursing the added weight. She quickly left the shop before Gráinne could bark any more instructions at her. Once she got around the corner she slowed down. What was she going to do about Ken? He would have no trouble finding her if he wanted to and then she would be in for it. She would probably end up like poor Dimitri.

That was it! Of course! Ken's lies and deception were all related to Dimitri's death! Why hadn't she thought of that before? It was the obvious explanation. And if he had something to do with Dimitri's death then it stood to reason he was involved in the murder attempt on her that first morning under the scaffolding!

Ciara realised she was in grave danger.

She decided the best thing to do would be to keep a low profile for the next couple of hours, then when the St Patrick's Day parade started she could hide herself in the mayhem, blending in with the other costumed figures. Ciara looked about her, wondering if there was anywhere for a giant rabbit to hang about for a couple of hours without arousing comment. Already the streets had a carnival air. Tourists in green scarves and hats mingled with families in from the country, their lapels displaying enormous outgrowths of shamrock. Among the milling, gathering crowds were outlandishly costumed figures obviously making their way to whatever bit of the parade they were attached to. This made Ciara feel less of a freak. In fact she felt that she could fit in quite well if she found out where the parade was assembling.

She noticed four men in gaily coloured band uniforms on the other side of the street. Ciara figured they must have a destination, someplace to pick up their instruments and warm up for the march through the city. Wherever they were going would be just the place for a giant rabbit to loiter unquestioned. She followed the men at a distance until they met up with the rest of the band in a carpark behind Christ Church.

Ciara spent the next two hours sitting on a wall watching groups of baton-twirling majorettes, Irish dancers and brass and bagpipe bands assemble. A few yards away from her a middle-aged man listened to the radio as he polished his vintage car, occasionally peering at the sky and willing the rain to stay away. Ciara listened to the eleven o'clock news which stated that the parade was scheduled to start at twelve from various points about the city. The strands would eventually converge on O'Connell Street as one big parade.

Ciara anticipated that she would meet up with Ruth and her 'giant automated gene-monster orbited by skull and crossbones helium-filled balloons' once she got there. By twelve o'clock she was stiff from sitting on the wall and glad to move when the groups started off in formation.

As the parade snaked its way on to Dame Street Ciara had settled into the spirit of things. She gave out the flyers and was even doing little dances for excited children thrilled at the sight of a giant rabbit. The streets were lined with people standing so deep on the footpath that Ciara was sure those at the back couldn't see a thing. She was just passing the bank when she saw another Easi-tel rabbit on the opposite side of the street. He was standing very close to the kerb, distributing flyers to the front of the crowd. Ciara held her breath for an instant. What if it was Ken? What if he had found out she was supposed to be on Dame Street and was lying in wait for her?

As she stared at him the other rabbit raised his hand in casual salute and went back to work. Ciara sighed with relief. It wasn't Ken, and even if it was how could he possibly know it was her when she was in full costume? Maybe she was being too cautious. After all, what was he going to do to her on a crowded street? They would have difficulty even having a conversation! It was almost one o' clock. She only had to avoid him for another couple of hours and then she could go home.

Consoled, she went back to work. At the rate she was going she would soon run out of flyers! Maybe she could go home earlier than three or at least go back to the shop for a sitdown. The idea of Gráinne waiting to say something disparaging had just put her off that idea when she thought she heard her phone ring. There was so much noise on the street around her she couldn't be sure. She took off her glove, reached into her pouch and pulled out the T2. It was definitely ringing. She pulled off her head and pressed the fluorescent button.

'Hello?'

'Ciara, where are you?' It was Ruth.

'Hey, Ruth, I thought that was my line,' Ciara teased.

'Yeah, yeah, never mind that now. Where *are* you?'

There was an unfamiliar note of urgency in her voice.

'I'm on Dame Street. Why? What's the matter?'

'Nothing. Look, there's something I need to talk to you about. It's sort of important. I'm in front of Trinity College, can you come up here to me?'

'Sure, Ruth, OK. Are you on a mobile phone?'

'Yeah. I'll explain when you get here. See you in a few minutes.'

Ruth hung up, leaving Ciara staring at the silent T2.

She had never known her sister to use a mobile phone. This was very strange.

She had just put the phone back in her pouch when it rang again. But that was just typical of Ruth. She would make a really rushed phone call and then have to phone you back immediately to finish off whatever message she had half delivered.

'Yes, Ruth, what can I do for you?'

'Hi, Ciara.'

It was John.

'Gosh, John, sorry, I thought . . .'

'Ciara, we need to talk.'

She had a feeling she knew what he wanted to talk about.

'Yes, we do . . .'

'Can you come over to the shop? I'll wait for you here. I'd pick you up but I can't get a car through the streets.'

'Well, I . . .' She didn't want to confess she had been about to stop work and skip gaily off with her sister.

'Don't worry about work, I'll explain to Gráinne. It should only take you a few minutes to get here. You're on Dame Street, right?'

'Yeah.'

'See you shortly then. 'Bye.'

Ciara was in a dilemma! Ordinarily there would be no question what she would do. She would go to Ruth, have whatever chat was at issue and then go to John with some excuse about getting delayed by the crowd, or a bus, or the river having burst its banks, or that she'd lost her way in the dark, or been whisked away by an alien ship. Anything that came into her head! But today was different. Because of what had happened between them earlier she didn't feel she should keep John waiting. This meeting might be the deciding factor in their relationship and to put John in second place to Ruth's malfunctioning 'giant gene' or burst balloon or whatever her problem was, would be too careless.

She had to go and talk to John.

Besides, maybe he would take her somewhere nice for lunch!

Throwing a wistful glance in the direction of Trinity College, Ciara turned left across Temple Bar and the Ha'penny Bridge. When she got to the shop on Henry Street John was waiting in the doorway. He didn't smile when he saw her. In fact his cold attitude of the morning didn't seemed to have changed at all. Ciara could sense this was not going to be an easy conversation.

'Hi, John.'

'Hello, Ciara.'

'Thanks for the call.' She was determined to make this as easy for him as possible. John did not answer but instead stepped towards the shop door as though to go inside. Ideas of a nice lunch started to fade.

'Do you want to go somewhere?' Ciara asked quickly, apprehensive about meeting Gráinne and not wanting to have 'that' conversation with John in a shop where anyone could barge in.

'I left my phone in the staffroom,' he said tonelessly. 'Come on through.'

Reluctantly Ciara followed him into the shop. It was quite empty, as though it was closed. Before she had time to ask him about this her phone rang. She quickly pulled it out of her pouch and answered it. As she did so Gráinne emerged from the staffroom and stopped suddenly, looking from John to Ciara and back.

'Hello,' Ciara said into the phone, making sorry-I-have-to-answer-it gestures at John and Gráinne.

'Ciara, where are you?' Ruth sounded worried this time.

'Yeah, sorry, I'm back at the shop. John ...'

Ciara stopped speaking in astonishment. Gráinne had brushed past John and, grabbing the phone out of Ciara's hand, violently pressed the disconnect button before dropping it into the wastepaper basket. It immediately started to ring again.

'Hey! What do you think ...' Ciara was so astonished she was surprised she managed to say anything.

'Shut up and get into the staffroom,' Gráinne snarled.

Ciara, even more taken aback, looked to John for support. Surely he wasn't going to allow Gráinne to talk to her like that?

He was.

'John?' Ciara assumed he must have just forgotten she was there.

John looked at the counter and mumbled, 'Do as she says.'

A thin triumphant smile flickered around Gráinne's lips as she made an exaggeratedly polite gesture towards the door at the back of the shop. Indignant but unsure how to react, Ciara allowed herself to be led into the staffroom.

'John, what's going on?'

He didn't reply.

And this time Ciara didn't notice. She was too busy taking in the scene inside the tiny room. It was crowded. The first people she noticed were two large threatening men dressed in dark tracksuits. They had the demeanour of thugs, standing with legs apart, heavyset shoulders harbouring equally heavyset heads with very short hair. Ciara might have taken them for a couple of rugby players if it hadn't been for the batons they held in their hands. Taking a closer look, she decided they were more cudgels than batons. The two men looked at her with open hostility.

Ciara averted her eyes and stared at the other people in the room. She gasped in surprise at what she saw. Elena was sitting on the edge of a chair, her face tear-stained, her breath coming in the jagged gasps of somebody near hysteria. For a moment Ciara thought she might be in labour. Then she noticed Sasha. He lay on the floor with blood pouring from a gash on his forehead. Anna the unfriendly Russian knelt beside him, her arm about his shoulder.

'What the hell . . . ?'

'Shut up.' Gráinne was determined Ciara wouldn't speak.

All eyes focused on her.

Ciara stopped talking. Gráinne strode into the middle of the room.

'Get up, Sasha,' she ordered the man on the floor.

Anna, tightening her grasp around his shoulders, sobbed, 'He cannot, he is too much hurt.'

Sasha, however, had already started to drag himself into a standing position, his shoulders hunched, hands clasping his stomach.

'Now, Elena, I want you to tell us once more what you told us earlier.' Gráinne's voice was hard and measured. Elena let out a sort of whimper, looking fearfully at Ciara, shaking her head. Then her face crumpled into fresh tears as she looked pleadingly from Sasha to Gráinne and back.

Everybody waited.

John leaned against the wall and folded his arms.

Gráinne nodded to one of the thugs and in a split second he had raised his cudgel and brought it down full force on Sasha's shoulder. He screamed with pain and fell back against the wall.

'Jesus Christ, what are you doing? Stop! What the *hell* are you doing?' Ciara flung herself across the room towards the groaning man. The other thug extended his arm and she bounced back almost to the door where she had been standing. Ciara turned to John, still leaning against the wall.

'Do something!'

His face remained expressionless. Gráinne for once did not interject.

'What do you want me to do, Ciara?' Even his voice was inexpressive.

'Stop this ... this ... travesty.' She waved her hand towards the frightening scene before her.

'The only travesty I see in this room, Ciara, is you.' John's voice was bitter now.

Ciara heard Gráinne laugh coldly behind her.

'What? John, this isn't about *me*!'

'Isn't it?'

She shook her head, determined to keep him talking because at least it stopped Gráinne from ordering another beating.

'This has nothing to do with me!'

'You used to say you would only marry a rich man. Well, my deadline on being rich was thirty and this is what makes me rich.' He pointed at the frightened group of people on the other side of the room. Ciara had no idea what he meant.

'John, I was joking about the rich man . . .'

He went on as though he hadn't heard her. 'But there's always something else with you, isn't there? You and your men. There was always somebody else . . . And if it wasn't that it was some whine, some imperfection you went on and on about . . .'

Ciara had a feeling they were having that chat they should have had this morning, and they were having it in a crowded room.

This was a nightmare.

A little strangled noise came from behind her as Gráinne's anger erupted.

'You bastard! You had something going on with her all along!'

John raised his hands. Still looking at Ciara he said, 'It was nothing, Gráinne, a mistake, part of my past. Let's just get this sorted, OK?'

As Ciara turned to watch Gráinne visibly swallow her fury she realised John had never broken up with her. Their intimacy in the pub had been the intimacy of lovers not of a couple splitting up. He had made up his story the night before to keep Ciara quiet!

Gráinne transferred her wrath to the Russians.

'OK. Last time. Out with it, Elena.'

She looked defeated now, staring at the floor.

'Ciara has it,' she whispered quietly.

This was news to Ciara who stared in surprise as all eyes turned to her again. She shook her head, puzzled.

'What?'

'The icon,' Gráinne snarled. This still meant nothing to Ciara who shook her head again. 'Elena, Elena.' Gráinne spoke in a disappointed voice and shook her head, then she nodded at the thugs. One of them took a step forward and slapped Elena so hard she fell off her chair on to the floor.

Realisation dawned on Ciara as she watched the thug work out where he would hit the young woman next. They were looking for the little holy thing Elena had given her. There was only one way to stop them beating Elena and that was by confessing she did know where it was. Or at least had been!

Anna was now reaching towards Elena, screaming, 'No, no!' but the other thug was standing firmly in front of her, ensuring that she could do nothing to help the pregnant woman.

'It's in my car,' Ciara tried to say above the noise.

But her voice was lost in the cacophony of everything happening at once. Only Elena seemed to hear and she was in no position to do anything about it. As Ciara spoke the thug glanced quickly at Gráinne who nodded again. He raised his foot to kick Elena in the stomach. Her pregnant stomach. Ciara, realising that shouting was useless, threw herself between Elena and the boot.

Just then a giant ear of corn burst through the door, screaming, arms and legs flailing as it ran straight into Gráinne who collapsed under its weight against the wall.

Ciara landed with a thud on the floor, covering her face as a boot came rapidly towards it.

She felt a searing pain in her head.

Everything went black.

Chapter Nineteen

'Has Ruth been in?'

'No, Mum.' Ciara didn't shake her head because it was far too painful to do so.

'You'd think she'd call in to see you, under the circumstances.'

'I'm sure she'll be in later. Have you any news? What's happened?'

'I have no idea. Your sister Karen rang to find out how you were. She'll be in this evening because of the children, you know. She said there was something in the paper.'

'What?'

'Now, Ciara, you know I don't hold with bringing that sort of thing into the house on a Sunday. "Six days shall work be done: but the seventh day is the

Sabbath of rest, a holy convocation: ye shall do no work."'

Ciara gave up and lay back against her pillows. Maybe one of the nurses could get a newspaper for her after her mother was gone. She wanted to know what happened in the Easi-tel shop after she got knocked out the day before. Were Elena and Sasha OK? Was John really involved in something horrible and violent?

When Ciara had come to in the hospital after arriving by ambulance the night before they had told her she was a little concussed but otherwise fine. Then they had wheeled her into the ward where she had woken that morning with an incredible headache. Her mother was her first visitor and she was revealing nothing.

Revealing anything or even mentioning the matter would mean she would have to admit she'd been wrong about John.

Mrs Bowe never admitted she was wrong.

She put the bag she was carrying on the bed.

'Ciara, I looked among your things at home for proper attire for you to wear in hospital but there was nothing. How many times have I told you to have something set aside in case of an emergency? I've brought you what I had in the drawer for myself. At least they're decent. That's what I'll get you for your birthday tomorrow: appropriate bed-wear.'

She slid two flowery garments out of the bag. The

velvet ribbons at their high gathered necklines taunted Ciara, demanding she admire and appreciate their feminine charms.

'Thanks, Mum. You might just leave them in the locker, I'll change later.'

'Be sure you do, you never know who might be walking through these public wards.' Mrs Bowe sniffed and glanced about. Even though the curtains were drawn almost the whole way around she could see a couple of patients at the other side of the room.

'That woman there on the left – I wouldn't say she'll be with us for long. She has the same pallor your grandmother had when she . . .'

'Mum, it's bad enough being here without a running commentary on the other patients.'

Mrs Bowe set her mouth into a prim line. 'I was just saying.'

'Yes, Mum, sorry. How was dinner yesterday?' Ciara moved the conversation on, hoping to get her mother to a safe subject. It didn't work.

'That television is very loud, you'd think they'd turn it down while visitors are here.' She craned her neck to see what was on. 'I don't think the noise is doing that poor woman any good . . .'

'Mum, please! Did Karen take the kids to see the parade?'

That worked. Her grandchildren were Mrs Bowe's favourite topic of conversation and she talked about them until Ciara was ready for another nap. So far that morning she'd had five naps. She didn't even hear her mother leave.

When Ciara woke up Ruth was standing beside her bed, obviously fighting the urge to nudge her. Unsuccessfully.

'You're awake! Brilliant. How're you feeling? The nurses say you'll live!' There was laughter in her eyes.

'Ruth. Great. Hi.' Ciara tried to pull herself into a sitting position but gave up because her head started to thump. 'Mum was in.'

'I know.' Her sister grinned mischievously. 'They told me at the ward office that she was here so I went to the visitors' room down the corridor and waited for her to go. I didn't think a Bowe reunion was something you needed in your condition, little Ms Hero!'

Ciara smiled shyly. 'What do you mean?'

'What do I mean? As if you didn't know! You saved Elena's baby and probably Elena as well by blocking that man's foot.'

'Really? How is she?'

'She's fine. I asked on the way in and she has just given birth to a little girl.' Ruth looked at her watch. 'She should be fifteen minutes old now even though she's a month premature. Pity she didn't wait a day, she'd have had the same birthday as you!'

Everybody was determined to remind Ciara that it was her birthday the next day. Her twenty-eighth birthday! She shuddered.

Once she got beyond that she was delighted to hear Elena was all right but there was so much more Ciara needed to know. What had happened to John? How come Ruth had turned up in her ear of corn costume when she did? What had it all been about? She was sorting out which question to ask first when a familiar voice came from behind the curtain.

'Knock, knock, is it OK to come in?' Ken's head popped around it. He looked at Ciara and smiled. 'Hiya, how're you feeling?' He stepped around the curtain, his arms full of flowers, and spoke to Ruth. 'No vases but they said they should have one later.' He gently heaped the flowers on the end of the bed.

Ciara was bewildered. What was Ken, liar and cheat, doing here with an enormous bunch of flowers, and on such friendly terms with Ruth?

Very friendly terms indeed by the look of things!

'What's he doing here, Ruth?'

She looked surprised. 'Ken? Why he's . . . he's . . . But of course, you don't know, do you?'

'No, I don't know.' Ciara stared at them defiantly. Ruth and Ken exchanged glances.

'Better start from the beginning then,' Ruth declared,

shoving the flowers to one side and sitting on the end of the bed. Ken reached around the curtain for a chair and sat down near her.

Ciara glared at him.

'Ciara, I'm afraid the Capitalist is one of the bad guys. I don't know how much you heard before you checked out but he and Gráinne created Easi-tel specifically to launder money.'

Ciara nodded, her mind in turmoil. She had more or less worked out for herself that John and Gráinne weren't engaged in charity work or even good clean business, but it was another thing to hear it confirmed. To know that John, her John, was a criminal who had lied to her and then left her at the mercy of thugs.

But she was still confused about everything that had happened in the staffroom.

'Yeah, but what's that got to do with the holy thing everybody was making such a fuss about?'

Ruth laughed. 'That "holy thing" as you call it is worth a fortune! It's one of a number of icons so valuable it's against the law for them to leave Russia. The Capitalist was smuggling them out of the country using refugees like Sasha and Elena and selling them on the black market. Elena refused to give him the "holy thing" because he was supposed to get her husband and sister to Ireland as well but he had reneged on the deal.'

'So she gave it to me,' Ciara said quietly.

'Yeah, you were her only option really. She took a risk because she couldn't give it to any of the Russians without putting them in danger. She knew the Capitalist would get violent so she gave it to you for safekeeping, so to speak, and ran.'

'And now it's missing with my car.' Ciara closed her eyes at the idea.

'But that's the thing – the guards found your car!' It was Ken who spoke now, the excitement obviously too much for him. 'And the icon was still in it. Everything was still in it except the radio. They found it in Bray so it was probably somebody who missed the last bus home and decided your car would do nicely!'

'Is Karman Ghia all right?' Ciara spoke to Ruth, unable to talk to Ken. She was still furious with him for lying to her and had as yet found no reason to let him off the hook.

'It's fine. A bit of damage to the door and wiring, that's all.'

Ciara heaved a sigh of relief. But she had more questions.

'What about Dimitri? Was he involved in this?'

Ruth nodded but it was Ken who answered. 'He had threatened to go to the police and report the icon scam so they killed him. It was Dimitri who asked me, as a journalist, to help but there was nothing I could do to prevent his death. He told me the day he died that they had tried to kill him that morning but nearly got you instead. You were wearing the wrong head. It had a blue ribbon so they thought you were him. That's why I spoke to you. I needed to find out whose side you were on!'

'And?' Ciara finally allowed herself to speak to him but her tone was still angry.

'I couldn't find out. You certainly looked as if you were involved. I saw you with John, getting into his car on the street, yet you never mentioned that you knew him. And you never said anything about the murder attempt so it did look suspicious.' There was a hint of embarrassment in his voice now.

Ciara had nothing to say to this. She was not going to admit that she had omitted details because she fancied Ken! However she could not let what appeared to be an accusation stand there pointing its finger at her.

'Well, you were hardly little Mr Truthful to me, were you?' she snapped.

Ken's expression was contrite but before he could speak Ruth interrupted. 'Ciara, he saved your life. If it wasn't for him you'd probably have been sold into the white slave trade or something by now.'

Ken looked bashful.

'What do you mean?' Ciara did not want to hear good things about Ken, she wanted to hate him.

'OK, I'll give you the abridged version, shall I?' Ruth said patiently. 'You see, after I saw Ken in the rabbit outfit I decided to give him a ring to see if he'd do an article on our anti-GM float. He arranged to pop over to meet us while he was working yesterday and I happened to mention that you were my sister and then it all came out. He knew that John and Gráinne had arranged Dimitri's death and they would stop at nothing to get that icon. That's why I phoned you to meet us, but you went off to meet John instead. When we found out Ken and I ran all the way to the shop with Ken on the phone to the police. They were just arriving when I burst into the room and knocked that po-faced bitch over!'

Ciara looked hesitantly at Ken.

'Thanks,' she said stiffly.

He nodded, a little of the light coming back into his eyes. 'Don't mention it.'

Ruth, having no time for meaningful looks, chattered on.

'Have you seen the papers?'

She reached into her bag and pulled out a newspaper. 'It's mentioned in most of the papers but this is the best one because the journalist was actually an eye witness!'

She dropped the paper on the bedclothes in front of

Ciara. The main headline stood out: BUNNY BUSTS BOGUS BUSINESS SCAM! By Kenneth Meagher.

Underneath the headline there was a picture of Ruth as an ear of corn. This wasn't relevant to the story but it made a very good picture! The article explained the whole Easi-tel affair and Dimitri's murder. At a glance Ciara saw that her name was mentioned more than once. She wanted Ruth and Ken to go away so she could study it in peace!

As though reading her mind Ruth popped off the bed. 'Better give you a chance to catch up on your reading then, hadn't we? By the way there are some of your clothes in that bag if you fancy a change.'

Ciara nodded at her gratefully, relieved not to have to change into the nightdresses from hell left by her mother.

'Ah, there's another thing, Ciara.' Ken stepped forward, fishing for something in his pocket. He pulled out a small piece of paper. 'This.' He handed the piece of paper to Ciara. She opened it up and saw it was a lottery ticket. 'When Elena identified the box last night she said this wasn't hers so I guessed it must be yours. It's a bit out of date but I thought I'd return it anyway.'

'Thanks.' She nodded. 'I don't suppose I won anything, I never do.'

'What's that?' Ruth reached out and grabbed the ticket.

She looked at it closely. 'How do you know you haven't won by matching five numbers? Did you check?'

Ciara shook her head, knowing it was useless to say anything when Ruth was like this. Ken was laughing at her optimism.

'Well, I'm going to check it on the teletext. If nothing else at least I can turn that television down while I'm at it.' Ruth disappeared around the curtain.

'It's all part of her grand plot to save the planet, you know, cut down on noise pollution and so on!' Ciara said to Ken as she rearranged the newspaper to cover her awkward feelings at being on her own with him. For the first time since he'd arrived in the hospital she looked at him properly. He was as stunning as he had been all week! She hoped she didn't look as bad as she felt. Ken stepped a little closer.

'Ciara, now that I have a chance, I just want to say I'm sorry for any misunderstanding. I didn't mean to hurt you ...'

She felt a stab of disappointment. This could mean only one thing: that he had tried to seduce her as part of his job. She had been just another source of information for him, that was all!

'That's fine,' she said shortly.

'No, it's not,' he said emphatically. Then stopped short as the television went silent and a grumble of protest went up around the ward. Ruth was having an effect. Ciara raised her eyebrows and looked at him expectantly. She didn't want him to stop now. Ken took a deep breath.

'I was going to tell you everything on Friday night but you never turned up. I couldn't bear the idea you might be involved – I needed to know, even if it meant losing my cover. But I . . . I'd really like a chance to make it up to you. Can I come and see you again tomorrow? Would you mind?' He broke into one of his Ken smiles. 'If you like, I could come to see you every day for as long as you want?'

Now that sounded more like it!

Ciara nodded happily and he reached out his hand to her. Before they could touch, however, there was a shriek from the other side of the curtain as Ruth burst through waving the lottery ticket.

'What did I tell you. What did I tell you? You've won five thousand pounds!'

'No?' Ciara was incredulous. Her mind was racing, trying to think what she could do with the money.

Ruth cut across her excitement. 'You'll be able to get your own flat now!'

'Yeah, I won't have to go back to Mum.'

'You can get Karmie fixed!'

'I can take a bit of time to find a proper job!'

'And you can take us out for your birthday tomorrow, if they let you out of here.'

Ciara nodded happily. She didn't say it aloud but she figured if there was any money left over she could hire a personal fitness instructor to sort out that little matter of her waist. Though the couple of days in hospital might have already done that for her.

The possibilities were endless!

Ken, laughing at the sisters' excitement, leaned over and kissed Ciara on the lips.

'Congratulations,' he said softly.

Ruth, at the end of the bed, raised her eyebrows at their easy intimacy.

Ciara grinned at her and shrugged.

Things were finally looking up for Ciara Bowe!